Mist
Walker

An Inspector
Green Mystery

Barbara Fradkin

RENDEZVOUS
PRESS

Cover art: Christopher Chuckry

Le Conseil des Arts | The Canada Council
du Canada | For the Arts
depuis 1957 | since 1957

We acknowledge the support of the Canada Council for the Arts for our publishing program. We acknowledge the support of the Government of Ontario through the Ontario Media Development Corporation's Ontario Book Initiative

Napoleon Publishing/RendezVous Press
Toronto, Ontario, Canada

Printed in Canada

07 06 05 04 03   5 4 3 2 1

National Library of Canada Cataloguing in Publication

Fradkin, Barbara Fraser, date—
    Mist Walker / Barbara Fradkin.

(An Inspector Green mystery)
ISBN 1-894917-03-0

    I. Title. II. Series: Fradkin, Barbara Fraser, date-. Inspector Green Mystery.

PS8561.R233M48 2003   C813'.6   C2003-902838-0
PR9199.4.F73M48 2003

Acknowledgements

Mist Walker deals with a complex, emotionally charged theme which deserves an informed and respectful voice. A number of experts willingly and graciously answered my call for help during the writing of this book. My thanks to Sergeant James Davies of the Child Abuse and Sexual Assault Unit of the Ottawa Police, Staff Sergeant Don Sweet, formerly of the Forensic Identification Unit, Dr. Brenda Saxe of the Centre for the Treatment of Sexual Abuse and Childhood Trauma, Margaret Lederman of the Forensic Psychiatry Unit of the Royal Ottawa Hospital, and especially Constable Mark Cartwright of the Ottawa Police for his ongoing advice and expertise in police matters.

I am also indebted to my writing colleagues, particularly Mary Jane Maffini, Robin Harlick, Madona Skaff, Jane Tun and Tom Curran, for their insightful support, and to my editor, Allister Thompson and my publisher, Sylvia McConnell, for their continuing belief in my work.

Mist Walker *is a work of fiction, and although the Ottawa Police Service and many of the Ottawa locales do exist, all the events and people, as well as the Rideau Psychiatric Hospital, are the invention of the author. Any resemblance to actual circumstances is purely coincidental.*

"...and many times beating with her hands on the earth abundant she called on Hades and on honoured Persephone... And Erinys, the mist walker, of the heart without pity, heard her out of the dark places."

-The *Iliad* of Homer
Book IX, 569-572

One

To Janice's surprise, the door was unlocked. Matthew Fraser, a man with five locks and a ten minute ritual for securing them, had left his apartment unlocked. She twisted the knob, pushed gingerly, and let the door drift open before her. Even before she stepped inside, the smell knocked her back two feet. Like mildewed carpet and week-old fish baking together in the heat. How could the man stand it!

A narrow, dimly lit hall stretched ahead of her, its brown carpet worn bare with age.

"Matt?" She tossed the word cautiously into the gloom. No response. She sifted the silence. Nothing. Not the whir of air conditioning, not the whisper of breathing, not even the distant hum of traffic from Merivale Road. With shallow breaths, she edged down the hall into the main room. At the entranceway, she froze, trying to make sense of the sight before her.

Lining the walls and filling every spare cranny were floor to ceiling shelves crammed with books, binders and newspapers curling with age. More stacks sat on the coffee table and the floor as if waiting for space. A vinyl couch and a computer were the only other occupants of the room. Dust danced in the slivers of sunlight that seeped past the blinds on the windows.

"Matt?" she ventured again, peering around a bookshelf into another hall. More bookshelves. More newspapers. An old-fashioned telephone table held a heavy black phone with its receiver off the hook. No wonder I couldn't get through, she thought as she hung it back up.

She'd been trying to call Matt for six days, ever since he'd failed to show up for their daily walk. He had seemed unusually skittish at last week's therapy group, and his old paranoia had been creeping back in. He'd been talking about conspiracies and about the futility of the little guy against the system. Just like bullies in the playground, he'd said, they own all the balls in the game.

He never stopped trying, that much was clear. Whatever obsessed him was right here in this room, labelled by month and year going back ten years. There was an entire bookshelf devoted to cross-examination and the testimony of minors, and another two bookshelves of *Ottawa Citizen*s and *Sun*s dating back a decade. He had bookcases on psychology ranging all the way from Sigmund Freud through cognitive psychology to recent texts on post-traumatic stress disorder. Other books lay splayed open on the coffee table and stacked on the floor.

Janice felt the hairs rise on her arms as she gazed at the clutter, which had a flavour of fanaticism. She liked Matt and thought him a lonely, wounded man who was struggling to put his life together. It had taken him weeks to say a word in the therapy group, more weeks to accept her invitation to coffee, and months to confide to her anything of his ordeal. At the beginning, she'd simply thought him shy and slow to trust anyone but his cherished Modo, a Lab-Rottweiler mix that he'd adopted from the Humane Society. Modo had been a reject like himself, found at four months old tied to the railway track on the outskirts of the city. She'd been ungainly and mismatched, all feet and monstrous head, but she'd suited his mood. He'd taken her in when he was at his lowest ebb, shut away from the world, fearing the gossip and the disgust.

Modo! Janice realized belatedly that the dog had not greeted her at the door. Modo had been well trained to scare off intruders and should have set up a thunderous barking the second Janice started fiddling with the door.

Matt must have taken his dog with him, Janice decided, which was hardly unusual, since the dog spent most of her time glued to his side. But where would he have gone, and what was he up to? He was agoraphobic; the mere glimpse of crowds and bustling streets sent him scrambling back to the safety of his apartment. On top of that, he was so paranoid that he never even raised the blinds on his windows and had bought himself the biggest, ugliest guard dog he could find. Yet today, he had left his front door unlocked.

Despite her trepidation, Janice forced herself down the hall to the kitchen, where the smell was even stronger. The room was neat, but flies buzzed around a plate of crusted food on the counter. Modo's food and water bowls sat empty on the floor by the fridge, and the *Toronto Star* was spread open on the tiny table. Matt said he read at least four papers a day. She glanced at the date. June 6, six days ago.

Janice frowned in puzzlement. Matt clearly hadn't been here for several days, but he appeared to have left abruptly. She felt a twinge of hurt along with her uneasiness, for he had not called her. True, he owed her nothing, because nothing had really happened between them. Just a few walks with the dog in the park, an amicable few hours over *lattes* at Starbucks, some friendly conversations and the first tentative sharing of private thoughts. But men didn't come into her life all that often—who was she kidding, one hadn't ventured near it in over fifteen years—so she'd allowed herself a faint hope.

But now he was gone, without bothering to pick up the phone.

Which was off the hook, she remembered with that odd chill again. Resisting the urge to clean up the dinner and throw out whatever garbage was creating the smell, she ventured instead towards a closed door at the end of the hall, which she assumed was the bedroom. He'd never invited her into his apartment, let alone his bedroom, and now she felt almost brazen. The door seemed locked when she first pushed against it, but then it gave a few inches, reluctantly, as if a huge weight was pinned against it. A fresh odour of feces wafted through the crack, and alarm galvanized her. Straining, she shoved the door back enough to squeeze through and stumbled over a huge limp object on the floor. She gasped at the sight.

Modo lay on her side against the door. At first glance, Janice thought she was dead, until she saw her eye move to meet Janice's.

"Modo!" Janice dropped to her knees at the dog's side. Modo mustered a cocked eyebrow and a faint thump of her tail. The heat in the room was sweltering and the air rancid. Janice glanced around quickly and saw soiled patches in the rug, but no sign of food or water.

"My God, you poor baby!" Janice hurried into the kitchen to fetch a bowl of water, but Modo was too weak to stand or drink. Janice began spooning water into the dog's mouth. The dog flicked her tongue feebly, but Janice knew it was not enough. She had to get Modo out of the stifling room and into a vet's care immediately, but the dog weighed at least a hundred pounds. It was a job which required a strong man. Much as she hated to admit it, her neighbour was the only one who came to mind. That was the trouble with years of rarely meeting another living soul.

As she grabbed a phone book to look up his number, she suppressed a tremor of fear. Something was very wrong. No matter how obsessed and paranoid Matt had become, no matter how distorted his ideas, he would never have left Modo behind to die.

*　　*　　*

As he rounded the block to the station, Ottawa Police Inspector Michael Green glanced at his watch in dismay. Almost six o'clock. Up ahead, southbound Elgin Street was still blocked solid with the last of the commuters exiting the downtown core. Police headquarters loomed on his right, a concrete bunker built in what Green had heard aptly described as the Brutalist style. Short on aesthetics, but no doubt designed so that a Scud missile could barely make a dent. The bunker was incongruously plunked amid the red brick Victorian townhouses of Centretown, a stone's throw from the yuppie pubs of Elgin Street and the flowerbeds and recreational paths of the Rideau Canal. Even more incongruous was its spectacular view of the Museum of Nature, which sprawled like a Scottish baronial castle in the middle of a grassy square. Only a moat was lacking, although the constant traffic swirling around it up Metcalfe Street did a passable imitation.

The view, however, was only enjoyed by the lucky few whose offices lined the north side of the building. Offices on the south side, if they'd had windows, would have looked over eight lanes of elevated expressway, complete with exhaust, noise and a constant stream of cars heading across the city. The theory was that police units responding to a call could reach even the farthest outskirts of the city in less than half an hour.

Except at six o'clock, Green grumbled as he saw the tide of cars inching westward in the stifling afternoon sun. The damn meeting with the RCMP had shot the entire afternoon, and while he was wasting his time learning about the latest policy initiative, a dozen fresh cases had probably landed on the various crime desks under his command. It was proving a busy summer for criminals in the nation's capital, for hot weather brought on the usual spate of domestics to add to the standard fare of drug-related assaults and armed robberies. Green needed to ensure that no new crises or screw-ups had surfaced while he was learning to play nice.

Yet he'd promised Sharon he wouldn't be home too late. She had just started a long stint of day shifts at the hospital, their son was getting yet another molar, and the air conditioning in their new home had succumbed to the heat for the third time this month. As flexible and forgiving as she was, today was not a day to put those qualities to the test.

Five minutes, he promised her silently as he pulled into the circular drive of the station, flicked on his hazard lights and ducked through the glass doors into police headquarters. As his eyes adjusted to the cavernous gloom of the foyer, he made out the tall, angular figure of a woman at the reception desk at the side of the room. Encased head to toe in a shapeless brown shift, she was pressed to the window, punctuating her tirade with short jabs of her finger.

Green glanced through the reception glass and groaned when he saw the florid face and triple jowls of Constable Dan Blake. Blake had thirty years on the force, during which he'd never advanced beyond beat cop, due to a lack of even the minimal requirement of intelligence, fitness and sobriety. He was an anachronism in modern policing, who regarded the hijacking of police work by youth, education, women and minorities with undisguised contempt. Green, as a university-educated Jew and, at forty-one, still young for an inspector, was not on his list of favourites.

The feeling was mutual, however, and Green gave a curt nod as he headed past on his way toward the elevator. A sudden smirk creased Blake's jowls, and he flicked a pudgy finger in Green's direction. The woman swung around instantly.

"Excuse me!" she cried, leaping into Green's path. "I want to report a missing person, but no one will take me seriously!"

Green stopped and shot Blake an angry glare just in time to see the man suck his smirk back in and hustle out of the cubicle. "Sorry, Inspector Green," he said, without the faintest hint of scorn. "Miss Tanner is concerned about a friend. Ma'am, if you'll come back here—"

The woman didn't budge. "Inspector? Finally, someone near the top!"

She was flushed and breathless, her eyes fixed on Green with desperate hope. With his five minutes ticking away, he seized on the nearest platitude. "Have you filed a missing persons report with—"

"Of course I have," she retorted. "It went into a computer database somewhere, and I'm sure that's the end of it. They said I'm just a friend, so how can I even be sure he's missing."

"Well," Green equivocated, "is his family concerned? Has any one else reported him missing?"

"That doesn't matter! I know he's missing, and not by his own choice. Something bad has happened to him."

Green caught Blake's quick rolling of the eyes and felt a spike of anger. "Constable Blake, would you doublecheck that the officer who took Ms. Tanner's report is aware of all her concerns?"

Before Blake could react, she clamped her bony hand on Green's arm. Her nails, he noted, were chewed to the quick. "But you're an inspector. His boss, right?"

"Inspector Green handles major criminal investigations," Blake added, ever helpful.

"I see," she retorted, snatching her hand back. "This isn't big enough for you, is that it? This is a major crime, I'm telling you. Something has happened to Matt. He didn't just leave."

"I understand your concern," Green replied, "and Constable Blake is going to follow up. But unless there's evidence of a crime—"

"What a ridiculous catch-22! How can there be evidence of a crime if you refuse to investigate?"

"The officer on the case—"

"—is a thick-headed twit!" She turned an unhealthy mottled pink, and her eyes sparked.

"Inspector Green is certainly no thick-headed twit, Miss Tanner," Blake interjected with a barely stifled grin. "He's one of the sharpest knives in the drawer."

Green's combination of brains, imagination and pure pig-headedness had earned him a fair reputation on the force, but coming from Blake, it was hardly a compliment. Green was just formulating an appropriate retort when Ms. Tanner renewed her grip on his arm.

"At least hear me out, Inspector. Let me tell you the evidence I have that worries me, and then tell me what you think I should do next."

The woman was shaking with apprehension, but her eyes met his with defiance and determination. Not unlike his own when he was on the scent, he conceded with reluctant admiration. Even at six o'clock, after a long, draining day, she deserved more than a patronizing pat on the head. Perhaps giving her five minutes of his time would soothe her fears and get him out of here faster than all the bureaucratic obfuscation they could fling at her.

Normally, he would have taken her into one of the interview rooms, but he hoped to save some of his precious five minutes by checking his desk while he listened. When he had her ensconced in his little alcove office, however, he realized that five minutes would barely get her off the ground. Janice Tanner prattled as if she hadn't had anyone to talk to in six months. Which may have been partly true.

"I'm agoraphobic, you see," she began, once she'd folded and unfolded her large hands several times. "I don't usually tell people that unless I have to. I mean, unless I'm about to bolt from a theatre or something. But in this case, it's how I met Matt—Matthew Fraser, the man who's missing. He's agoraphobic too, and we were in this therapy group together. Once a week Tuesday afternoons, at the Rideau Psychiatric Hospital. For most of us, especially in the beginning, just getting to the group was half the cure." She gave a little laugh, then must have misinterpreted Green's frown of impatience as puzzlement, for she asked him if he knew what agoraphobia was.

Even if his wife hadn't been a psychiatric nurse, Green would have known, for in twenty years on the force, he had encountered just about every human frailty, but before he could intercept her, she launched into the topic.

"It's more than just fear, it's pure, paralyzing panic. It hits you unexpectedly in a mall, in a coffee shop, in the street outside your front door, and pretty soon you panic at just the thought of going out. In the group, we talk about ways to survive the panic, and we give ourselves little homework chores to do—open the front door, walk around the block, make a phone call to a store—"

"I understand, Ms. Tanner, but what makes you think something has happened to Matthew Fraser?"

"Well, you have to know the whole picture. The group supported one another, that's the thing. We egged each other on. Most of us haven't many real friends, so we grew close. We

9

went together on the bus rides, to the mall—"

Green tried again. "And you did this with Mr. Fraser?"

"Several times a week, like clockwork. Routines are good for agoraphobics, because they help us get mentally ready. With Matt, it began by accident." She blushed. "Well, not quite by accident on my part. I discovered he took his dog for a walk every morning really early, before most people are up. Usually he'd walk down by the Lemieux Island Bridge, where he'd found a deserted little beach. Modo liked to retrieve from the water, and Matt would sit on the beach tossing sticks in the river."

"Modo?"

"Quasimodo, his dog."

In spite of himself, Green smiled. The story was beginning to take on colour. "The man has a warped literary sense of humour. Either that or an ugly dog."

"An ugly dog." A smile softened her tense features briefly. "I began joining him in the mornings, and soon I persuaded him to walk at Dow's Lake too, where there are a lot more people around."

"Did your relationship progress beyond walks?"

She shook her head, turning blotchy again. Not for want of desire on her part, he thought. "We're just friends," she murmured. "He's a lonely man."

"Can you give me a physical description of him? Age, height, weight?"

"I told the other officer I thought mid-thirties, five-ten. Sort of medium everything. Longish brown hair that looks like he cut it himself at the bathroom sink."

"Good looking man?"

Green's skepticism must have shown, for she stiffened. "What's that got to do with it?"

"Perhaps there are other women friends?"

She shook her head emphatically.

"Other friends, period?"

"You're missing the point! Matt is a social recluse! There are no friends."

"What about family?"

"No family that didn't cut him off years ago."

"Why?"

Her anger deflated. "I'd rather...I'm not sure."

He felt a tweak of curiosity. Secrets drew him like magnets. "I can't help if you don't tell me everything you know."

"It's not that. It's just I don't know what was real and what ghosts were just in his imagination."

Ghosts. *Oy veh*, he thought and hastened to steer her back toward reality. "So what leads you to believe something has happened to him?"

"First, he missed the group, and then he didn't show up for our walk."

"What day was that?"

"Last Wednesday."

"So he's been missing six days. Did you call him or check his work?"

"Well, I don't know if he works, and I didn't—at least he never told me where he lived."

Green sat back, his skepticism even stronger. He felt he was going in circles, wasting precious time. "So he never told you where he works or even where he lives. Sounds like a man who likes to keep people at a distance. Maybe he just doesn't want to see you as often."

"No, Inspector, it's more than that. I went to his place today—"

"I thought you didn't know where he lived."

The blotches on her face deepened, but she drew herself up, salvaging her dignity. "I followed him once, but that's irrelevant. The apartment stank. There was half-eaten food rotting in the kitchen where he left it."

"Any signs of a struggle? Things broken or out of place?"

"No. It was very cluttered, but—"

"Maybe he's just a slob. A single man, living alone—"

"He left his dog shut up in his bedroom to die, without food or water. Matt would never do that."

"He could have forgotten, had an emergency out of town—"

"Oh, you're as thick-headed a twit as the first man!" She clutched her head in her hands in exasperation, then her eye caught the photo on Green's desk. She stopped in mid-exclamation and stared at it. "That's Sharon Levy."

Before he could stop her, she had picked up the photo, which depicted Sharon cradling their baby son in the park. "Sharon Levy's your wife?"

Green removed the photo firmly and laid it face down on his desk. "Ms. Tanner—"

"I knew her slightly, from the hospital. And that's your little boy? Oh, I feel better. Sharon is such a sensible, understanding woman that you must have something going for you."

In spite of himself, Green almost laughed. Thanks for the compliment, he thought, although at times he wondered how true it was. Twenty-two years on the force, fifteen of them in criminal investigations, had left him with a pretty battered soul, and sometimes, in the face of suffering, he had to dig very deep to find compassion and hope.

Belatedly, Janice Tanner seemed to hear herself, for she blushed. "Matt's a good man, Inspector. Yes, you're right, he does keep people at arms' length, but the one creature he loves without reservation is his dog. Matt's very meticulous and orderly. He would never have left the apartment unlocked, the food half-eaten and the dog shut up." She leaned forward, her bony elbows on the edge of his desk. "I'm not a detective, but I think someone came into his apartment, locked the dog in the bedroom to get her out of the way and took Matt away. Either kidnapped or killed him."

Green tried to keep a straight face. In the years shut up in her apartment, this woman had obviously watched too many soap operas. "Why?"

"I don't know, but in the last while, Matt seemed to think there was someone out to get him."

Green's eyes narrowed. "Who? And why?"

"He never said. But I had the impression it was from a long time ago."

*   *   *

After Janice Tanner left, Green remained at his desk, torn between the phone messages on his desk and the computer sitting idly in the corner. The story of Matt Fraser piqued his curiosity, not so much because the man had disappeared while leaving his dog behind, but because he had chosen a secret, reclusive life and there were hints of darkness in his past. Furthermore, the name had a familiar ring to it; Green was sure he'd encountered it before. Perhaps somewhere in the police records, there was information that might shed light on that past.

Green knew he shouldn't even be contemplating the search. He should be beating a hasty path home. It was nearly six-thirty; Sharon would have been home for two hours, fending off Tony's demands and, in the stifling heat, trying to whip together something passable to feed them all. She was probably already sharpening her nails for the fight. Or more likely erecting the barricades for a week of the famous Levy silent treatment.

The last time she'd left him, exactly a year ago, she'd almost not come back. He'd earned another chance with abject apologies and solemn promises to reform. Plus the purchase of a house in the suburbs, which had proved too sterile for his inner city soul. It was now up for sale while they renewed their search for their dream house. The quest was off to a rocky start, as evidenced by the phone messages accumulating on his desk from Mary Sullivan, their real estate agent. Mary would have given up on them long ago had she not been the wife of Green's oldest friend on the force. Mary's latest message, logged in at four o'clock that afternoon, promised she had finally found them the perfect house.

Green debated his options. They had been searching for six months, but so far either he or Sharon had vetoed everything Mary had found. For him they had all been too far from town, too plastic, or too expensive. For Sharon they had all been too cramped, the street too busy, or the neighbourhood dubious. Sharon had flatly refused to look at another house until he became more reasonable, and hence Mary, herself a lover of antique dwellings, had taken to tipping him off at work so that he could check out possibilities without raising Sharon's ire. In the mood Sharon was likely to be in tonight, it might not be wise to even mention the subject of houses. But on the other hand, if he checked out the house on his way home and it was as wonderful as Mary claimed, perhaps the news would be enough to distract Sharon from the late hour of his arrival, and make her forget the silent treatment.

It was worth a try. And it would also give him a few spare

moments to run Fraser through the system.

He activated the computer and phoned home while he waited for the internal police database to load up. Sharon answered on the first ring, sounding harried and out of breath. A bad sign. He tried for his cheeriest tone.

"Hi, honey, I got a note from Mary, and I want to swing by an address she gave me, just in case. It's probably nothing, but—"

"Green, it's six-thirty. I'm starving."

"I could pick up something from Nate's Deli on my way home." Nate's was nowhere near his way home, but their succulent smoked meat might be enough to distract her.

No such luck, he thought, as he heard her irritated sigh. "I've got supper. Hamburgers. On their way to being charred."

"Okay, well—" He stalled for time. The program had loaded, and he clicked buttons to access the search. "Just put mine in the fridge. I'll check with Mary and be home in less than an hour." Not that the commute home to the Dreaded Vinyl Cube ever took much less than an hour, except with the siren on.

"Whatever." She hung up.

He entered Matt Fraser's name, hit search and then returned to the phone. Judging from the background clatter, Mary was in the kitchen preparing dinner when he called, but like a good business woman, she dropped everything when a potential client was on the hook. Highland Park, she said as if to set the hook well. Highland Park was an old residential neighbourhood in Ottawa's west end, a lattice of quiet streets lined with tall trees and houses with broad verandas and ivy covered brick. Highland Park was suburban quiet within walking distance of urban life. It was grace and character, and usually totally out of their price range.

"What's wrong with it?" Green wanted to know.

Mary laughed. "Well, it's had the same owners for over sixty years."

"Meaning it hasn't been updated since before the war."

"But you can do so much with it. Brian's all excited. He's dying to help you fix it up."

Green didn't doubt it. In all the years he'd known Brian Sullivan, the man had always been working on some home improvement scheme or another. He claimed it was his way of keeping sane in the mad world of Major Crimes in which he spent his days. By now there was probably nothing left to improve on his own home, so he was itching to start on Green's.

"Sharon's going to hate it," Green said. "Prehistoric plumbing. Tiny kitchen, fuses that blow all the time, closet space for a midget."

"Mike, just drive by for a look. You'll love it."

"I probably will. But Sharon will hate it."

"Well," Mary sounded undeterred, "the address is 62 Londonderry. In case."

"What are they asking?"

When Mary told him, he had to suppress a surge of excitement. The price was manageable, even allowing for the astronomical cost of renovating. It was the first manageable price he'd encountered in his search for a house that wasn't made out of plastic twenty-five kilometres out of the city. Did he really want to get himself all excited, get his hopes up that he had finally found a way out of the tangle of treeless suburban crescents he was condemned to? A quick drive by, that's all he had to do, to see the crumbling heap of bricks that would dash his hopes as quickly as they'd been raised.

The quick drive by would add less than ten minutes to his schedule, and he'd be home before Sharon even missed him.

That resolved, Green turned back to the computer, which had generated a list of Matthew Frasers with police contacts in the city of Ottawa. One was clearly too old and two were too young, but three names remained. Green selected the first and frowned as the man's lengthy record of police contacts scrolled up onto the screen. Mostly D and Ds and occasional contacts as witness or victim of assault. Likely a regular joe with a weakness for alcohol and some nasty drinking buddies. The second Matt Fraser had been an abusive and threatening husband whose circle of intimidation had extended not just to his wife but to her friends and family as well.

That one was possible, although Green had never known a bully to turn phobic.

The third Matthew Fraser was born in 1967, which made him thirty-six. Furthermore, his list of police contacts was very brief, hardly the stuff of a career criminal. A handful of charges but only one victim. One trial. One acquittal.

For sexual assault, ten years earlier.

Two

Even before Green set foot in his hot, airless kitchen, he extended a silver gift bag through the archway and slipped it onto the kitchen table. Sharon was on her hands and knees beneath the high chair, rescuing Tony's hamburger, and she peered up at him through damp locks of black hair. Her gaze was frosty. Propped in his high chair, the toddler wiggled with delight at the sight of his father and shouted to be picked up. Sharon's frown dissolved into a smile as she pulled the gift bag towards her.

"Offerings to the gods, Green?" She peeked inside, then extracted a tub of Ben and Jerry's New York Super Fudge Chunk ice cream. Her smile widened. She rose, slipped her arms around his neck and kissed him. "The gods are pleased."

He lingered over the kiss, savouring the pressure of her soft, petite body against his. "Sorry I'm late."

She extricated herself to put the ice cream away while he scooped his son into his arms. "So what was Mary Sullivan's latest catastrophe like, anyway?" she asked.

He hesitated. How to describe the house he'd just seen, with its broad veranda, steeply pitched roof and trademark Ottawa red brick? How to capture its promise and keep Sharon's mind open? Tony was squirming, Sharon frazzled, and with the air conditioner on the blink, their new house was a sweltering 28°C. Such a description was best left until after Tony's bedtime, when Sharon had her feet up and a glass of wine in her hand.

"Oh...interesting," he replied as he set Tony down and cracked open an ice cold coke from the fridge.

"Interesting good or interesting bad?"

"Both. But we can talk about it later."

Tony had pulled open a bottom cupboard and was happily banging pots together. Ignoring the racket, Sharon snatched Green's coke to take a long swig. "Both. That sounds ominous."

Green took another coke from the fridge and rolled the cold can across his brow. The sodden summer heat hung in the air, and although Sharon had opened the windows as far as she could, in the treeless pasture where they lived, the sun beat down all day, and the air barely stirred. He thought of the house he'd just seen in Highland Park, so overgrown with brush that it barely saw the light of day. What a welcome thought.

"Not ominous. It just...needs work."

"Uh-oh." She eyed him warily. "I sense slanting floors and a ventilated roof. Green, I'm not moving into a place with kerosene lamps and an outhouse."

"Oh, I think there's electricity. Maybe a few other surprises—"

"Green!" she protested, obviously too hot for humour. She dove to rescue a glass bowl from her son's grasp. He began to shout, and barely missing a beat, she gave him a pot and wooden spoon. "God, Mary's having a field day with you!"

He laughed. "Speaking of surprises, someone who knows you came to my office today. Another reason I was late. A woman named Janice Tanner, a patient at Rideau Psychiatric."

Sharon looked blank, so he supplied another clue. "She's in an agoraphobic therapy group."

"Oh, that's Outpatients. But the name's familiar." Sharon

took a deep swig of cola and closed her eyes gratefully. "Janice Tanner. About forty? Tall, thin, nervous-looking? Short, greying hair and glasses?"

He shook his head and raised his voice over the banging spoon. "Tall and thin, yes, but she has red hair and no glasses."

"Then she's fixed herself up somewhat since I knew her. I think she was an inpatient on my ward a couple of years ago, admitted because she was too terrified to leave her apartment, and she was slowly starving to death."

"Could be her."

"I'd say she's come a long way if she made it all the way to your office on her own. Either that or she's desperate."

"A bit of both, I think. She was certainly persistent. Insisted one of the other phobic patients had met with some serious harm. Was she the type to overreact?"

"A phobic overreact? Unheard of." She sobered as she watched Tony, tiring of his spoon, run out into the hallway. "You put the gate up, eh? No, Janice was a shut-in, and she'd had very little contact with people for years. I remember nobody ever came to visit her in hospital. But she did have a good heart, and after she'd settled in, she took a couple of our more fragile schiz under her wing."

Not necessarily a good sign, Green thought, and voiced his misgivings. "Did she have a preference for fragile schiz? I mean, was she drawn to weirdos?"

"Not weird for weird's sake, but I think she felt more comfortable with people who needed her. Why? Who was the patient she's worried about? Maybe I know her."

"Him. Matt Fraser."

Sharon's eyebrows shot up. "A 'him'? My, Janice really has made progress. I don't know him, though."

"Who would know him at the hospital?"

"The therapist who runs that group, and I have no idea who that is. And his treating psychiatrist." She smiled slowly. "Mike, you didn't promise her you'd look into it."

"No, I didn't. You'd be proud of me, I didn't promise a thing. Well…maybe that I'd check with the officer on the missing persons file. But the case has a curious feel. I don't know what it is."

"The fabled Inspector Green intuition?"

"Something like that. Could you maybe, subtly, ask around about this guy? Find out if he's missed any appointments or left word about his plans?"

She paused with her coke can to her lips. "Subtly?"

"Okay, forget subtle. Find out who his therapist is. Find out what kind of guy this Matt Fraser is."

She raised one eyebrow slowly in silent rebuke that he would ask her to violate patient confidentiality. He raised his palms in a classic Yiddish shrug which said it was the furthest thing from his mind. Both of them dealt with confidential material all the time, and he knew no further words were necessary. She would make casual inquiries about Matt Fraser at the hospital, and if, in her judgment, anything suspicious or worrisome emerged, she would quietly pass it on to him.

In the meantime, because curiosity had always been one of his greatest failings as well as his greatest asset, he decided that when he got bored in the morning, he would pull the police file on Matt Fraser and see what he could learn.

*   *   *

The file on Fraser's old case proved to be voluminous, suggesting that although the man had only had one criminal charge, it had been a complicated one. It was all on microfiche

21

in the records department, and over the phone, the records clerk implied that Green shouldn't hold his breath waiting for her to print it out.

After he'd hung up, Green eyed the clutter on his desk and the list of unread emails stacked up in his electronic inbox. A rooming house fire in Vanier during the night had claimed at least one life and drawn a team of Ident officers and Major Crimes detectives out to the scene, including Brian Sullivan. The Staff Sergeant in Youth wanted a meeting to discuss the rise of swarmings in Ottawa's south end, and Superintendent Adam Jules had asked him to review the agenda for yet another meeting. The last thing Green needed was fifty pounds of microfiche print-outs dumped on his desk as well.

He drummed his fingers on his desk as he considered other approaches. Barbara Devine had been the lead investigator on the Fraser case. Plain Detective Devine back then, Inspector now. After her stint in sex crimes, she'd made the rounds through the departments on her way up the ladder and was now ensconced in an office one floor closer to the gods than his, pushing paper and keeping company with the senior brass. Backroom gossip held that she'd once been an idealistic, hard-hitting detective who'd soured on the nobility and purpose of what she was doing and turned her attentions instead to the cause of her own advancement. Although he'd never worked directly with her, she was a contemporary of Green's with a string of relationship disasters that eclipsed his own. Currently, having burned her way through three husbands, she'd set her sights on Superintendent Adam Jules, the austere and resolutely celibate chief of CID. The thought made Green's lips twitch irrepressibly.

Counting on the lure of an old case to draw her into his quest, he grabbed his notebook and headed up the stairs to her office. Devine owned an array of power suits from Holt Renfrew, and today she had packaged herself in dark red with fingernails and lips to match. The door to her spotless office was ajar, and he could see her typing furiously away at her computer. She scowled at him dubiously as he strode in. Probably afraid I'll want her to do some actual police work, he thought and cut off any incipient protest by dropping into a chair and tossing his notebook on her desk.

"Barbara, I need to pick your considerable brain. Remember Matthew Fraser?"

She sat back, her fingers still poised over the keyboard and her eyes slitting warily. "Certainly. One of the most frustrating and disappointing cases I've ever worked. Why do you ask?"

"His name's come up. Tell me about the case."

"What's he done? Offended again?"

"No, he's been reported missing."

"In that case, good riddance," she said, brushing non-existent dust from her desk and straightening a stack of reports. "I wouldn't waste too much energy on it."

He grinned and propped his feet on the edge of her pristine desk. "That's why I'm here. The file is going to be several truck loads, so I'm looking for an executive summary before I put any manpower on it."

She eyed his feet in silence for a moment, her red nails tapping the desktop, and he could almost see her weighing how much to cooperate. "You must remember the case, Mike," she said eventually. "Two of our officers quit the force after the trial. They had little children themselves, and they couldn't stomach working for a system that gives the villains all the breaks."

Finally the penny dropped. Matthew Fraser had been an elementary school teacher accused and ultimately acquitted of sexual abuse, and Green could still recall the bitter divisions the case had engendered not only within the school and community but within CID itself.

"Did you think he was guilty?" he asked.

Her eyes flashed and her mouth grew hard, but she restrained herself. "I'd never have brought the case forward if I'd doubted that. I was the one who took the girl's initial statement. I watched her face that first time in the station, I heard her crying and saying 'I just want him to stop.' She was very credible before the lawyers and the Children's Aid got into the act, and the whole courtroom circus froze her up."

"So she recanted on the witness stand?"

Devine shook her head vigorously. "If I had dropped all the cases where the abuse victims had second thoughts, I'd have had precious little work to do. But Rebecca Whelan didn't really recant. She just got confused, the defence chipped away at her recollections, and the judge was 'See no evil, hear no evil' Maloney, who wouldn't recognize sexual abuse if it was—" She pressed her lips together as if to prevent further indiscretions from escaping.

"Shoved up his ass?" Green said. "Was there any other evidence? Any other complainants?"

"You're not the only one on the force who knows how to build a case, Mike. We had plenty of circumstantial evidence. I had doctors and abuse experts who swore she had all the classic signs, I had other little girls who alleged touching or grooming types of activity, but it was either too vague or the parents wouldn't let them testify. So in the end, what it boiled down to was this six-year-old all alone in the courtroom, sitting on a telephone book so she could see over the witness box, with the judge staring down at her and the high-priced lawyer from the teacher's union hammering away at her every word. She crumbled."

Green made a face, inwardly grateful that he had resisted the pressure to do his turn in sex crimes. Adults killing each other were bad enough. "What was Matthew Fraser like?"

"He was one sick bastard," she replied, her discretion lost in the heat of her recollections. Her lips formed a harsh red slash of emotion across her carefully made up face. "One of those quiet, unreadable types. You know, the type who plots murder without ever changing his expression. He acted so concerned for the little girl, but he put her through six weeks of active trial while he paraded all his teacher friends across the stand one after another to say what a great guy he was. Of course, I hear they all dropped him like a hot potato afterwards. For the cameras it was union solidarity rah, rah, and all that, but out of the public view, that was another story."

"He apparently told a friend he was being followed recently. Any threats on his life after he was acquitted? I imagine there were people in the girl's family who would have liked to see him suffer."

"And half a dozen guys on the force eager to do the job for them," she countered. "But it's been ten years, Mike. That's not exactly heat of the moment."

Ten years is nothing in the life sentence of the victim's family, he thought. Or of the little girl herself, who would be almost seventeen by now. "Do you know what happened to the girl?"

Devine's face darkened abruptly, further marring her studied Holt Renfrew finish. "That man put her through hell. The doctor said the abuse had happened repeatedly, but the bastard pleaded not guilty, virtually accused the girl of lying, and then dragged the case through the system for over two years. Two years of motions and postponements on every technicality in the book, two years that little girl had to hang in limbo, with everybody whispering about her. She had to change schools and move to a new neighbourhood, so she lost all her old friends. I did my best, but..." She threw up her hands. "Damn, it still gets to me!"

Her passion and moral outrage surprised him—even attracted him—and she moved up a few notches in his esteem. "Yeah, you do this job long enough, and there are always a few that stick with you. But think of it this way, Barbara, if it still gets your blood boiling after ten years, how does the family feel?"

Her anger cleared as she weighed his question. "They hate him. That will always be there. But I think you should be looking for more recent victims. Believe me, men like Fraser don't stop once they get a taste."

He shrugged easily. "I'm just exploring ideas here, Barbara, not putting anyone on trial. What was the family like?"

She played with her left earring as she considered his question. "Her family was right in the thick of things, but they were basically good people. Mother, father, stepfather. Even her grandparents showed up for the verdict."

"Any worrisome signs?"

"Nothing you wouldn't expect. I mean, a lot of people despised the man. Even some of the other parents, who were afraid he might have abused their children too. Fraser had a classic pedophile profile, Mike. Soft-spoken, shy, liked to hang around with children, and he had this gentle manner that hooked them right in. Children couldn't see the manipulation behind his overtures, so I couldn't get anything more solid than a twisted feeling in my gut. Who knows, maybe if I had, the guy would have been put away where he belongs, instead of out roaming the streets, where he's probably raped three dozen other little girls in the time since."

That unsettling thought stayed with Green after he returned to his office. It lent a greater urgency to the mysterious disappearance than did a ten-year-old settling of accounts. Perhaps there was a more recent score to settle, or a more recent danger to flee. Shortly after eleven, telling himself he'd earned a decent lunch break after weeks of car seat dining, he headed out.

For a man who lived in fear, Matt Fraser had chosen to reside in an unsavoury part of town. Built upon the vacant lumber yards of J.R. Booth's old empire, Carlington had once been a modest, house-proud working-class neighbourhood first settled by World War II vets returning to civilian life. It was now a hodge-podge of post-war shanties, welfare townhouses and massive high-rises, a neighbourhood where new refugee families were sandwiched in with drug dealers, blue collar retirees and the working poor. Petty crime flourished, and bands of youth prowled the streets with restless contempt. Green suspected that poverty, not preference, had dictated Fraser's choice.

Fraser's apartment was on the third floor of a squat brick low-rise, surrounded by decrepit parking lots. Weeds sprouted through the broken asphalt, and against one wall were the rusted shells of two cars. The apartment's security was a paranoid's nightmare—a row of buzzers just inside the front door, which had been propped open with a stick to encourage some flow of muggy air. Inside, the odour of onions mingled with a stench of rot in the fetid air. After much knocking, Green roused the building super from his midday siesta in his basement apartment. The TV was blaring, and the man opened the door wearing nothing but a scowl and rumpled boxers hitched high over his sagging gut. But one flash of

Green's badge sent him shuffling back inside for a pair of overalls and a set of keys to Matt Fraser's apartment.

"Nice guy," the super observed two minutes later as he laboured up the narrow staircase. "Wish all the tenants were as good as him."

Green peered at him through the gloom. New light bulbs were evidently not part of the landlord's budget. "What do you mean?"

"No noise, no late-night visitors, fixes everything hisself. Won't even let me in to do the repairs. Even the dog's quiet. Big bugger, and quite a few people are scared of it, but it wouldn't hurt a flea."

"Does he get many visitors?"

"None that I seen. Sticks to hisself. Why, what's he done?"

"He's missing. When did you last see him?"

The man grunted at each step with the effort of lifting his bulk. "Not in a few days. But he's usually out really early walking his dog, then again late at night. You think something's happened to him?"

"I've no idea. Did you notice anything or anyone unusual—say, in the last six days?"

"Unusual? Well, yesterday, yeah—" The super broke off as he reached the third floor, and he groped for the wall, chest heaving. "Fuck, it stinks up here. What the hell? Is he dead?"

"No, I believe the apartment's empty."

The super tried the door with obvious trepidation, and it swung open, unlocked. Both men stepped back as the stench hit them.

"Fuck!" The super hustled over, snapped up the blind and tried to open the tiny window, which was crisscrossed with spider webs. "Fuck! He's nailed it shut. Must drive him crazy in this heat." He turned, and his pig-like eyes rounded in shock as he noticed the mess for the first time. Books and newspapers were scattered everywhere, flung haphazardly over the floor as if by a rampage. "Fuck! Who is this guy?"

Green slipped on nitrile gloves and moved rapidly through the rooms checking for intruders and obvious signs of trouble. Twenty years of police work had inured him to most human oddities, but even he found the crammed bookshelves unnerving. Any possibility that Fraser had simply been a nice, normal guy wrongly accused of child abuse vanished from his thoughts. Barbara Devine was right. This was one sick bastard. Not the shy, vulnerable man Janice thought she was drawing out of his shell, but a man whose whole life had but a single focus—the subject of the hundreds of books and newspapers which were catalogued along every wall.

"I'm going back downstairs for a hammer to get those nails out," the super muttered, tripping over himself in his haste to get out the door. Left alone, Green continued his search. All the windows were nailed shut, but in the bedroom he found a small air conditioner, which he turned on gratefully. It would take several hours to cool the place adequately, but at least it might soon be tolerable.

In the kitchen, he noted that Janice hadn't even attempted to clean up but had left a note for Fraser on the kitchen table to explain that Modo was safe with her. Apart from the half-eaten food and open newspaper on the kitchen table, Matt Fraser kept a fastidiously tidy kitchen. His fridge gleamed white inside and out, full of food in neatly labelled rows of Tupperware containers. Sliced carrots, diced peppers, chopped lettuce, boiled rice and single-serving portions of left-overs. A health nut too, to top it off. Not a processed cheese slice or frozen dinner in sight. The cupboards were the same. No empty potato chip bags or lidless ketchup bottles, no duplicate boxes of Cheerios to give Green a sense of kinship. The man was seeming less human by the moment.

Yet he clearly had left the scene without bothering to clean up. Without even bothering to finish his food. This suggested two things. First, something very urgent and compelling had taken him away, and secondly, whatever it was, it had occurred at a meal time.

Had he gone on his own, or had someone forced him?

Green's eyes fell on the dog dishes on the kitchen floor. A big bugger, the super had said, surely capable of making any intruder think twice about breaking in, and capable of making enough racket to rouse the dead if he did.

When the super came huffing back into the room with his toolbox under his arm, Green turned to him. "Have you heard the dog barking any time in the past few days?"

The super wheezed as he bent over to paw through his toolbox. He seemed to be thinking, and Green gave him time. Finally the man shook his head.

"But I'm way down in the basement. I don't hear much that goes on up here."

Especially with your television on full blast, Green added silently. "How long has Mr. Fraser lived here?"

The man found a hammer and straightened up, his face dangerously red from the exertion. Sweat poured down his temples and disappeared into the folds of his chins. He squinted as if that would help him muster his thoughts.

"Three, four years?"

"What does he do for a living?"

On this the super was no help. He knew nothing of the man's private life beyond that he rarely went out except to shop or walk the dog, and he had no visitors.

"None at all?"

The super started to shake his head, then paused, sweat flying. "Recently, yeah. There was a lady come yesterday—I seen her hanging around before. Outside, like. And I think someone else came last week. I didn't see much, just heard them go up to the third floor, and they didn't go to Crystal's place. Crystal probably seen them, though."

"Crystal?"

The super fidgeted, his pig-eyes squinting almost shut. "The woman next door. She's the only other tenant on the third floor."

Green made a note to get to her later. Since she lived next door, she might have some useful information about Fraser's habits or recent visitors.

The super swept away the cobwebs and pried all the windows open, billowing humid air into the already stifling room. Looking eager to get away, he asked Green if he were still needed. When Green declined, the super handed over the key with relief.

"Lock up when you're done," he tossed over his shoulder as he hustled out the door.

Green stood in the living room, trying to soak up Fraser's presence. From what he could see, the man lived an existence entirely without comforts. No television, no CD player, not even a comfortable arm chair. Just a computer, a desk with utilitarian chair, and a hard vinyl couch whose main purpose seemed to be for spreading out papers. There were endless shelves of articles and text books on law and psychology, but not an action thriller or hobby book among the lot. Nothing that might engender joy.

As if the man were doing penance. Perhaps he was.

Once Green's eyes grew accustomed to the bizarre character of the room, he realized the incongruity between the various rooms. The kitchen and the bedroom, apart from the rotting food and the dog mess, seemed meticulously ordered, indicating that the man kept a neat house. Even the organization and labelling of each shelf attested to a fastidious mind. Yet in the living room everything had been turned upside down; books and papers had been pulled out and impatiently cast aside.

Janice Tanner had made much of the rotting food and the abandoned dog, but had not mentioned a ransacked living room. Surely this would not have escaped her notice. Could someone have been here since yesterday? Fraser? In Green's house, it was not uncommon for him to turn the place upside down for something he'd misplaced, but Fraser seemed as if he'd know where every slip of paper was. Had someone else been here? Whoever they were, whatever they were looking for, they'd been in a hell of a hurry. Or a hell of a temper.

Intrigued, Green examined the books that lay on the floor. The Child and Family Services Act, which detailed the law governing child abuse, as well as its predecessor. There was a heavy tome called *Child Witnesses*, and another with the lurid title of *Breaking the Silence*. The latter looked well thumbed, with pages dog-eared and passages underlined. Green began to read.

"Fuck! What stinks!" The querulous shriek came from the hallway, and Green glanced up just as a young woman stumbled into Fraser's doorway, shielding her eyes from the daylight and clutching a man's extra large cotton shirt over her scrawny frame. She recoiled slightly at the sight of Green, and glanced down as if to ensure the shirt covered her crotch.

"What the fuck is that stink?" she repeated.

Green took a guess. "Crystal?"

Her eyes slitted warily. "Who the fuck are you?"

Extensive vocabulary, Green thought. Matches the super's.

He introduced himself and steeled himself for hostility. She looked like the type whose encounters with police might have been less than amicable. When the hostility came, however, it was not directed at him.

"What's he done? What's the pervert done?"

"Disappeared," Green replied. "When did you last see him?"

"He gives me the creeps. Always sneaking around with that freaky dog of his, locking himself in with six locks like he's got the crown jewels in there. Won't even say hi, but I know who he is anyway and don't want him anywheres near my daughter, so I stay away from him."

Green shifted gears quickly. "Has he ever acted suspiciously around your daughter?"

Crystal held her hand under her nose with a grimace. "What the fuck stinks? I thought I smelled something weird, but I figured it was just lazy Laslo not bothering to throw out the garbage. Smells like shit."

With a sigh, Green decided he might never get a straight answer to his questions. Her mind was as jumpy as a spooked cat, and she looked as if she were in dire need of her next dose. He steered her back into the hall and shut the door on the offending odours.

"When did you last see Mr. Fraser?"

She chewed at her fingernails. "What day is it? Monday?"

"Tuesday."

"Tuesday." She frowned, as if with the effort of rallying her wits. "I don't think I seen him since last week. Wednesday, maybe? He was going out, all dressed up."

"You mean—"

"For the office. Grey suit, tie, briefcase."

"He didn't usually dress that way?"

She snorted. "He wore the baggiest, ugliest pants and sweatshirts you could find. Even the Sally Ann has nicer clothes. He couldn't look dumber if he tried! I mean, he wouldn't be a bad-looking guy. He's got wide shoulders and a nice tight—" she paused and twisted her thin lips into a smirk, "butt on him, still got all his hair, even if he wears it like a dork. Way long in the back."

"What time did you see him leave in the suit?"

"I don't know. Lunchtime? Yeah, "Young and Restless" was on."

"Did he seem in a hurry? Did he act strange in any way?"

"Yeah, he was walking fast. Usually he kind of slinks along, never looks at you, you know? This time it was like he knew where he was going. Plus he didn't have that ugly dog with him."

"Did you see him return?"

She shook her head. "But he did. I heard him later. Six locks make a lot of noise, and that time he wasn't quiet about it."

"What do you mean?"

"I mean he slammed the door and banged all the locks real quick."

"What time was this?"

"I don't know," she whined, wiping her nose. "All these fucking questions. Six, maybe? "Much MegaHits" was on, so what time was that?"

Unfortunately, the hectic pace of both Sharon's and his lives left little room for television, but the music channel's broadcast schedule would be easy enough to check, and if the show aired at six, the timing was interesting indeed. Six o'clock was close to dinner time. "Did you see or hear anyone else come just before or after him?"

"Well, I don't spy on him, you know. My TV was on, and my daughter was talking to me."

"Did you hear the dog bark?"

Her pinched face cleared. "Fuck, yeah. A few minutes after the guy got home. Just about shook the walls down. Then it didn't shut up for days!"

And you didn't bother to check why? Green thought but knew better than to ask. In Crystal's world, it didn't pay to be too curious. He held her gaze in an effort to keep her focussed. "Did you see anyone else hanging around outside or in the hallway?"

She was edging back toward her own door, which she'd left open. "Look, that's all I know. I mind my own business, take care of my daughter, and I figure what other people do—"

"Are you talking about Matt Fraser or someone else you saw?"

She scowled and stepped backwards through her doorway. "I didn't see anyone. Not then."

He thought of the time span between Janice's visit and his own, during which someone had apparently ransacked the place. "Some other time? Last night or this morning maybe?"

"I was half asleep. I can't swear to anything."

He pressed his advantage. "But you did see someone. A glimpse at least."

"A glimpse is no good in court, I know, and I don't need the aggravation. I gotta go. That's all I can say. Maybe someone else saw more." She swung her door shut and left him standing on her doorstep, staring at the peeling paint. But there was no sound of footsteps from within, and he sensed that she was watching him through the peephole. Merely curious, or something more?

He jotted down the interview, making a note to catch her again when she was more mellow. Crystal's "glimpse" might be the only solid lead he found. When he returned to Matt

Fraser's apartment, it smelled none the sweeter for the fifteen minutes of fresh air. Now he began to snoop in earnest. In the bedroom he found a sparsely filled closet of bulky, styleless clothes, among them a navy suit and a handful of skinny polyester neckties, but no grey suit. The dresser contained rows of jockey shorts and neatly rolled black socks, as well as stacks of the shapeless sweatshirts and T-shirts Crystal had described. On his bedside table was an empty glass and a tape recorder but no sign of bedtime reading.

With his pen tip, Green pressed the play button and heard the soothing strains of harp music and a hypnotic voice inviting the listener to close their eyes. Recognizing it as a relaxation tape not unlike the one Sharon sometimes used after a hard day, he turned it off.

In the bathroom, the man's compulsive neatness astounded him. One toothbrush, not the half dozen elderly ones sprouting from the glass that he and Sharon shared in the bathroom. One tube of toothpaste rolled from the bottom, folded towels and a shelf of the latest herbal remedies like ginseng and Vitamin K, plus a half full prescription bottle labelled Zoloft. Green tipped one of the pills into a small evidence bag from his pocket and jotted down the prescribing doctor's name.

In the kitchen, the fridge door was pristinely clear, and the wall calendar was blank except for weekly appointments on Tuesdays. Presumably that was his therapy group. But in a drawer, Green finally found something out of place. Or at least oddly placed. He was searching the drawers hoping to find the man's stash of personal papers—letters, bills, bank statements or even a wallet or day book. He found linens, cooking utensils, tools and then unexpectedly, a small black book, curled and grimy with age. It was peeking out from under the tray in the cutlery drawer as if it had been hidden deliberately. Green pulled it out and flipped through its pages, which were filled with names and addresses in a small, neat hand. He slipped it into another evidence bag, put it in his pocket and continued his search.

The man had to have some personal papers. There was no sign of a filing cabinet anywhere, but surely a man as paranoid as Janice described would hoard everything and probably squirrel it away in some secret hiding place. To search the whole living room would be a mammoth task. Papers could be hidden in plain sight, mixed among the newspapers, or hidden behind some volumes in a dusty, unlit corner. It would take a search team hours to comb this place, and that for a case that was not even his. In fact, not really a case at all.

He flicked on the computer and waited as it hummed and clicked slowly to life. Not exactly state of the art, Green observed, but then the man had little to spare for extravagance. Windows eventually appeared on the screen with a prompt for a password. Green groaned. He should have known that a privacy fanatic like Fraser would use that feature. On a hunch he tried Modo. Invalid. Quasimodo. Also invalid. He pondered his chances of plucking the right name or code from the air with almost no knowledge of the man's life or interests. He made one last try—Hugo—and to his astonishment the screen lit up with icons. Pulling up a chair, he hunched forward and began to search. It was a short search. Other than his internet browser, Fraser had no software beyond an old-fashioned word processing program and a database. The application files were in place, but there was not a single data file in either program.

Curious to see who the man communicated with, Green connected to the internet and pulled up his email screen. Not a single email in his inbox. Same story with his "sent" box and his "trash". Green was astounded. What mere mortal had a completely empty email account? Certainly no one in his acquaintance. Either this man stored all his files in a secret place, or someone who knew computers had wiped his entire system clean.

Green clicked through subdirectories in search of hidden files, uncovering mostly folders with recognizable program names. Under "web", however, one folder name stood out from the rest. Mistwalker. Eagerly he clicked on it. Wiped clean. Green sat back in puzzlement. Mistwalker was a peculiar word. Even mysterious, and certainly whimsical for a man as obsessive and analytical as Fraser. But tantalizing as the puzzle was, Green was stymied, for he'd exhausted all his admittedly primitive computer skills. This was a job for the younger guys on the force.

Yet his snooping had paid off some dividends. He now had the little black address book and, with it, access to the people in Fraser's life. On his way out, Green paused at the door to examine the locks. Crystal had exaggerated; there were only five. Plus a peephole. Each was sufficient to keep out an unwelcome caller, and two of them could only be locked and unlocked from the inside. There were no scratches or chips to suggest that any of them had been forced. If Matt Fraser had had a caller that night, after he'd arrived home and barricaded himself in, then he had checked through the peephole and opened the door of his own free will.

Pretty reckless stuff for a paranoid agoraphobic who rarely left his apartment except to walk his dog.

Three

"Yessir!" Sergeant Lonsdale sat ramrod straight and spread his hand to encompass both the paltry stack of paper on his desk and the computer humming in the corner. "Any case you want to take a look at, you're more than welcome, sir."

He was a squeaky clean man with slick hair and a glossy smile, but beneath the joviality, his tone was tinged with anxiety. Although he might be happy to have his docket lightened by one file, Green knew he was nervous about such close scrutiny of his turf. Justifiably. Green suspected the rookie sergeant was just passing through Missing Persons on his way towards a comfortable desk in the upper echelons, so keeping his image buffed and his butt covered ranked at least equal to the cause of justice. Green's unsolicited involvement in a case often presented a risk to both image and butt.

Ignoring the man's discomfiture, Green scanned the woefully short file containing nothing but Janice Tanner's report and the results of Lonsdale's interview with the building super, which he'd probably conducted by phone without even looking up from the business section of the *Globe*.

"Did you contact any relatives?" Green asked.

"Not yet, sir. No one else has reported him missing, and the man was of age with no suggestion of ill health. He probably just wanted to drop out of sight. Besides, the complainant was a little..." Lonsdale started to twirl his finger but Green's frown stopped him short.

"Do you know who he is?" Green asked.

Lonsdale's hand strayed to his tie, perhaps hoping that a perfectly centred knot would make up for the slight indiscretion Green had caught. "Yessir, I ran his name. It seemed all the more reason to drop out of sight, in my opinion. People like that don't change their ways, if you know what I mean. Maybe he was afraid he was about to get caught again."

Green considered the idea. It was certainly one explanation for Fraser's hurried arrival home that afternoon, and for the rapid locking of his door; he'd been one step ahead of some irate father's boot. It did not, however, explain Modo's being left to die.

"Or maybe," Green countered, "he has been caught again, by someone interested in a more direct form of justice." He jotted down the case number and turned toward the door. "I'll just make a couple of calls."

Lonsdale made a grasping gesture, as if to retrieve the file for a second look, but Green was already out the door, pondering his next step. Which was to track down an actual next of kin, so that he had more tangible grounds on which to pursue the case. Lonsdale's file listed the next of kin as unknown, and when Green thumbed through Fraser's old address book back in his own office, he found no listing for a Fraser or a Mom or Dad. There were, however, some possibilities. Almost all entries were carefully recorded by first and last name, telephone number and address, including postal code. But one was simply a name. Rose. Plus an address in the far eastern suburb of Orleans.

Several minutes of searching through computer databases yielded a last name to go with Rose—Artlee, not Fraser as he had hoped—and an age. Forty-four. An older sister perhaps, whose name had changed through marriage? On a chance, he dialled the number, and when the cheerful woman who answered the phone confirmed she was Mrs. Rose Artlee, he introduced himself and blithely asked if she were Matt Fraser's next of kin.

Complete silence.

"Hello?" he prompted.

"What's happened?" she asked in a voice so low it was barely audible. All trace of cheer was gone.

"Are you a relation?"

"Why do you want to know?"

It was a strange game of cat and mouse, but he supposed she'd earned the right to be suspicious. No doubt the press had been merciless during the trial.

"He's been reported missing by a friend, Mrs. Artlee. I'm following up to see whether his family knows of his whereabouts."

"Oh, no!" she breathed, not a denial of his question but an exclamation of dismay, as if something she'd long feared had come to pass.

"Do you know something?"

"No," she replied as if hastily collecting her wits. "I haven't seen him in years."

"Mrs. Artlee," he said, "perhaps I should drop around for a quick chat."

"I told you I don't know anything!"

"But you sound worried."

"Because you said he's disappeared. Of course I'm worried. If you find him, tell me—" She hesitated. "No, I'll call back in a few days."

He sensed she was about to hang up. "Just a quick chat. I'll be there in twenty minutes."

"No! I—I mean I'm on my way out. I'll meet you…" He could feel her haste through the wires. "At the Tim Hortons on Montreal Road, just off the Queensway."

She'd hung up before he could get in a word, and he glanced at his watch in dismay. This was not a high priority case. In fact, it was hardly a case at all, and meanwhile, several active cases were bubbling in the major crimes squad, demanding his attention. Not the least of which was Brian Sullivan, who'd been trying to contact him since before noon about his rooming house death in Vanier.

I'll drop by the Vanier scene on my way back from Tim Hortons, Green promised himself as he buckled on his radio and headed out his door. Tim Hortons doughnut shops were proliferating across the city like mushrooms, and Green wasn't sure which one Rose referred to, but luckily it was easy to spot amid the strip mall scenery just north of the Queensway. Inside, a handful of workers lingered over lunch, but Green was able to pick out Rose without difficulty. Only one woman was sitting alone in a booth, with her back against the wall and her eyes glued to the door, a heavy-set woman with a doughy face and short, spiked hair which seemed to be her only attempt at fashion. Round glasses accentuated her moon face, and behind them her eyes were pale and wary. As a peace offering, he picked up two ice cappuccinos before approaching the table. She launched into a pre-emptive strike before he could even introduce himself.

"I don't know what I can do for you. I haven't seen Matt in years."

"Why?"

She looked taken aback. "Why? Because of what he did. I have two daughters, and even if I didn't, I—"

"But he was acquitted."

"Because it was the word of a six-year-old against him and a whole slew of his teacher friends."

"So you're saying he was guilty?"

Her jaw jutted out, and the wattle beneath her chin quivered. "Is that so wrong of me? He may have been my brother, but I don't shut my eyes to right and wrong."

"Do you think a whole slew of his teacher friends would? Just because he was a colleague?"

"Teachers stick together. But the proof was, afterwards, they wouldn't give him the time of day."

"But you're saying they all lied to protect one of their own. And left a six-year-old to twist in the wind."

She mixed her drink with short jabs of her straw. "I sound bitter, don't I? Well, I have a right to be. Ten years ago, my brother dragged our family through the mud. Vandals broke our windows so many times we had to move, my little girls got picked on in school, I got let go at the day care where I worked, because—hey, I must have had the same screwed up childhood, right? By the end, my husband couldn't stand the stress and took off to Calgary. He came back, but not before I'd been through three years of hell on welfare. My brother molested little girls, but we're the ones who paid the price. So yeah—" she barked out a short laugh, "I guess I'm bitter."

"You've more than earned the right," he replied. "And I'm not reproaching you for your feelings about your brother, believe me. But when I called, you said 'oh no' as if you were worried about him."

His ploy had the desired effect, and some of the fight died from her eyes. She rummaged in her purse and extracted a package of DuMaurier cigarettes. Ignoring the "no smoking" signs plastered around the walls, she lit up and sucked a grateful breath into her lungs.

"My brother and I were never what you'd call close. I'm eight years older than him, our dad left us when I was twelve, and we had to leave the farm and move to the city so our mother could work. I lost all my friends and got stuck in a crappy little apartment taking care of Matt. He was delicate as a kid. Always had colds or asthma. He cried if you yelled at him, but the kid had brains, and he was really good at making me take the blame for whatever went wrong. Mom never took the time to listen to my side. I was trouble, I admit it. I mean, look at me. I was a big, fat, ugly kid with attitude, and I'm still a big fat, ugly broad. Attitude? In spades. I've never been in trouble with the law, I don't mean that. But I never caught on to the finer points of how to win friends and influence people. Matt did. But that was his downfall too. He never toughened up. He'd rely on his helpless act, and people would rescue him left, right and centre."

She blew out a lungful of smoke before resuming. "That's why this trial thing killed him. Sure, he got all his colleagues to rally around, and he played his poor-little-me-wouldn't-hurt-a-fly routine, and he got off. But then it all came apart. Suddenly he was alone. I'd had enough, and anyways if I'd tried to help him, my husband would have killed me. His teacher friends dropped him, the school board fired him, and everywhere he went, people pointed fingers. Hell, his story had been plastered over the news for months, and nobody believed for an instant that he was innocent. If this had been farm country and not Ottawa, he'd have been strung up by the balls behind a barn somewhere within days of the verdict."

She stopped as if suddenly realizing she'd lost her place, and her eye caught the frown of an employee behind the counter. Muttering, she busied herself mashing out her cigarette on the floor. Green waited patiently. He knew what he'd heard when he'd told her Fraser was missing, and no amount of blustery denial on her part would convince him this woman didn't love her brother. And sure enough…

"Well, you know," she resumed, and her eyes didn't meet his, "old habits die hard. I mean, I've been taking care of Matt since he was four, and I knew him inside out. I wanted nothing to do with him because what he did makes me physically sick, but I did wonder how the hell he was going to carry on when everyone dropped him. I mean, it was justice in its own funny way, right? I did figure he deserved it, but I got to wondering. I never contacted him, I never answered his calls, and pretty quick he got the message and stopped."

"Where was your mother during all this?"

"Oh, Mom was in Florida with her new man, pretending she was twenty years younger than she was, and certainly never admitting she had any son at all, let alone a fully grown pervert."

"Are you the only other family he has?"

She nodded, then stopped herself. "Well, Dad showed up for the trial. That was a treat. I hadn't seen him in over twenty years, and Matt didn't know him from Adam. 'Just wanted to show my support, son', and all that crap. I sent him packing." She chopped at her drink with a vigour that shook the table. "All slick and polished like that, he'd do more harm than good to Matt's case, and Matt just about came apart at the seams when he met him."

He propped his chin in his hand and smiled at her slightly. "So you really did look out for him, didn't you. It's second nature. And privately, even now, you still worry."

"Well… I wonder. I mean, ten years is a long time, and I got to wondering if he'd gotten himself together. After the trial, he tried to go away and make a new start, but the word always seemed to spread, and anyways he was no good at starting new. Matt was a kid who liked the same thing for dinner every night, and if you changed the brand of frozen orange juice, he'd notice." She paused as if caught in the memory. "Anyways, I heard he came back here and found himself an apartment." Her jaw jutted out again. "But I don't know what he was doing with himself, and I don't care. I almost forgot about him."

"But?" he prompted, not believing her for a second. She said nothing but chewed her lip as if wrestling with how much to reveal herself. He gave her a gentle push. "Something reminded you?"

Her eyes grew shuttered. "He did. He phoned last week."

"What day was that?"

"Wednesday."

Green's pulse jumped, but he was careful to keep his tone neutral. "What did he want?"

"I don't know. I refused to talk to him." She paused, her fingers gripping the cappuccino cup so hard it dented. "Look, he took me by surprise, okay? I hung up on him. I was thinking of calling him back."

"And now you're worried that perhaps he was in trouble?"

"Well, even Matt had his pride, you know? We hadn't talked in eight years, so for him to pick up the phone, it had to be something important."

"You think he needed your help?"

She frowned at him. "I don't know. How could I know what the hell was on his mind? He sounded all earnest and desperate, like in the old days when he needed me to bail him out. He said, 'Rose, I have something to tell you', and I hung up."

"He had something to tell you. Like, news?"

"I thought it was a confession. That's why I hung up. All those years, he never once admitted he did it. Even just between us, when the truth wouldn't have hurt him. But I didn't want to hear it now, just 'cause it suited him. Fuck, it was over eight years ago, I'd put it all in the past, and no way was I letting him drag it all out again."

"But now you're worried perhaps it was something else entirely?"

She didn't reply. Around them, the doughnut shop was empty and the staff was cleaning equipment. A Celine Dion ballad wafted over the air waves, crooning about love. Wrapped within herself, she seemed oblivious. She'd never been a pretty woman, but he saw there was a maternal strength to her when she wasn't trying to bluster. Worry pinched her brows and quivered at the corners of her mouth. Again she seemed to be debating the wisdom of revealing her softer self. Finally, she sighed. "No, I thought maybe the guilt had been eating at him for ten years, until he'd finally gathered up the courage to tell me. So when I hung up on him, maybe it was the last straw. You see, I've always thought that some day, when he finally faced what he was, my brother was going to kill himself."

*   *   *

Green was driving down the Queensway, halfway to Rideau Psychiatric Hospital, when he remembered Brian Sullivan's rooming house death in Vanier. He cursed. Sullivan had wanted him to look at the scene before the body was removed and use his fabled intuition to see if he could detect anything amiss. The staff sergeant had already dismissed the case in his own mind and urged his subordinate to do the same. Death by misadventure. Specifically, setting your bed and yourself on fire by smoking while intoxicated—a tawdry but common enough end to a vagrant's life. But obviously Sullivan was not so sure.

Brian Sullivan and he had been rookies on patrol together over twenty years ago and had remained friends ever since, despite their differences in temperament and rank. Where Green was impulsive and fanciful, Sullivan was practical and meticulous. Green made wild intuitive leaps, while Sullivan steadfastly filled in the gaps. In the past, before the changing face of police work and Green's promotion to the senior ranks had drawn him further and further from the trenches he loved, the two had made a perfect investigative team. Now, Sullivan and his colleagues from Major Crimes conducted all the routine investigations without need of Green's input, while he sat on planning committees and chafed with frustration. Sometimes he bulldozed his way onto a case out of sheer boredom, or the fear that no one else on the force knew what they were doing. Occasionally, Sullivan took pity on him.

Perhaps Sullivan was simply taking pity this time, but he had sounded as if he really did want Green's opinion, and a request from Sullivan was not to be taken lightly. Green glanced at his watch. It was almost two-thirty, which meant that after this detour he wouldn't reach Rideau Psychiatric until after four. That was cutting things close, but still within the realm of possibility. Surely most of the doctors and therapists on the day shift would still be at work at four.

He took the next exit ramp off the Queensway and headed back east, deftly skirting around road construction and through side streets on his way deep into the city's shabby east end. Historically, Vanier was the home of Ottawa's francophone working class community, with roots back in the lumbering days, and it had retained a strong French Catholic flavour. Like much of the inner city, however, it had become an uneasy mix of indigenous French, transients down on their luck, aboriginals from up north, and immigrant families from all over the Third World. Proud shanties stood side by side with cheap apartments and rooming houses which saw a constant turnover of tenants with uncertain pasts and even more uncertain futures.

On a dingy side street off Montreal Road, Green spotted Sullivan's unmarked blue Taurus parked outside a structure that ought never to have passed its building inspection. The ancient, three-storey rooming house squatted in a patch of sodden weeds, its mottled grey bricks steaming in the mid-afternoon heat. The only evidence of its recent fire was some blackening around the second storey window and a thorough soaking from the fire hose. In a line behind Sullivan's car were the red fire marshall's vehicle, the Forensic Identification van, the black coroner's van, and another police-issue Taurus which Green suspected belonged to the arson squad. Sullivan has really called out all the troops, he thought as he pushed through the crowd of curious locals, logged in with the uniform on guard, slipped paper shoes on his feet and ducked under the police tape.

The reek of burnt chemicals and charred flesh assailed him even before he stepped over the threshold, and involuntarily he covered his nose. In the street, the afternoon heat had been oppressive, but inside it was a sauna. Within seconds, he was damp with sweat. He could hear voices and footsteps milling throughout the building, but he followed the boom of a familiar Scottish brogue up the stairs and into the front room on the second floor. The room was bare except for a partially burned crate under the window and a mattress on the floor whose charred springs poked through the residue of blackened cloth. Three men were bent over the mattress, conferring in low tones and affording Green only a brief glimpse of burnt sneakers hanging off the edge of the bed.

Sullivan was a big man, and his shoulders seemed to fill the tiny room. He'd left his suit jacket in the car, and his white shirt was drenched with sweat. Above the collar, his neck and face were an unnatural crimson that Green hoped was only from the heat. Drawing in a cautious breath, Green stepped through the door. At the sound, Sullivan swung around and a smile of relief lit his florid face.

"Mike, about time! Dr. MacPhail was about to give up on you and take the body away."

The tall, rangy Scot laughed and clapped Green on the shoulder with his gloved hand. "Worse luck, lad! I'm still here, trying to get some ideas from what's left of the poor bugger."

The Ident Unit had turned a strong spotlight on the bed, and Green recognized one of their senior officers bent over his camera, photographing every section of the body. The bright light spared nothing. Curled fetus-like on the bed was the remains of something human of indeterminate age, sex or even colour. Most of the body was charred beyond all recognition, and on the upper body not a scrap of skin nor a single hair was left intact. The rank stench of burnt meat was choking.

Black spots laced Green's sight, and he forced shallow breaths to fight down the bile in his throat. Dead bodies had never been his forte, but he was determined not to give the pathologist further fuel to mock him. MacPhail had spent the last twenty-two years awash in corpses and whiskey, and his sense of humour was decidedly off-kilter. Green forced his attention to practical details.

"Have you got an ID?"

Sullivan shook his head. "Still working on it. It's an adult male, MacPhail's guess is medium height and weight, but he'll know more after the autopsy. As usual, nobody's talking in the building here, at least not to the cops. This is a rent-by-the-week room, cash in advance, no questions asked. Nobody knew who he was, and he didn't talk to anybody. He just signed in last week under the name Jake, but that's all we've got to go by. We'll be checking missing persons reports and canvassing the street, but it will probably come down to dental records or DNA once we get some possibles. Not much left of the fingers."

Green heard the weary resignation in Sullivan's voice, and he sympathized. This was a pointless and unlamented end to what had probably been an aimless life. They'd both seen them countless times before, life's losers who drifted from one dive to another and from one high to another, until fate and their own stupidity stumbled upon each other, leaving the police force with the job of mopping up. Perhaps, even after all their hard work, they would never identify this one, and worse still, perhaps no one would even care.

Yet Sullivan had clearly not called him here to offer his sympathies. Green turned away from the body briskly. "Let's go outside, and you can fill me in."

To his dismay, however, Sullivan shook his head. "I want you to look at this body carefully and tell me what you think."

Green sighed. The request was vague, but he knew it was not trivial. Sullivan thought the body was telling them something, and he wanted to know if Green saw it too. Green forced himself to turn back to survey the scene. Even through the water and soot that covered everything, Green could see that the room was almost bare. On the floor lay a few blackened objects, one of them recognizable as a glass bottle. The remains of the bed sat in the corner, burned away to bare springs. On it, the body was curled on its back, grotesque but almost peaceful in repose. The skin and clothes were burnt away, leaving nothing but a blackened shape. Smoke and flame damage was extensive around the body, but quite limited in the rest of the room.

Green was not an expert in fires, but he sensed what was bothering Sullivan. Something seemed unnatural. He'd seen bodies burned to death before, and usually they were found huddled on the floor by the door, making a last desperate effort to escape. Even drunks who passed out in bed and lit the mattress on fire usually woke enough to try to get to the door. Green pointed this out dubiously, but Sullivan was ready for him.

"We do see it sometimes, Mike. The guy was smoking in bed, fell asleep, and the cigarette dropped on the mattress right beside him. Smolders a while before it catches, and it's the smoke that kills them before they wake up."

"That's just it. It looks like this burned hard, suggesting maybe an accelerant helped it along. Otherwise the mattress would probably have smoked a lot more."

Sullivan nodded. "The fire investigators and Arson are looking at it." He pointed to the empty bottle which an Ident officer was just slipping into an evidence bag. "The label's burned off, but it might have been some cheap brew."

"Alcohol doesn't burn hot enough for this."

"No, but maybe something homemade, or even something more flammable. If the guy was lying down and tried to drink from the bottle, he'd spill some on himself and the mattress. The fire investigators have taken their samples, and we'll have to wait for their findings."

"Then what started it?"

"Most likely a cigarette. He could have dropped the cigarette in the booze, and it went up so fast he had no time to react. It's a theory, anyway. But..." Sullivan's rugged, square face creased with dissatisfaction. "What do you think, Mike?"

Green's eyes roamed the room, studying the layout and the position of the body on the bed. MacPhail had begun cautiously bagging what was left of the hands, and his impatience was showing. "It's possible, I suppose," Green replied. "But it looks set up to cause maximum damage to the body. Damn convenient."

Sullivan nodded. "Convenient how?"

"Because it makes it hard to identify him. Plus—I'm trying to imagine how a guy, lying in bed, spills booze, sets himself on fire, and then lies back to enjoy the blaze. The pain should have driven anyone up out of the bed in two seconds flat."

MacPhail straightened up and nodded to his assistant. "Well, I'm taking him away, lads, before he decomposes in this heat. Michael, we'll be checking him upside down and sideways to determine what substances he had in his system, and whether they were sufficient to render him unconscious entirely. In the meantime we'll wait for the fire investigators to complete their investigation before we draw any conclusions about accident, suicide, or what have you."

Sullivan glanced at Green, whose mind was already tracking a new possibility. In her missing persons report, Janice Tanner had estimated Matt Fraser's height as five foot ten and his weight about one hundred sixty-five pounds, figures which came pretty close to MacPhail's estimate of medium height and weight for the dead man. Of course, it also fit half the men in the city, and why Fraser would leave the sanctuary of his apartment and the protection of his dog to hole up in a roach-ridden room in Vanier was a mystery. And if he had come here to die anonymously, why had he waited six days before doing the deed? Gathering the courage?

Sullivan seemed to read Green's puzzlement. "You got a theory?"

"Rush the DNA, and keep your eyes open during the post mortem that this guy might have taken a lethal overdose."

"DNA takes at least three weeks, Mike, no matter how much

53

you try to push it through. And besides, we have to have some family members to compare it to, in order to establish who it might be."

"I know." Green was already ahead of him, thinking of Rose Artlee, the tough-tender woman he had left in the Tim Hortons booth, defiantly smoking her second cigarette and lost in her own private thoughts. No doubt worrying if her final rejection had been more than her brother could bear.

DNA comparisons with a corpse would cheer her up no end.

Four

Sharon Green stepped onto the hospital elevator and heaved a sigh of relief as she punched the button for the main floor. Home. A thousand things awaited her there, but at least she could close the door on the soul-sapping depressives, the fragmented schizophrenics and the compassion she had to find within herself all day long. She leaned against the back of the elevator, shut her eyes, and didn't open them until the elevator jerked to a stop and the doors rattled open. Then she found herself face to face with her husband, who looked slightly smudged and smelled awful.

"Oh, good, you haven't left yet," he said as he drew her out.

She wrinkled her nose. "God, what have you been rolling in?"

"A case. A fire. That's not important. I need your help." He had that glint in his eye she'd come to recognize as Mike on the hunt. She thought of her swollen feet, her aching back, her son pining at the sitter's, and the unmade dinner still to come. She groaned.

"Green, no chance this can wait till tomorrow?"

He flashed his most disarming grin, the slightly crooked one that had first brought her into his arms five years earlier, despite all her friends' and family's advice to the contrary. "Probably, but I'm here," he said, taking her elbow and steering her to a chair in the lobby. "Matt Fraser. I need to talk to his doctor, and I figure I'll step on fewer toes if you give me an introduction."

"I don't know who his doctor is."

"Then find out."

"It's four o'clock. Everyone is getting ready to go home now."

"That's perfect. On his way out, the good doctor can spare me five minutes to answer one simple question."

She folded her arms stubbornly. "Green, spill it."

"Could Fraser have killed himself? That seems to be his sister's theory on his disappearance."

"Well, if he's already done it, there's hardly an urgent reason for violating his right to confidentiality, is there?"

"But what if he hasn't done it yet? What if he's wandering around trying to screw up the courage?"

She couldn't resist a smile. When he wanted, he could manipulate with the most accomplished psychopath, and it was society's luck that he, unlike the psychopath, never used the talent for personal gain. "For six days?" she said.

He pulled a face that might have been sheepish. "It's an arguable point, isn't it? At least let me run it by the doctor and see if he buys it."

She weighed the idea, intrigued in spite of her aching feet. There was no harm in at least finding out who the doctor was, and that would give her a hint of their receptiveness to Mike's dubious plan. When she cajoled the medical records clerk into checking the database, however, her heart sank. Matt Fraser's doctor was Bradley Emmerson-Jones, psychology's imitation of Fort Knox.

"I'll run this by the doctor myself," she told Mike as she returned to the lobby.

He stood up. "But you don't know enough—"

She placed her fingers on his lips to restrain him. "Green, I do. Trust me."

She had sounded more confident than she felt as they took the elevator to the third floor. En route, she steeled herself to confront the prissy little man whom she'd met only at the occasional hospital function, although he'd been working at the hospital as long as she had. He was currently the senior psychologist assigned to the Mood and Anxiety Disorders program, and he cut through his patients' fears with a ruthlessly behaviourist knife. "Show me the data" was his favourite cry, which sent the social workers and other newly minted students of the human soul scurrying elsewhere for mentorship. Thus, over the years, he had collected around himself a small but dedicated cadre of like-minded neo-Skinnerians, but found himself rarely consulted by the mainstream clinical staff.

Sharon found him sitting alone at his computer, peering over the rim of his reading glasses at some blips on the screen. His office made little attempt at a cozy, supportive atmosphere; besides his massive desk, it contained nothing but a large bookshelf crammed with journals, and a pair of utilitarian armchairs placed on either side of a small work table, as if to stress the business nature of the interaction. Not a single knick-knack, picture, or even professional degree graced the walls. Emmerson-Jones swivelled at the sound of her knock and arched his eyebrows questioningly.

"Dr. Emmerson-Jones? I'm Sharon Levy from Six West." She tried to keep the uncertainty out of her voice, but there was something about his imperious eyebrows that tipped her off-balance. "May I have a word with you about a patient?"

The brows arched further, but still the man said nothing. All right, so don't ask me in, Sharon thought, and her annoyance made her brave. She strode in uninvited and took a seat in one of the armchairs. Stick to the facts, she told herself. He loves facts.

"Matt Fraser," she began as he still did not react. "He's been missing from his apartment for almost a week, and a missing persons report has been filed with the police. Because of his past, and some suspicious evidence at his apartment, the police are concerned about revenge and are taking the disappearance seriously. His sister, however, believes he may have finally decided to kill himself. I was hoping you—"

"Just a minute!" He pulled off his reading glasses with a sweep of his hand, the better to glare at her, she suspected. "By what authority do you believe you can ask me any questions whatsoever?"

"The man's life may be in imminent danger. Under such circumstances, the law—"

"And who are you? The police? The court-appointed psychiatrist? His next of kin?"

"She's my wife." Mike strode into the room and flipped open his badge. "Detective Inspector Green, Criminal Investigations, Ottawa Police."

Sharon fought back the urge to kill him and the equally strong urge to laugh. She knew Mike as the boyish, impetuous, mercurial and infuriating lover in her life, but had never seen him play inspector. He was good. The two men sized each other up, Emmerson-Jones from over his half-moon glasses and Mike from behind a mask of brisk authority. The psychologist didn't move, but Mike settled smoothly into the chair opposite Sharon.

"Sharon is helping us with our inquiries," he said. "At present my prime goal is to ascertain if there's been a crime committed or any risk of imminent harm to a member of the public, including Mr. Fraser himself. That's the extent of police involvement, doctor, and the extent of the cooperation I'd appreciate from you. I don't need to know if this man has decided to relocate to another town in order to escape an unpleasant person or situation here in town. I have two simple questions for you. One, should we be worried about suicide in this case, and two, if so, can you provide some suggestions as to where we should look for him?"

Emmerson-Jones hesitated. His eyes were unblinking, and Sharon could almost see him mentally riffling through the legalities in search of guidance. The issues were not black and white, and Sharon knew how much he hated grey. Not surprisingly, he asked for clarification.

"Is there evidence beyond his sister's opinion that he may have been contemplating suicide?"

"There is evidence that his past still haunts him," Mike replied.

Emmerson-Jones shook his head. "That's a chronic stress, hardly a new condition or a recent shift in behaviour."

"There's also evidence that he left his apartment abruptly, without ensuring that his dog was taken care of."

The psychologist's brows arched slightly, betraying his surprise before he could bring them back down. "That suggests something unplanned or unintended. It's not the careful planning of a suicide that's years in the making."

"Some suicides are impulsive," Mike pointed out.

"Not Matt Fraser's kind. His would attend to every detail. So it's unlikely—" the psychologist's lips parted in what could have been a smile. "It seems I've answered your question after all, Inspector."

Mike's face was deadpan, but Sharon knew he was having fun. Outwitting pomposity was one of his favourite sports.

"Normally, I'd agree with you," he replied. "I've seen the man's house, and he sets new boundaries for the term obsessive. But I also had the feeling that his grip on reality wasn't what it should be, and once that begins to go, a lot of details can get lost in the haze."

Sharon took great satisfaction in the look of astonishment on the psychologist's face. She'd always known Mike had a wonderful intuitive sense, but he'd also been an adept pupil who'd picked up a lot of wisdom about human failings from discussing work with her. Now she wondered how Emmerson-Jones, the quintessential rationalist, would handle Mike's poetic bent.

"You're implying he's delusional," he replied sharply, as if to bring the discussion back to a more prosaic plane.

To her surprise, Mike laughed, further rattling the man. Then he gave a cheerful shrug. "I like 'haze' myself, but yes. The poor man had all his windows nailed shut in thirty degree heat and dark blinds blocking out every sliver of the outside world. He had five locks on his door and—I kid you not— enough newspapers and photocopied articles to fill a tractor-trailer. All about his case. Either he was really thorough, or the real world had ceased to exist for him."

Despite his best efforts, the psychologist grew visibly pinker with each point, then after a moment's deliberation, he picked up his phone and dialled zero. "Have Leslie Black paged for me, please. Extension 6083."

As the name blared over the hospital intercom, he hung up and rose to his feet. "Would you both step outside for a minute, please, while I deal with a private matter."

Outside in the hall, Sharon gave Mike a playful swat on the rear. "Thanks for letting me handle it, schmuck."

He raised his finger to his lips and positioned himself outside the door. "That doctor didn't know a damn thing about his patient," he whispered. "It's time for some ass-covering."

"Or buck passing," she responded. "Leslie Black's a friend of mine, and she runs anxiety groups. She probably ran the group Janice and Matt attended."

"In other words, the one who really should know what was going on in Matt's head."

Sharon nodded. "She's a nurse with some graduate psych training. She's really experienced, but she never got her degree, so technically Emmerson-Jones has to supervise her."

"And technically, he's accountable." He grinned. "Some serious ass-covering."

Inside, the phone rang, and Sharon heard Emmerson-Jones's gruff hello. A moment later, his voice rose sharply. Sharon joined Mike pressed against the door, but she could distinguish only a few words.

"Police…kill…did you…responsibility… What do you mean, no!" His voice dropped to a low murmur, and for some time they could make out nothing. With a smile, Mike steered her back towards the waiting room.

"I think we may get lucky," he murmured. He settled into a chair and was looking the picture of cooperation when a frazzled middle-aged woman burst out of the elevator and hurried into Emmerson-Jones's room. Five minutes elapsed.

"He's getting their stories straight," Sharon said.

"And he's telling her what she can and can't say. I wish I was a fly on the wall."

Emmerson-Jones's door opened, and he beckoned them back in. "This is Mrs. Black, one of our therapists. She's been treating Mr. Fraser in group therapy, and I thought her input might be useful."

Sharon glanced at Leslie, who was sitting beside Emmerson-

Jones's desk and whose flushed face and erratic breathing belied her pose of pleasant calm. Emmerson-Jones sat down, folded his hands, and embarked on his speech.

"Neither Mrs. Black nor I had any evidence to suggest that Mr. Fraser was at significant risk for suicide. Nor have I heard anything today from you two that clearly suggests otherwise. However, preferring to err on the side of caution, I'm prepared to admit that there may be certain risks of which we were unaware, and in the interests of protecting my patient—as well as others, of course—I'm prepared to share some details of his treatment. I trust this information will be treated with discretion."

Mike nodded and extracted his notebook, which was his favourite dramatic prop. Sharon knew inwardly he was celebrating his victory, but his expression was the essence of respect. With a flick of his hand, Emmerson-Jones invited Leslie to speak.

Leslie was a petite woman whose delicate features belied her strength. There was a stubborn set to her finely chiselled jaw, but her voice was flat and precise. "Matt's been in my group for almost a year now. He's as conscientious and punctual as clockwork, he records all his assignments in his therapy binder, and he attempts to do each one to the best of his ability. Which is unlike some of my patients, who've been avoiding social challenges and making excuses for themselves for so many years, that the habits are hard to break. Matt always tries. But within the group, he says very little. We always have a few who monopolize—"

"Like Janice Tanner?" Mike interjected.

"Well, yes, actually—" She managed before Emmerson-Jones stopped her.

"Mrs. Black, please confine your remarks to Mr. Fraser."

Leslie nodded, but not before Sharon caught the flash of

anger in her eyes. How she hates this forced subjugation, Sharon thought.

"So Matt is a private person?" Mike encouraged, ignoring Emmerson-Jones.

"Private, but also very shy. Some private people talk endlessly about everyone else's problems but their own. They try to take over my job, in fact. But Matt simply listened. He was intelligent, I could see that, and quite intuitive, but he kept his opinions to himself."

"So he seemed rational, right until the end? No hint of strange obsessions or delusions?"

Here Leslie wavered. "Well, in truth... Dr. Emmerson-Jones just told me what you said about Matt's apartment. I had no idea. If I'd known, I would have checked into his mental state further. But he always presented as organized, neat and clean. He was OCD, of course—sorry, that's obsessive-compulsive—but lots of people are. He looked poor, and his clothing sense was horrendous, although I think the baggy sweat clothes were part of his protective cover. But he was always able to keep track of group activities and follow the conversation." Her voice faded, and she gazed into space, chewing her lip as if remembering some worrisome point. Sharon itched to pursue it, but Mike had the interview so well choreographed she didn't dare disrupt it.

In the next instant Mike, as if reading her mind, picked up the thread himself. "But now, in retrospect, there were some signs?"

"Some of his comments were odd. One of the other patients has paranoid tendencies and was talking about being followed in the street. Matt asked him if he'd ever done anything bad, and then he said sometimes it's not our imagination. Sometimes people do follow us, and it can be for things that happened long ago, that nobody else even remembers."

"Did he elaborate, or did you ask if he was talking about himself?"

She shook her head. "His comment was off topic. Worse than that, it was feeding this individual's anxieties. The fear that everyone is looking at you and thinking bad things about you is a core component of social phobias."

"Was it usual for Fraser to say things like that?"

Leslie glanced across at her supervisor, and again Sharon had the feeling she wanted to say much more. "Matt tended to be more cynical than most, but given what he's been through, that's hardly surprising."

"Did the others know about his past?"

"He never spoke of it. Of course, Dr. Emmerson-Jones and I knew, and—"

"It was not relevant to his treatment," Emmerson-Jones cut in. "He needed to get out into the world again. That takes a well-planned series of small steps, not a whole lot of talking about the past."

"Still, I imagine it was hard for him to just turn the memories off," Mike said in an affable tone beneath which Sharon could recognize the sarcasm. "Did he talk about it indirectly? Allude to any strange worries or thoughts?"

Leslie was shaking her head. "In retrospect, I can see he's been getting more agitated in recent weeks, as if he couldn't get his mind off things. The last session, he kept scribbling furiously in his binder, he shifted in his chair and twirled his pen, he just couldn't seem to relax. I was surprised when he missed the group last week, because he's usually so conscientious."

"Looking back at what you know about him now and what he revealed in discussions, have you got any idea if he felt he was being followed, and by whom?"

Emmerson-Jones silenced Leslie with an abrupt slice of his hand. "This is clearly beyond the issue of public safety, Inspector. You're trying to pry information out of us to further your investigation."

"They're one and the same," Mike replied, with an edge creeping into his voice. "Somebody might have been stalking him and waiting for the chance to settle accounts. In which case he may be in danger. Or dead."

Emmerson-Jones and Leslie Black exchanged looks, and Sharon saw a sudden uncertainty in his. He doesn't know what to do, she thought, because he doesn't know his patient from Adam, beyond the anxiety rating scales Fraser had probably filled in during the initial consult. In clinical matters, Emmerson-Jones was not one to venture out on a limb. If he didn't have his numbers and his data to support his opinion, he said nothing. Yet here, to say nothing might land him in serious professional trouble. In that glance to Leslie Black, he was asking her to go out on the limb for him. Clever little prick, Sharon thought with gritted teeth.

But if Leslie was aware of the dual purpose she served, she seemed unfazed. Sharon sensed she loved limbs, perhaps because she knew the clearest and farthest views could be had from them.

"Yes," she said without a moment's pause. "He did believe he was being followed, and he did say that some people would stop at nothing, even after years, and so he—"

Belatedly, she checked herself with a look of dismay, but Mike was not to be denied.

"He what?"

Leslie shifted in her chair, clearly reluctant. "Well, I don't want you to take this the wrong way. Out of context, it sounds ominous, but I'm sure he didn't mean it that way."

Mike waited patiently, his pen poised.

As the silence ticked on, Leslie obliged. "He said he might have to stop them first."

"Oh, *really!*" Emmerson-Jones interjected. "Idle talk in the therapy group, nothing to base a suspicion on, Inspector. People say all kinds of things!"

Mike's eyes remained on Leslie. "But you think he was serious?"

"I don't think he was being glib," she replied slowly. "Matt spoke so rarely that when he did, you knew it was something he'd been worrying over for weeks."

"Mrs. Black!" the psychologist exclaimed. "If you knew of a possible threat, you should have come to me at once!"

"I didn't see it as a threat," she countered, flushing. "Not in the context. I had the impression he meant he'd consult a lawyer."

"For a restraining order, you mean?" Mike asked.

"It sounded like something of that sort."

Mike's eyes narrowed. "If he went to a lawyer and not the police, then chances are he knew who was following him. Did he give a hint? Someone from the trial?"

Leslie sat a long while in silence as if she were mentally reliving the group discussions. Finally, she sighed and shook her head. "The group didn't know about his past, and so his comments were always circumspect. It might have been—"

"I think that's enough speculation, Mrs. Black. The police need evidence, not your subjective interpretation of what a patient might have meant." Emmerson-Jones rose and reached for his suit jacket. "I believe we've helped you much more than we're obliged, Inspector. Let's hope this whole matter is resolved quickly and with happy results." He held open his door and extended his hand. "Good day."

"Arrogant putz," Mike muttered as he followed Sharon out the door. She punched the elevator button and swung around with a mock glare.

"Yes, and thanks to you, he's going to nail me with the Director of Nursing tomorrow morning. I was handling it my way, Green. How's he ever going to believe I had no control over you?"

The elevator door slid open, and she stomped in. Once inside, he gave her his crooked grin. "He's a shrink. That should be obvious to his finely-honed intuition."

"Yeah, right. Some cops get hunches, and others plod through the facts. Shrinks are no different. Emmerson-Jones has no intuition, but what he does have is a very stiff poker up his ass."

He laughed, caught her hand and pulled her into his arms. "Sorry. Will you be in big trouble?"

"What can they do, fire me? They can't afford to, with the shortage of nurses and my ten years' experience. So they'll sweep it under the carpet, I'll stay out of Emmerson-Jones' way for a while—which will be my pleasure—and it'll be business as usual. However, you won't get off that easily. You owe me big time, Green, and a tub of Ben n' Jerry's isn't going to do it."

"So what's your pleasure this time?" He bent to nuzzle her neck. "Maybe...?"

She pushed him away. "Not smelling like that! Cooking dinner would be a start."

The elevator jolted to a stop on the main floor. As the doors opened, he kissed her lightly on the nose. "Okay, I just need to make one quick stop back at the station—"

"Green! It's past five o'clock!"

He led the way through the heavy glass doors into the

garish afternoon sun. Just ahead, his car was parked illegally at the curb with a police sticker slapped on the dash. He paused with his hand on the handle. "This will only take a minute. I have to look something up."

"For this case?"

He nodded and slipped into the car. "Leslie Black got me thinking of something. Half an hour, I promise, and then I'll whip up the meanest Kraft Dinner you've ever had. And to while away the time..." He fished in his wallet and held out a scrap of paper. "You could always take a peek at this house on your way home and see what you think."

Without making a move, she grinned. "In half an hour? No time. Wouldn't want my Kraft Dinner to get cold."

Five

As he drove back towards the police station against the rush hour, Green glanced at the gridlock stretching along the Queensway in the opposite direction and ruefully acknowledged that his promise of half an hour had been hopelessly optimistic. Especially since he had to travel all the way out to the end of the earth to reach his new home.

The squad room was deserted when he arrived, but fortunately in his absence the records clerk had delivered the Fraser file to his office, where it sat in two large boxes on his desk. Inside were pages of reports, witness statements and interview summaries, in no particular order as far as he could tell. Sitting at his desk, Green resisted the urge to get sidetracked by the interviews and instead riffled rapidly through the pages until he found the name he was looking for.

In his therapy group, Matt Fraser had hinted that he was thinking of consulting a lawyer in order to stop some harassment, real or imagined. Perhaps he had, and perhaps he had used the same lawyer who had defended him so successfully ten years earlier.

Josh Bleustein.

Green groaned. Over the past fifteen years, Green had not won many popularity contests with the Ottawa Defence Bar, mainly because the cases he handled rarely made them look good, but Josh Bleustein had tangled with him more than most. Bleustein was a brawler who took more pleasure in eviscerating a witness on the stand than in arguing the finer points of law. Nearing sixty, a two-pack a day and six-pack a night man with three chins and a paunch to rival Buddha, Bleustein continually surprised people by turning up each Monday morning still alive and well.

And ready to scrap. Josh Bleustein would sooner throw him out of the office than cooperate with him about a confidential case. Green pulled out his day planner, flipped it open to the next day and contemplated the mass of blue ink that filled the page. He had a full day of meetings with his counterparts in urban police forces around the province. The bane of middle management life. The event was about the growing threat of biker gangs, and it included lunch to facilitate networking, as the corporate luminaries called it. He couldn't skip it, because Superintendent Adam Jules, no doubt with tongue firmly lodged in cheek, had volunteered him to present CID's new computerized geographic profiling system.

Fortunately, Green had learned a few middle management tricks of his own over the years, and he'd hastened to draft into service an eager-beaver new detective who actually knew how to operate the thing and who would happily demonstrate his superior wisdom to a room full of inspectors in exchange for a few brownie points in the eyes of the brass. But Green knew that he himself would still have to be there, to look as if he knew what was going on.

But all of this smoke and mirrors technical wizardry paled in comparison to a real live case, and Green was getting an increasing sense that Matt Fraser's disappearance was serious stuff. There was no body or blood stains to point to foul play, but Green knew something bad had happened. He was like a dog on the scent, and right now the trail led to Josh Bleustein.

A phone call to Bleustein's firm netted him an answering machine and an after-hours emergency number at which there was no answer. Like it or not, meeting Bleustein would have to wait until tomorrow, until he could find time to sneak out of his seminar.

Outside his little alcove office, a door slammed and footsteps thudded across the carpet. Then Green heard a sigh. He peeked out to see Brian Sullivan drop into his chair and flick on his computer. Green glanced at his watch, which read almost six o'clock. He'd left Sullivan at the rooming house over two hours ago, and he wondered what Sullivan could be trying to do on the case at this point. The body had been removed to the morgue to await post mortem in the morning. Ident and the fire investigators would almost certainly still be at the scene, completing their painstaking collection of physical evidence. In the morning, there would be plenty to do chasing down the results of the physical search and canvassing the street again for witnesses. Maybe, as a break from that plodding and often futile exercise, Sullivan might like to slip in a quick visit to everyone's favourite defence attorney.

Green picked up his notes and Josh Bleustein's office address and sauntered out of the office. Except for Sullivan, the squad room was empty. The huge former linebacker hunched over his keyboard, sweat trickling down his temples and his sausage fingers dancing nimbly over the keys. His florid complexion had faded, but a dusky hint of high blood pressure remained, reminding Green of the price they all paid for the job. Sullivan was searching the internal police database, and when a mosaic of tattoos filled the screen, he leaned forward to squint at them.

"What are you working on?" Green asked.

"MacPhail and I found part of a tattoo still intact on the

victim's hip just above his groin. Most of it is burned away, but I can make out part of what looks like a young girl. I'm checking to see if it's on the system."

"Girlfriend tattoos are pretty common," Green observed doubtfully. "Part of the love and possession theme of the jailhouse."

"Yeah, but this is a pretty sophisticated job. Curly ringlets, sort of like Shirley Temple, if you remember your old movies. MacPhail's going to try to clean it up, so it might help us get an ID on the guy. Ident's hit a big fat zero with usable prints. Fingers are too burned, and the empty bottle had nothing but smudges."

"So we'll be looking at teeth or DNA."

"But the tattoo might give us some possible relations to check it out against."

For a moment, Green felt a surge of excitement. Shirley Temple had been a precocious child star with a girlish innocence and a coquettish flair that would be perfect fuel for a pedophile's dreams. But Green was reluctant to subject Fraser's sister to the experience of DNA comparison unless he had something more substantial than intuition. No tattoo had been listed among Fraser's distinguishing marks at the time of his arrest. It was possible he'd had it drawn since then, in which case his sister probably wouldn't know about it. On the other hand, how likely was she to know about a little girl on his groin anyway?

In the silence, Sullivan rubbed his bloodshot eyes and suppressed a yawn. "Jesus, I'm getting old. These screens are getting harder and harder to see."

Green clapped him on the shoulder. "We're on the slippery slope, buddy. Put Gibbs on it. He's ten years younger than us, and you know how he loves this detail stuff. Besides, I've got something else I need you to do."

Sullivan glanced with alarm at the paperwork in Green's hand. "What, now?"

He knows me too well, thought Green, no matter how casual I try to be. He knows that when I'm on the scent, I forget to eat or sleep, even forget that a day has only twenty-four hours in it. "Tomorrow. It shouldn't take long."

"But Mike, I have to go back to Carillon Street tomorrow. I ran into complete stonewalling today. None of the neighbours saw a thing. In fact, no one can remember ever seeing the occupant of room 2C."

"Maybe that's true."

"And maybe I'm the Queen of England. I figure a visit bright and early in the morning before they've had time to get too seriously into the sauce, I might get fewer faulty memories. Give it to Watts and Charbonneau, their manslaughter just took a guilty plea."

Inwardly, Green grimaced. Watts and Charbonneau were standard-issue detectives, long on plod but short on imagination. Cases with twisty trails were beyond the agility of their brains. "I'd even do it myself," he muttered, "but I'm stuck in that smoke and mirrors—I mean geographic profiling thing."

"Hey, don't knock that. I'm planning to use it to study the pattern of muggings in the east end."

Green nodded with what he hoped looked like encouragement. In truth, he had no quarrel with geographic profiling. Like behavioural profiling, in the hands of an intelligent investigator, it helped narrow down the search, so that the proverbial needle was in a far smaller haystack. What bothered him was spending precious hours showing off a new toy when he'd rather be out grappling with a real live case. So he tried another approach.

"There's a remote chance this might be connected to your John Doe anyway and save you plowing through all those tattoos. Plus you get to butt heads with Josh Bleustein."

"Bleustein? Now for sure I don't want—" Sullivan started to protest, but broke off when Green plunked Bleustein's address down on his desk. Rarely did Green actually pull rank on him, but there were times like this one, where despite their friendship, his authority was implicit.

*   *   *

Despite her misgivings, Sharon's curiosity got the better of her on the way home and lured her on a short detour past the house in Highland Park. She cruised slowly around the neighbourhood and parked outside for a few minutes, soaking up impressions. Her first reaction was one of horror, followed by intrigue and finally a begrudging twinge of hope. The house was in wild disarray; lilacs heavy with blooms choked half the yard, and a massive maple towered ominously over the roof. The parts of the house that could actually be seen through the underbrush all seemed to need replacing, from the curling roof shingles to the sagging veranda and the grimy windows. It would cost a fortune. Yet the street was quiet, and the small park on the next block had a play structure and benches beneath the graceful boughs of gnarled old trees.

She wasn't going to admit it to Mike yet, but the place had potential. All they had to do was win the lottery.

The clock on the dash of her Chevy Cavalier read six-thirty by the time she finally picked up Tony from the sitter, dropped by the grocery store and reached their little home. No Corolla. No Green. "Schmuck," she muttered, thinking of the sweltering house, the dinner to be prepared and a crabby baby to be fed before she could even consider resting her tired feet.

She heard the phone ring before she'd even reached the front door. Swearing, she plunked Tony and the diaper bag down on the front step while she scrounged in her purse for the keys. Two rings. She found her keys and wrestled with the lock. Three rings. She shoved the door open, swooped up her son and dashed into the kitchen to snatch up the phone just before the answering machine kicked in. If it was her husband, he was going to get an earful.

It was Leslie Black. Apologetic, agitated, tripping all over herself. Most unlike the Leslie Black Sharon knew. Leslie said she'd spent the last two hours worrying, because she couldn't leave things as Emmerson-Jones insisted they be left. Not if Matt Fraser's life were in danger, or indeed someone else's, as unlikely as that seemed.

Jamming the phone into the crook of her neck, Sharon dumped her son on the kitchen floor, where he instantly began to shriek. She opened the fridge and began to hunt for some cheese.

"Sharon?" Leslie prompted into the clamour. "I'm sorry, I don't mean to intrude at the crazy hour."

"You're not," Sharon said hastily. "My son has just become very definite about his wants these days. Like his father. But I'm listening." She cut up some cubes of cheese, and through Tony's clamour she tried to focus on Leslie's voice. The woman was clearly worried.

"Matt may have been further over the edge than I thought. When he told the group he would have to put a stop to this harassment, I told your husband I thought he meant a restraining order. And maybe he did. But I've been reviewing my notes and replaying the session in my head, and there was definitely a creepy flavour to it. Matt's a very quiet-spoken guy, he doesn't ever show much affect, but there was an eerie intensity to his words. He didn't look at me—he rarely does maintain eye contact for long—but he was inspecting his hands. Of course, Dr. Emmerson-Jones dismisses any notion of the subconscious, but to me it looked like subconsciously Matt was relaying a message to his hands. To his fists."

Tony ran out of cheese, and Sharon rummaged in the cupboard for a cookie to silence him long enough for her to consider Leslie's theory. It was a bit too fanciful even for her clinical sense, but she'd seen too many bizarre twists to the human psyche in her ten years in psychiatry to discount it completely.

"What about his thinking? Do you think he was paranoid?"

"He was definitely paranoid," Leslie said without the earlier doubt in her voice. "But I put that down to some type of post-traumatic stress reaction. Traumatized people see threat or danger in the most innocuous event and interpret ambiguous or neutral behaviour as negative. After what happened ten years ago, Matt has always seen condemnation or retaliation in the least little thing. If someone bumps into him in a grocery store or looks at him twice, he thinks they know. He doesn't trust anyone, and he sees himself as an easy scapegoat. And really, till we've walked in his shoes, we can't judge how paranoid he should be, can we? The whole world hates a sex offender, and a pedophile is the lowest of the low. It doesn't matter that he was acquitted. People remember the accusation and don't believe the acquittal. He's a permanent pariah, and emotionally Matt was never equipped to be a pariah."

Sharon looked at Tony's big trusting brown eyes and his dimpled cheeks, at the mop of chocolate curls and the gooey cookie clutched in his fist. She felt a rush of protective love.

"On the other hand, you can hardly blame people. An acquittal doesn't mean innocence. It means reasonable doubt. Would that be enough for you? Would you let him around your own children?"

"Absolutely. At least as far as the risk of pedophilia is concerned. But as far as the paranoia business…" Her certainty began to fade. "I'm not sure I could trust him. Matt felt trapped. He felt betrayed. And deep down, I think he had an incredible amount of rage. That's what scares me."

Sharon knew little about the case or about Matt Fraser himself, but she knew what could happen when a shy, timid man felt cornered, or nurtured a rage deep inside for ten years.

It was a chilling scenario, except for one small point. "But if he was guilty of the molestation and got away with it, he'd have a whole different set of emotions," she said. "Then every funny look or small slight would be a reminder of what he in his heart knew to be true. Surely he wouldn't feel angry or betrayed. Trapped and cornered, perhaps, but mainly by his own guilt and shame. If he has a normal conscience, that is," she added, remembering that many pedophiles do not see themselves as villains but as lovers of children giving natural expression to that love. Lost in these thoughts, she became slowly aware of the silence at the other end of the line.

"Leslie?"

"I don't think he's guilty," Leslie replied, so softly Sharon barely heard her. "Sharon, you must never tell anyone that I told you this. Neither Dr. Emmerson-Jones nor I think he's guilty. Matt had a sexual behaviours assessment, you see. When he came back to Ottawa three years ago, when his life was falling apart and he was sinking further and further into his panic attacks and paranoia, he went to his doctor and asked for a referral to Dr. Pelham. He said he needed someone to believe him, to prove to the world that he wasn't aroused by children. So he took Pelham's tests."

"You mean with the plesthmograph and the whole bit?"

"Yes. And he passed."

"I don't remember any news about that," Sharon said. "Did he tell anyone?"

"No. That was the odd thing. Dr. Emmerson-Jones and I only learned it because we read it in his file. Sharon, I'm telling you this because I don't know what to do, and I'm scared to be the only one who knows."

Now it was Sharon's turn to be silent. Although she had never worked in the forensic unit at the Rideau Psychiatric Hospital, she knew the forensic psychiatrist Dr. Pelham's reputation as an expert in sexual deviance. He had provided testimony at countless trials across the country on the sexual proclivities of accused men, which he assessed not merely by skilled interviewing and standardized questionnaires but by measuring the amount of blood flow to their penises in response to pictures and stories depicting different sexual themes. Matt Fraser had willingly submitted himself to the humiliating experience of having his erections measured while he looked at pictures of all sorts, including children. It would be like opening the curtain on his most intimate, private dream world. Why would he do that seven years later, when he'd already been acquitted? When people had begun to forget.

Was it to prove his innocence once and for all, or more sinisterly, to add further weight to his deception? Sharon didn't know if the test results could be faked, or if treatment in the interim could have suppressed the urges. He had been away for several years; maybe he had secretly enrolled himself in a treatment program where he'd learned to control his fantasies, and then returned in the hope of clearing his name beyond all doubt.

In which case, why had he told no one? Surely, with his deep-rooted cynicism, he would not have trusted others to get the message out through word of mouth or staff room gossip. Regardless of whether he was truly innocent or guilty, he should have trumpeted this finding from the rooftops. Something didn't make sense, but before she revealed any of this news to Mike, she needed to doublecheck the whole story. Because if what Leslie said was accurate, then Mike might need to look in an entirely different direction and possibly for an entirely different crime.

"Leslie, would you do me a big favour?" she asked on impulse. "Could you requisition his file tomorrow and let me have a peek at it?"

There was utter silence at the end of the line. Inwardly Sharon cringed, for she knew what she was asking. Her request violated every mantra of confidentiality they'd ever been taught to recite. Leslie would not only have to go out on a limb, she'd be twisting in the wind.

"I know it's asking a lot," Sharon added as the silence lengthened. "I promise I won't ever let on how I got the file, but it's important."

"I have to think about it," Leslie replied. "I'll call you at noon tomorrow."

Six

Trying to be unobtrusive, Green inched his sleeve up to sneak another peek at his watch. Superintendent Jules had placed him at the head table so that the thirty-five pairs of eager middle management eyes seemed to catch his every move. For the occasion, Green had even put on a proper suit, which bunched at his crotch and pulled across his back. His tie chafed, and despite the frigid climate control of the windowless conference room, perspiration beaded his brow.

An OPP officer droned on in a dusty monotone as he led the group through a series of computer slides on the pattern of drug crimes in the Province of Ontario. The lights were dim, adding to the challenge of staying awake.

Green's watch read 10:22. An hour and a half until lunch, but only eight minutes until break time. Thank God. No doubt Sullivan had already finished his canvass of the streets around the rooming house, and with any luck he was just winding up his visit to Josh Bleustein. One quick phone call to Sullivan during the break, and Green could be back in his seat at the head of the table before anyone noticed he'd gone.

The lights came on and a buzz of conversation rose around the table. Spotting an inspector from Montreal plowing a path towards him, Green jumped to his feet and brandished his cellphone as if to imply he had an urgent matter to attend to. He took the stairs two at a time on his way to the privacy of his office, but when he reached the Major Crimes squad room, he stopped short. Sullivan was already back at his desk, hunched over his computer.

"What are you doing here?" Green demanded. "I wanted you to see Bleustein ASAP."

Sullivan straightened slowly from the keyboard, and Green had the sense he was counting to ten. Green knew tact was not always his strong point, but the fifteen-minute break was slowly ticking away. He held back his impatience.

"Bleustein threw me out," Sullivan replied. "Barely let me in the door. 'That's attorney-client privilege, Sergeant! You should be ashamed of yourself.'"

"Did you tell him Fraser was missing?"

"Of course I did. Attorney-client privilege was all I got back."

"But—"

"I tried everything I could, Green, and that's what I got. A goddamn giant clam."

"He knows something. Fraser's been to see him, and whatever it was about, Fraser wanted nothing to do with the police."

"I didn't get that impression. I think old Josh Bleustein was just getting a big charge out of being obstructive."

"In that case, he better be prepared for round two, with me. And he might be sorry he wasn't nicer to you." Green glanced at his watch irritably. Two hours minimum before he could get away. Two more hours of beady middle management eyes and droning lists of names, photos and stats. Still, he could use that time to figure out how he was going to tackle Josh Bleustein, all the while appearing to listen to the speaker with rapt attention. An art he'd perfected years ago in the back row of his high school classrooms.

Sullivan grinned. He was built like a bear, six inches taller and fifty pounds heavier that Green, and at first glance he might appear the more threatening of the two, but only to those who didn't know Green. "And when are you going to fit in this rematch?"

Green shrugged. "Lunch. I never was much for small talk anyway, and I don't want anyone to ask me how the profiling program actually works." He glanced casually at the computer screen. "Any progress on your John Doe?"

"Almost no one saw the guy. The rooming house is owned by some Indian guy who works for Nortel and hasn't been near the place in months. He hired a management firm to take care of it, and those guys have new building managers every month or so. There's not much job satisfaction in running a flophouse, evidently. So I tracked down the manager, some Iraqi refugee who drives a taxi too, and he does remember the renter paying cash for a week in advance, but he doesn't remember much else. Describes the guy as a businessman."

Businessmen wear grey suits and carry briefcases, Green thought excitedly. "Then he really should stick in the guy's mind! Why don't you—"

Sullivan seemed to read his mind. "Yeah, yeah. I've got the Iraqi coming down to the station this afternoon to try to work up a composite, but businessman or not, I'm not hopeful. The guy's English isn't great, and he's going to be damn uncooperative because he didn't want to miss his fares at peak time."

Green retrieved Fraser's police file from his desk and took out the police photo. "Show him this in a line-up. It might speed things up. This is ten years old, but it's worth a shot."

Sullivan took the picture and studied it in silence a moment, his brow cocked in surprise. "You think Matthew Fraser's our John Doe? What would he be doing holed up in this dump?

Doesn't he have an address off Merivale somewhere?"

"Maybe he was hiding from someone."

"And then after a week with the roaches, he suddenly flips out and torches himself?"

Green hesitated. His mind was already leaping ahead, spinning wild theories, but it was too early even for him to speculate, at least aloud. "Not necessarily."

"Okay, so he drinks himself into a stupor and sets himself on fire by accident?"

"Or so someone wants us to think."

*   *   *

True to character, Superintendent Jules adjourned the conference for lunch on the stroke of noon, and Green was just beating a hasty path to the door when Jules caught his arm. Jules had one of the beady-eyed inspectors in tow, although at second glance, this one's eyes were more bloodshot than beady, and everything about him drooped. His moustache, his jowls, his rumpled suit—everything sagged as if under the weight of years in the trenches.

"This is Inspector Alain Levesque of the Montreal Police. He's interested in setting up a joint initiative against the Hells Angels, and I thought we could talk over lunch."

Levesque's eyes regarded him with sorrow, as if he fully expected to be turned down, and Green's heart sank. The one thing he dreaded almost as much as meetings was initiatives—in tandem with "proactive", it was one of the favourite buzzwords of the brass. Not that crime prevention and strategic deployment of resources were not worthy ventures, but let someone else have the visions and the paradigms. In the end, criminals still committed crimes, someone had to catch them, and that was all Green had ever wanted to do.

But with Jules' pressure on his elbow, he allowed himself to be steered upstairs to the cafeteria, where Jules ensconced them at a quiet corner table while they debated the expansion of the Quebec-based biker gangs into the nation's capital, where the newly wealthy high-tech industry had opened up lucrative drug opportunities. The biker gangs had their own decisive enforcement methods which kept Montreal's homicide division hopping, along with its drug squad.

It wasn't until the afternoon break-out sessions that Green was able to escape. As he approached the squad room, he heard a chorus of voices arguing heatedly in some guttural foreign tongue. Inside, he found a senior Ident officer and Sullivan seated at the computer, surrounded by a knot of excited men. That must be the Iraqi building manager and his support group, Green surmised, here to develop the composite of the rooming house DOA. Refugees rarely went to meet anyone official, especially the police, without a bevy of advisors.

"What's going on?" Green demanded over the din.

Sullivan looked up wearily. "Mr. Ahmad has brought some taxi-driver friends to help him, and they're having trouble being specific enough about the features."

"Well, did any of his friends even see the man?"

Sullivan shook his head, and Green raised his hands in exasperation. "Then clear them out."

Sullivan gave him a "been there, tried that, how stupid do you think I am" look, but held his tongue. "He wants them here. Anyway, I don't think I'm going to get anywhere with the composite."

"Did you show him the mug shot?"

"Not yet. I was saving it to see if I could get anything unprompted first." Sullivan reached into the file by his side, pulled out the photo line-up he'd worked up and placed it on the desk. He gestured to the man nearest him, a tall, emaciated man with dark flashing eyes and a broken tooth. "Do you see the man among these? He may be older now, with different hair."

The man picked up the page of photos, and the others clustered around to peer over his shoulder. Arabic flew back and forth, and Green tried to read Ahmad's face. The man looked uncertain as he studied the photos, frustrated as he listened to his friends, and decidedly reluctant to be in this position at all. The other men sliced the air with their hands, gestured to the photo and shrugged expressively until finally, with one last examination, Ahmad tossed the sheet down on the desk. His finger landed on Fraser.

"This is the man."

Green felt a brief stab of regret at the death of the sad, tormented man he'd been tracking, but this was superseded, in spite of his finer instincts, by triumph. Someone up there is looking out for me, he thought, as he thanked the men and left them to Sullivan while he headed down to his car. At noon, when he'd originally planned to go into battle against Bleustein, he'd had nothing but a lot of bluff and bluster, but now he had a real weapon. Attorney-client privilege was irrelevant now, because the client was dead, and surely even Bleustein would cooperate with the police in the attempt to solve his death.

*   *   *

It took less than one minute for Bleustein to disavow him of that notion. Bleustein's law firm occupied half of a renovated brick Victorian off Elgin Street, across the street from the court and a short stroll to the roast beef house and the pubs where he spent the rest of his time.

"Green!" the man roared through his open office door before Green had even finished introducing himself to the pretty young secretary sitting outside. "Don't even think I'm going to help you with that damn case! After all the shit you've given me?"

Green stepped over and poked his head through the door. Inside, Josh Bleustein's office was a reflection of the man. It was oversized and expensively furnished in black leather and cherry wood, but it looked like Miami after a hurricane. Stacks of papers littered every surface; some had toppled and cascaded onto the floor. His jacket and tie lay in a heap on a chair, and his court gown had been tossed over a four-foot bronze statue of Lady Justice as if she were nothing but a cheap coat rack. Bleustein himself was kneeling on the floor, pawing through a stack of files. His white shirt was rolled up to his elbows, damp with sweat, and his jowled face was bright red. From behind folds of fat, his eyes skewered Green. Green had never met the man on his own turf, and he had to suppress a twinge of awe.

"Josh," he replied, leaning against the door frame casually, "you dish out as good as you get, and I'm still talking to you. It's business, right? And speaking of shit, how do you get any clients with the place looking like this?"

"Because I win, that's how."

"And so do I."

Bleustein paused, then hauled himself to his feet and pulled his trousers out of his crotch. He approached to loom over Green. "Well, don't expect a mutual admiration society."

Green kept his own gaze steady. "Luckily, we're both on the same side on this one, so don't unsheathe your sword just yet. I'm worried about your client."

"Ex-client."

"In fact, I'm afraid he may be just that. I'm afraid he may be that burned body in the Vanier flophouse."

"With all your fears, you should see a shrink."

Green grinned. "Give me a break. I was talking to one yesterday, and I think I'd do better just drinking myself silly like the rest of the world. Matthew Fraser's been ID'd as the man who rented the room."

For the first time, Bleustein's gaze flickered, as if he couldn't hide his surprise at the news. Green pressed his advantage. "The death is looking like a homicide," he said, deciding that the situation called for tweaking the truth slightly. "I know Fraser was worried someone was following him. I know he was hoping to get a restraining order, but there's no record of an application. Did he come to see you, or should I start hunting down your competitors in the yellow pages?"

Bleustein had recovered his footing, and his face was deadpan. "Be my guest. The guy's a nutbar anyway, and I'm surprised no one bumped him off earlier." He gave a dismissive shrug as if the matter were no longer of importance to him. "Yeah, he did come here—maybe a week ago? Sandy!" He shouted in the general direction of the outer door. "What day did that wacko kiddie diddler come to see me? The one with the briefcase that weighed fifty pounds?"

There was silence for a moment, broken only by Bleustein's dangerously asthmatic breathing. "Monday, ten a.m.," came the sweet reply.

Green did a quick mental check. Fraser's neighbour Crystal had seen him leaving the apartment the previous Wednesday about noon, dressed as if for a business appointment. But it was obviously not with Bleustein. He waited for the lawyer to continue.

"Yeah, he'd been collecting pages and pages of crap from books and off the internet about sexual abuse and psychopaths, and he'd put together this really insane theory about what happened, and about how someone was out to get him because he knew."

"Knew what?"

"That's what I kept asking him, but you could never cut to the chase with this guy. He took out all these photocopied pages and newspaper clippings, all covered in yellow highlighting, and he wanted to show me every little step along the way. He was talking a mile a minute, saying he knew they knew he knew, and if he didn't put a stop to it, he'd be six feet under."

"You're saying he thought someone was trying to kill him?"

"The guy's a head case, Green! I never thought for a moment there was any truth to it."

"Who did he figure was out to get him?"

Bleustein hesitated, and again his conviction wavered. "He talked in riddles, like he thought the room was bugged or the phone was tapped. That's all I figured this was—the crazy thoughts of a paranoid. I didn't take the case. The guy looked pretty tapped out—the suit he was wearing had seen a good fifteen years' service—and I didn't want to be the one to take his last dime."

I'll bet, thought Green. It wouldn't go far towards keeping you in single-malt and Cuban cigars. No rich teachers' union to bankroll you this time.

"Of course not," he replied, careful to rein in the sarcasm.

"Anyway, I held my nose and defended the guy once, but to tell you the truth, I agree with the guys on the inside— pedophiles are the slime of the earth. So I packed all his crap back into his briefcase, told him if he had a complaint he should go to the police, and I turfed him out of the office."

"Well, he never came to us."

Bleustein shrugged. "I guess he and I shared one view in common."

"So who was he talking about?"

"That I don't think I should tell you. The guy was ranting and frankly, in my opinion he's put enough people through enough grief already."

"Josh—"

Bleustein held up his hands. "Hey listen, I've given you ten minutes more than you deserve. I'll give you one more thing for free. I also told him if he knew something, he should take it to the Children's Aid. So try them. They might give you more than I did."

Green's pulse leaped. The Children's Aid was the agency responsible for setting Fraser's whole nightmare into motion in the first place! Had it been them Fraser had headed off to see at noon on Wednesday? What on earth would make him walk back into the lion's den?

"Thanks for the tip," he replied, keeping the excitement out of his voice with an effort.

Bleustein was already lowering himself back down onto his knees, and he acknowledged the thanks between grunts. "Now fuck off, before someone sees me actually talking to you."

*　　*　　*

Thursday morning arrived with a deafening crack of thunder and a cloudburst of torrential rain under a charcoal sky. Cars slowed to a crawl, and pedestrians dashed recklessly from shelter to shelter, windblown and drenched. But Green's spirits were still high when, at nine o'clock sharp, he presented himself to the main receptionist of the Children's Aid Society and requested to see the Executive Director. It took George Kirkpatrick precisely two minutes to extricate himself from his morning staff meeting, scurry back down to his private office, and straighten himself up in preparation to receive him. Kirkpatrick was still buttoning his jacket as the receptionist escorted Green in, but his smile was firmly in place.

"Inspector Green, is it?" he asked as he strode around his desk with his hand extended. His grip was firm but warm, as if he'd practised for years to convey just the right blend of authority and welcome. Today, however, the grip was slightly damp, and the smile looked ill-at-ease.

Over the years, Green's work in major crimes had brought him into periodic contact with the child protection agency, although fortunately not too often, for adults usually confined their killing, robbing and bludgeoning to one another. He'd never envied the agency its job of finding that fine line between the rights of a family to be together and the need to protect children from harm. And no one was ever satisfied. With its every action scrutinized and decried by one side or the other, with lawyers snapping at its heels, the CAS was always looking over its shoulder to watch its back, and the mere appearance of a high-ranking police officer would be enough to send anxiety levels through the roof. Kirkpatrick herded him nervously to one of the easy chairs grouped around a coffee table and perched himself on the one opposite as if it were a bed of nails.

"How can I help you, Inspector?"

Since his meeting with Bleustein the day before, Green had been pondering what approach to take. His visit actually had a dual purpose, and he wanted to ensure the atmosphere remained amicable enough to get the answers to both questions, each of which might send the agency into defensive retreat. For an agency which dealt with highly sensitive, confidential material and operated under a perpetual mood of siege, defensive retreat would almost be the automatic response.

"Mr. Kirkpatrick," Green began, "this is not an official visit. That is, I'm not investigating a crime in which any of your staff or clients are implicated, and I'm not here to question any of your agency's decisions or activities. I need your help—your opinion, if you like—on a case I'm investigating, in order to make sure I'm not following the wrong path."

Kirkpatrick sat perfectly still, but a small pucker formed at the centre of his brow. He was clearly not reassured but rather waiting for the other shoe to drop. At that point, Green knew that only a head-on approach would work. Anything less, and the man would be looking for traps in Green's every remark.

"Do you remember the Matthew Fraser case? The teacher accused of molesting a six-year-old girl ten years ago?"

Far from looking puzzled or thoughtful as if searching his memory, or simply agreeable as if the memory were at his fingertips, Kirkpatrick looked startled. He covered it quickly.

"Certainly I do."

Green took an educated guess as to the cause of his surprise. "Mr. Fraser came to see you last week, I understand."

"No. No, he didn't."

"I'm not trying to pry into confidential matters, but Matthew Fraser disappeared the day he came to see someone here at the agency, and he's not been heard from since. It's our belief that he may be the victim of foul play."

"I don't understand. Are you suggesting someone at the agency—"

Green shook his head. "But I believe he had some information he wanted to discuss with you, and that information may be important in determining what happened to him." He explained about Fraser's visit to Josh Bleustein and his request for a restraining order. "Mr. Fraser clearly felt in danger because of something he knew. So if you have any knowledge about what he thought or who he felt in danger from, please tell me."

"I'm afraid I can't help you."

It was said with regret rather than defiance, but Green still sensed the man was watching his step. Still protecting confidentiality, or something else?

"Are you saying you didn't hear from him at all?"

"We heard from him, yes. That is, one of my workers did. Mr. Fraser phoned him some time last week. Just a minute, I'll see if he's in his office." Kirkpatrick dialled an internal extension and asked the person who answered to drop by his office. As he hung up, he turned to Green with a smile. "You're in luck. Jean-Paul Landriault is at his desk, and that's rare. I was surprised that Mr. Fraser contacted him, of all people. JP was the worker on the case ten years ago, and he worked like the dickens to see Fraser put away."

"You're saying Mr. Fraser specifically asked for him?"

"I don't think he said no one else would do. He simply asked for JP, and JP was sufficiently intrigued to take him up on it."

"And what did he want?"

"I'll let JP tell you about it." Kirkpatrick walked restlessly to the door to peek out into the hall. Green heard the clicking of heel studs against the hard tile, and a few seconds later, Kirkpatrick ushered his subordinate into the room.

Jean-Paul Landriault could not have presented a greater contrast to his boss. He looked as if he'd just rolled into town on his Harley, his short, squat form decked out in black leather jacket, cowboy boots and skin-tight jeans, and his long, greying mane slicked back into a ponytail. His teeth were stained nicotine yellow, and one was chipped, creating a sinister impression. Green couldn't help wondering what effect he had on the vulnerable, traumatized children he was meant to help.

But all doubt vanished as soon as the man smiled. His grin reached from ear to ear, and his eyes crinkled almost shut with silent laughter. He had a gentle, friendly handshake and a deep, melodic voice with just a trace of a French accent.

Green felt ludicrously prim in his sports jacket and tie, which branded him as just another featureless bureaucrat. He leaned casually back in the armchair and draped his arm over the top. No notebook, no officious fuss. A voice-activated tape recorded all his conversations for his own private reference, and the notebook's importance was mainly for the official record. In this case, he suspected the social worker might speak more freely without an official record.

"Mr. Landriault," he began. "I'm concerned for a man's safety, and I'm hoping you can help." Quickly he outlined the facts, and Jean-Paul's smile faded abruptly.

"Matthew Fraser called me, certainly, and he made an appointment to see me..." He flipped open an over-stuffed pocket agenda, causing a cascade of loose bits of pink paper to float to the floor. Absently, he retrieved them and shoved them back between the pages. "Last Wednesday at two o'clock. But he didn't arrive."

Crystal had observed Matthew Fraser leaving his apartment around noon, dressed as if for a formal appointment, so he had obviously intended to keep his meeting with JP.

"Do you know why? Did he call to explain?"

Jean-Paul shrugged. "I heard nothing. Lost his nerve, I imagine. I was surprised that he called me anyway, because he hated me. He thought I changed the little girl's words and made her all mixed up, so it was my fault she made those accusations against him. Which was bullshit. Becky disclosed them first to the school psychologist, and it was a spontaneous disclosure. The woman wasn't asking anything about that, just conducting a routine assessment, because Becky was having behaviour problems at school. Later, I had a female police officer right with me when I interviewed the child, but still Fraser thought I put the ideas into her head." Jean-Paul flushed as if reliving the outrage, and his hand drifted to his jacket pocket, where Green could see him toying longingly with a pack of cigarettes. Then, catching Green's eye, he grinned his merry smile again. "Like there's not enough work, so I invent some."

"Last week, did he tell you why he wanted to see you?"

Jean-Paul shook his head, but Green sensed he was withholding something. Surely, given the emotions of the case, Jean-Paul must have speculated. Green prodded him further, and Jean-Paul cast a quick, uncertain look at Kirkpatrick. The latter nodded.

"Well, he's still on the Ontario Child Abuse Register. Even when he was acquitted, we kept him on it, because we believed there was sufficient grounds. It's not accessible to the public, but it can red flag him to us if his name appears in another investigation. He was perhaps trying to have his name removed, if he wanted to teach again or work with children again."

Green pondered the possibility, which didn't seem enough to explain Fraser's sense of urgency, for the man would have been on the register for ten years. He explained Josh Bleustein's idea that Matt Fraser feared for his own safety. "Did he mention anything about that?"

"He just said he could not talk over the phone, and he would not meet me at the office here either. Asked me to take Rebecca Whelan's file and meet him on a park bench some place, for Christ's sake. That was too bizarre for me, so I said it was here or nowhere."

"When did he make this call?"

Jean-Paul pawed through a pile of crumpled pink telephone slips. Finally, he freed one and unfolded it. "Monday afternoon. Pretty short notice, actually. I had to put him into my lunch hour, and after all that the little prick doesn't show up."

"Did you try calling him back?"

Jean-Paul's jaw tightened, and without his smile, the sinister look returned. "He did not give me a number. Anyway, I was just happy to let the whole affair disappear. The girl's family's been through hell because of what he did, and their lives have been messed up forever. Rebecca—" he sliced the air in angry finality, "damaged forever. The parents' marriage almost fell apart, the mother's a closet alcoholic, the brother is in and out of drug programs. They don't deserve to have this guy bring everything all back again."

"Do you think that's what he was going to do?"

"What other reason would he ask me to bring the file? I told him no way I would discuss Rebecca's file with him. He said I didn't have to talk, just listen."

"Listen to what?"

A dull red crept up Jean-Paul's neck. "I told you I don't know. He sounded very paranoid, and when I saw him, he was running down the street clutching his briefcase—"

"Wait a minute. You actually saw him?"

"Through the window. My office looks on the street, and I had a quick look of him down the street. Like I said, taking off."

"Towards this building?"

Jean-Paul shook his head. "In the goddamn opposite direction. Freaked out of his mind, like he had an army of Hells Angels on his ass."

Seven

With his windshield wipers flapping and his CD player belting out The Tragically Hip over the drumbeat of the rain, Green was half way back to the station before he realized the significance of Jean-Paul's remark.

"Clutching his briefcase!" he said aloud and struck his forehead in amazement. How could he have missed something so obvious? Bleustein had mentioned the briefcase too, saying Matt Fraser had arrived at his office with a briefcase stuffed with clippings and notes. Even Crystal had mentioned it when she described her glimpse of the man heading out of the apartment that last day, dressed in a suit, carrying a briefcase and hustling purposefully as if he had an appointment.

Yet Green was certain there had been no briefcase at Fraser's apartment when he'd searched it. No briefcase, no personal papers, nothing remotely like the clippings Bleustein had described.

When Green reached the squad room, he was relieved to see Sullivan at his desk, poring over a computer screen of tattoos again. The big detective had perched a pair of half-moon glasses on the bridge of his nose, and the effect—professorial truck driver—made Green burst out laughing. Sullivan scowled at him red-eyed over the rims.

"Your time will come, Green. Spend hours staring at these

damn screens, and you'll be down at the drugstore yourself soon enough."

"That's why I avoid paperwork like the plague. What are you bothering for? You should be tracking the victim's recent movements. You have a likely ID on the body, and all we need to do now is wait for the dental results."

Sullivan rubbed his eyes. "Just cross-referencing. The Iraqi's ID was a little shaky, and there's no mention on Fraser's file about a tattoo."

"The info in his file is all ten years out of date, though. By the way, you go to the autopsy?"

Sullivan pulled a face. "Ident did. I figured it wasn't necessary, and I wasn't keen to watch this one."

"Don't like your bodies crispy?"

"You should talk!"

"True." Green rarely survived an entire autopsy without losing his last meal. "Did you get his report?"

"MacPhail was backed up, and in a bear of a mood. I'll call later."

"When you do reach MacPhail, let me know what he says." Green eyes drifted to the screen of girlish tattoos. Pretty ringlets of all description. "Tell me, was there a briefcase among the victim's effects in the rooming house?"

"Briefcase?" Sullivan arched his brows in surprise. "He didn't even have a wallet or jacket. Nothing but a bottle of scotch and the clothes on his back, which were completely burnt, of course. So unless someone stole his stuff, he came to the rooming house completely empty-handed."

Green pondered the information. Even homeless people acquired belongings—their own favourite blanket, an old hat to ward off the night chill, knick-knacks plucked from garbage cans, a cherished magazine or grimy deck of cards. If Fraser had checked into the rooming house to hide out for a week, surely he would have brought something, if only a toothbrush and a pair of clean underwear. Fraser's toothbrush was still sitting by his bathroom sink.

"Did the Iraqi say when Fraser rented the room?"

Sullivan flipped through his notebook. "He thinks last Wednesday. They don't keep good records, that way they can slip a few bucks past the tax man, but I think I scared him enough that he gave up Wednesday."

"Time of day?"

"That he was clearer on. Five o'clock, just at the peak of rush hour."

Green frowned to himself as he tried to make sense of the time sequence. Fraser must have booked the room before Crystal spotted him returning to his apartment. Presumably he'd gone home afterwards to pack and take care of his dog, which might explain why he no longer had the briefcase when he was found in the fire. Yet back at his apartment, something had obviously interrupted him before he could get ready.

Something interrupted him... Green felt a grim satisfaction as he headed on to his office. His reconstruction of Fraser's last days was beginning to take on flesh. Fraser had become more and more convinced that his life was in danger. He'd gone to Josh Bleustein on Monday to seek his help, and upon being rebuffed, he had made an appointment at the CAS with the very man who had accused him of sexual assault ten years earlier. Why? To censure him? To demand restitution or exoneration?

Or as Bleustein had suggested, to tell JP what he thought had really happened? What he'd pieced together, from bits of evidence stuffed in meticulous detail into his briefcase?

If his neighbour Crystal was to be believed, Fraser had set off as planned for his meeting with JP. He'd reached the CAS office in plenty of time, but when he got off the bus, he'd run headlong in the other direction. Had he simply lost his nerve? Had he remembered something else? Or had he seen something, perhaps someone, that had frightened him off?

Whatever it was, he'd never returned to the CAS. Three hours later, he'd turned up at a rooming house across town, where he rented a room under an assumed name. Then he'd returned home and had only enough time to change and begin his dinner before something drove him from the apartment again.

What had happened that afternoon to change his dogged determination into desperate flight? And what had he done in the three hours between his aborted CAS visit and his arrival at the rooming house? Had he learned something else? Had he tried to figure out another way to pursue the investigation? Had he approached another source of support? Not Janice Tanner or anyone in his therapy group, nor his therapists for that matter. Perhaps his family?

Green took out his notebook and flipped back to his conversation with Fraser's sister. Ah-ha! Fraser had called her Wednesday, the very day he disappeared. It was all beginning to fit! He had called her after all these years of silence, not because he wanted to confess as she believed, but because he needed her help. But she too had rebuffed him. Who else could he turn to? After living so long as a recluse, what friends did he have left?

Out of the fringes of his memory popped the peculiar word "mistwalker". It might be a code or a title, but it might be a nickname. Green flipped through Fraser's address book, which was crammed with meticulous lists of people, none of them mistwalker. On a whim, Green accessed his favourite internet search engine and ran the keyword mistwalker. To his astonishment, nearly three thousand references came up. He scrolled through the first page rapidly; someone had written a fantasy book by that title, other instances seemed to refer to a character in a fantasy game and still others to Celtic mythology. As Green explored a few sites, he felt he was searching for the proverbial needle in an alien, unpronounceable universe. This was a job for Detective Bob Gibbs, the quintessential detail man, when he had nothing but time on his hands. Green needed a more practical way to track down the important people in Fraser's life.

Because of Green's woeful administrative skills, the print-outs from the Fraser case were still strewn in piles on his floor. He picked up a fistful with a smile of triumph. This is why I never put anything away, he thought, not because I haven't the patience, but because I know I'll need it again.

He began scanning reports, and within half an hour he had ferreted out the names and addresses of half a dozen people who had testified on Fraser's behalf, mostly teachers but hopefully also friends. He spent a further fifteen minutes cross-referencing the names with the Canada 411 database to make sure the addresses were up to date. Two people had disappeared from the database, and still another had too common a name to trace, but three teachers were still at the same address. Perhaps even at the same school, he thought.

Glancing at his watch, he saw it was already twelve o'clock. If he hurried, he'd catch the teachers still on their lunch break. He pocketed his notebook, holstered his radio and gun and grabbed his sports jacket off his chair. Downstairs he signed out an official car and headed outside, where a wall of heat assailed him. As quickly as it had come up, the storm had blown over, leaving a mist rising off the rain-slicked ground. It had brought no relief from the heat, however, and the harsh sun seared his eyes as it glared off the cars. He turned up the air conditioning and squealed the tires as he accelerated into the traffic.

In his fifteen years of frontline investigative work before he found himself increasingly relegated to his desk, Green had perfected an interview style based on the element of surprise. Never let a witness know you're coming, never let him know what you're going to ask next. Without benefit of forethought, people rarely produced clear and carefully constructed answers, and Green hoped a little more of the truth would slip out.

In this case, others might argue that after ten years, the innocent witnesses on his list would have no reason to suppress the truth and might benefit from some forewarning in order to hunt back through their memories for the details he needed. But Green was less interested in the events of ten years ago than those of last week, regarding which the innocence of the witnesses, if Fraser had contacted any of them, was far less assured.

Green ducked around cyclists and in and out of the sluggish noon hour traffic, which was further choked by tourists lost in the maze of Ottawa's one-way downtown streets. He swung under the Queensway and backtracked alongside it over the historic Pretoria Bridge and up to Main Street. Here the traffic opened up a little as he headed out of the downtown core towards Old Ottawa South, an eclectic residential neighbourhood tucked in between the canal and the Rideau River. Green knew that the narrow, cluttered streets, the cramped lots and the aging brick houses were deceptive. Young urban professionals with double incomes, nannies and bright futures lived there with their fully equipped minivans wedged into narrow drives and their bicycles chained to front porches. He and Sharon had looked at properties here before emigrating to the Dreaded Vinyl Cube in the cow pasture, but they'd found they could barely afford the front porch. He was now secretly grateful, because he wasn't sure he'd feel any more at home among this Birkenstock and *latte* crowd of civil servants and academics than he did among the high-tech hopefuls in Barrhaven.

At the time of his arrest, Fraser had taught a Grade One/Two class at the Duke of York Elementary School, which proved to be an ancient, listing brick edifice nestled in the heart of Old Ottawa South. Despite its threat of imminent collapse, it had been rescued from closure numerous times by its articulate and fiercely loyal parent community. Green parked the Taurus at the curb outside the main door and sat for a minute watching the children squealing and chasing each other around the muddy school yard.

His job didn't take him into schools very often, and now he found himself thinking not so much of his pre-school son, but of his estranged teenage daughter, whose girlhood was little more than a conjuror's figment in his thoughts, coloured by distant memory fragments of his own boyhood. Memories in which school yard laughter had more often sounded malevolent than innocent, in which the chasing had felt predatory and the little jabs had turned painful out of sight of the teacher's indifferent eye. Now, however, as a testament to the changing times, a sharp-eyed teacher immediately detached herself from a gaggle of girls and approached him with a questioning frown.

"Can I help you?" she demanded.

In spite of his twenty years' experience as a competent adult in authority, he felt a twinge of small-boy humiliation. Guilty until proven innocent, the way he'd always felt at school.

"Inspector Green, Ottawa Police," he said, opening his ID. "Who's in charge here?"

The woman's eyes flashed in momentary alarm. She brushed a sweaty strand of hair back from her forehead and shielded her eyes from the sun as she searched the playground. "There's Mrs. Allen, the principal."

Another woman, older and immaculately sheathed in a blue dress with matching high heels, was already striding across the yard towards them.

"Can I help you?" Mrs. Allen asked, and there was no mistaking the frosty edge to her courtesy. This school staff was certainly on stranger alert, Green thought, and wondered if it was a legacy peculiar to this school or a reflection of modern times.

He repeated his introduction and suggested they continue the discussion in her office. Clearly unnerved but determined to appear in charge, Mrs. Allen led the way up the front steps and through the heavy wooden doors. As soon as he stepped into the creaky hallway and took his first breath of the stifling, mildewy air, Green wondered why the parents had fought so hard to salvage the place. It had narrow halls, cavernous ceilings, steep, dark staircases and more twists and crannies than a haunted house at the fair. The wooden floors sagged as if they'd borne the tread of a million little feet and creaked as if they could bear no more.

The principal squeezed her way between the desk and filing cabinet that passed for a secretary's office and entered the tiny room behind, in which there was barely space for her desk and two chairs. She had made the best of it, though. The room was as immaculate and colour-coordinated as herself, with pale green walls, dark green desk and bookcase, grey chairs and a tasteful array of nature photographs on the walls. The bookcase held rows of binders bearing the school board logo, and on its top sat a tea tray with china pot and matching cups. Only the woman's desk betrayed the frenzied demands of her job; it was covered with files, notes and memos which were rustling in the breeze from the fan she'd propped on the filing cabinet.

Mrs. Allen stacked the files hastily on the side of her desk as she shoehorned herself in behind her desk. "Final report cards," she said with a tight smile.

Green thought of his own report cards, manila cardboard affairs filled with ominous Ds and comments about his wandering focus. "Looks like my desk," he replied affably, as much to put himself at ease as her. "Makes me feel right at home."

She was not reassured. "What can I do for you—Inspector, is it?"

Green opened his notebook. "There are three teachers I'd like to speak to who worked here a number of years ago. I'm not sure if they're still here."

"What's this about?"

Green made a show of consulting his notes. "Linda Good, Virginia Pender and Ross Long. Are any of them in the school?"

She met his gaze. "I'd prefer not to divulge personal information without knowing the purpose of the request."

He sighed. Pissing contests with men were annoying enough, but why did some women, especially those fighting for the mantle of authority in what had always been a man's game, feel they had to piss longer and further than everyone else? He decided to give her a morsel.

"I'm hoping they may have some information in a police inquiry which has nothing to do with the school, I assure you."

"Nothing to do with the school," she repeated, her eyes fixed on his. He knew she wanted more, but he said nothing. For a long, irritated minute she waited him out, then shrugged as if she'd lost interest.

"I don't know the others, but Ross Long is here. He teaches Grade Five/Six, and you'll find him upstairs in the class at the end of the hall. But I warn you, the bell rings in less than ten minutes."

Green squeezed past the outer desk and made his way up the creaky staircase to the third floor, which was even hotter than the second. In the small, cluttered classroom at the end of the hall, he found a short, balding man with a walrus moustache and a stubby, pear-shaped body that jiggled as he scribbled science notes on the blackboard. He had opened all the windows and had two fans going, but still the room was an oven. The whir of the fans and the shrieks from outside obliterated all hope of a quiet interview.

Green introduced himself, and mindful of his ten-minute limit, cut directly to the point. "I obtained your name from the records of the Matthew Fraser investigation, and I saw that you testified on his behalf. Have you heard from him or had any dealings with him in the last couple of weeks?"

Green thought Ross Long flinched at the mention of Fraser's name, but his denial was quick and sure.

"When did you last have contact with him?"

"Oh, not for donkey's years."

"In human terms—months, years?"

"God, yes. Must be going on eight years. I've hardly seen him since the trial."

"Why is that?"

Long's gaze shifted nervously outside, where the students were still cavorting on the soggy grass. A trickle of sweat ran down his cheeks and dripped onto the collar of his golf shirt. "Well, you know...went our separate ways, I guess."

"But I thought you two were friends."

"Not really friend friends. More like colleague friends. Hell, when you're the only two guys in a staff room of women, you kind of stick together. What's this about?"

"Did you work together long?" Green knew they'd taught together for four years, because it had been in the man's statement, but he was curious to see how Long would characterize it now. In his official statement, Long had implied he and Fraser were close buddies who had lunch together, went for beers every Friday after work and even went on weekend fishing trips together when Long's wife let him off the leash. Now Long was putting as much distance between the two of them as he could.

"He wasn't here that long. Three or four years? He came here as a rookie out of teacher's college, and I've been here since before the great flood."

"How long ago was that?"

"What?" Long looked startled, then gave a nervous chuckle. "I've been here twenty-eight years. That seems like before the flood. I've seen lots of fads come and go, but now it's gotten so you almost forget you're supposed to be teaching kids because you're so busy filling out forms. What's this about, anyway? I thought all that stuff with Matt was long over."

Green pondered what response would elicit the most cooperation without feeding the rumour mill. "There are some new concerns—" he began.

"You mean he's done it again?"

"Again? But you said you thought he was innocent."

"I did!" Long clamped his jaw tight, and his gaze flicked toward the door. "And—and I do. You just caught me off guard."

"Off guard, sometimes the truth comes out."

"It's not that. It's just you never really know, do you? Afterwards, all of us were looking back over the things he'd done. Picking apart all the innocent little things and—"

"Like what?"

"Well, like volunteering to run the intramural sports so he could spend lunch hours with the kids, and even organizing a coaching system so the older ones could help the little ones. He was always with the kids instead of in the staff room. We all thought it was because he was shy, and for a young single man, the staff room can be like walking into a room full of piranhas. But afterwards we got to wondering…well, you know."

"You mean after the allegations?"

"No, after the trial, when he got off and I realized perhaps my testimony—our testimony—made the difference. During the trial, I said to myself, 'I'll just tell what I know, and the truth will come out in the end.' And all I knew was that he was a nice guy, he seemed to love the kids, he devoted boundless time and energy to them, and they seemed to like him too. I never saw a single sign of trouble. There wasn't a kid who didn't want to play on the teams he coached, not a kid who came out of Grade One worse than they went in. Even the kids he drove home—"

A bell shrilled through the building, setting Green's hair on end and nearly derailing him from the significance of Long's comment. He waited for the sound to stop.

"What kids? There's no mention of that."

Long paled, and his moustache twitched. His gaze flicked between the window and the door. "There wasn't. I mean, I didn't. Ah, it—it slipped my mind initially, I guess, and the policewoman who was investigating was so pushy, she threw us all on the defensive. She seemed hellbent on railroading Matt, and I wasn't about to give her any ammunition."

"So you withheld information from the police?"

Long thrust back his shoulders and sucked in his paunch. "She withheld stuff from us! Wouldn't even tell us what the accusations were, or who the kid was! How were we supposed to know what to think? We ended up looking at every kid with suspicion, wondering is that the one? Am I going to be next? So I figured, if she was going to play it like a star chamber witch hunt, I wasn't going to make her case for her. Not against a fellow teacher whom the parents were ready to hang by the balls anyway. You have no idea the hysteria that took over this place back then, detective. Parents scrutinized our every move—every teacher who ever had a kid on a behaviour mod program to reward good behaviour, every teacher who took a kid aside for a private discussion, our every motive was challenged. Plus our loyalty was questioned. Parents accused us of covering up and of putting their little kids at risk to protect one of our own. Teachers who'd known families for years and done their best to help their children over the years felt betrayed. So yeah, I saw the look in your eye when you said I withheld information. I didn't know a damn thing for sure, except that every little fact I raised would be inflated with hysteria, so I figured let the cops build their own damn case."

Outside, a hush had fallen as the yard emptied of children. Inwardly Green cursed and hoped Long could continue his tirade long enough to come to the meat of the matter. The man was growing red from indignation and lack of breath, and Green suspected he'd been saving up this tirade for ten years.

"Matt drove a few kids home sometimes after rehearsals or games," Long continued, "when it was dark and their parents were too damn busy to pick them up. If he was guilty of anything, it was naïveté for thinking that trying to help children was the right thing to do and that the parents wouldn't sue the ass off him if anything went wrong. Nowadays we don't hug kids, detective. We don't meet them alone to give them private advice or encouragement, and we sure as hell don't put them in our own car without a million waivers protecting us from here to China."

The hall below filled with the thunder of a hundred feet, and children's chatter reverberated off the walls. Long broke off his diatribe and moved toward his door. "I've got to get to my class now, detective. So if you've got more questions, they'll have to wait."

"That'll do for now." Green flipped his notebook shut. "I appreciate your honesty."

"Yeah, well, you know—" Long paused in the doorway and watched as the upstairs hallway filled with students. Sweaty, red-faced, and irritable from the heat, they jostled one another noisily. "It was a difficult time for everybody, and we just wanted to be fair. Frankly, we didn't think that was true of everyone."

Those words stayed with Green as he plowed his way through the crowds back down the stairs. Crime always aroused strong feelings in those it touched, and as a police officer he'd often borne the brunt of the public hysteria and finger pointing that followed. And nowhere were the feelings more intense and personal than when the victim was a child. Teachers, like police officers, could change from protector to traitor in the public eye on the strength of one word.

Once downstairs, Green headed back toward the principal's office to inform her he was done and found his way blocked by a massive woman in a purple and yellow floral tent dress and a straw hat. She overflowed the secretary's chair and took up all the remaining space in the little outer office. She eyed Green with a chilly stare no doubt designed to make the most rebellious student rethink his approach. When Green introduced himself, the stare grew shrewd.

"Oh, it's you. Mrs. Allen said to keep an eye on you. She's gone to a meeting, and she said if you had more questions, you should give her a call." The woman reached a pudgy arm across her desk to pick up a dish of mints. She offered one to Green, which he declined, before popping one into her mouth. "Waste of time talking to her, anyway," she continued, sucking noisily. "She's only been here three years."

Changing his mind, Green reached over, selected a mint, and regretted it the instant it hit his taste buds in full force. He propped himself as casually as he could against the edge of her desk. "How long have you been here?"

"Twenty-three years. And you're right, I remember it all."

"Remember what?" Green asked in surprise. Ross Long hadn't had time to tip off the office, even if he'd wanted to.

"The Fraser case. That's what this is about, right? Those teachers you wanted, they all testified at the trial."

Shrewd doesn't do the woman justice, Green thought, and gave her an appreciative smile. "Did you testify?"

The woman looked askance, her jowls shaking with the vigour of her denial. "Hell, no. I had to work with these people. Back then, I was on my own with three kids to support, no car, no child care, and this job was around the corner from my house."

"So you thought you'd better not take sides?"

"Listen, this community's got some powerful people in it. There are parents who are crown attorneys themselves, or justice lawyers, or work for big firms with lawyers up the yingyang. Consider this school's been slated to close three times—look at it, it's a dump!—but if the school board closed it, the kids would have to be bussed out of their community, maybe even meet the big bad world in the Glebe. So each time, the parents had enough clout to make the board, the trustees, the director and his backroom boys all back down."

The mint was slowly burning a hole in Green's tongue, and he eased it carefully into the corner of his mouth, trying to look attentive. "And were they out for blood on this case?"

"Blood? No, the kid's balls. And the balls of the principal, who didn't act fast enough on the first complaint, and the balls of the board, who didn't fire the kid on the spot."

"By kid you mean—?"

"Matt," she exclaimed, crunching her mint and sending spittle flying. "He was a kid from where I sat. One of those nice, soft-spoken guys who loved teaching and who had a special touch with the timid ones. He started off in Grade Six, but the big kids walked all over him, so the principal moved him down to Grade One. He loved the little ones, and they loved him."

"No hanky-panky?"

She hesitated and eyed him dubiously from under folds of flesh. Then, with excessive care, she leaned forward and took another mint from the bowl. "Who's going to know all this?"

Green, who hadn't even extracted his notebook, gave an exaggerated shrug. "Maybe nobody. We're not reopening the case, if that's what you're worried about. I'm just trying to fill in some holes. Are you suggesting there may have been some hanky-panky?"

"Not that I ever saw, mind you. I wouldn't have kept quiet if I really knew something. I mean, I have kids myself, and the parents would have had to get in line behind me to get a piece of his balls. But—" She paused to tug on her dress and to redirect the overflow of her breasts. In the heat, she sweated freely. "There was something weird about Matt. You know those soft, gentle kinds of men? They seem to feel safer with kids, maybe even sexually, you know? This is just my feeling. I mean, the sex drive is there, right, and the guy's got to make it with somebody, and if he's too damn shy to try a woman and he gets tired of going solo—well, it makes sense, eh? And that's what creeped me out. I didn't have a thing to go on, I never saw him look at a kid funny or sneak one off to a back room somewhere, but he hung around with the little kids, and he didn't show much interest in the pretty young thing we had here at the time who was trying to catch his attention."

Just as well you kept these thoughts to yourself, Green thought. Without substantiation, your speculation about Fraser's sexual inclinations probably wouldn't have done much to enhance Barbara Devine's case, but it would have been chewed to bits by defence council.

"Is that what most of the teachers thought? That he was a bit strange and just might be guilty?"

"The teachers?" She snorted. "They weren't allowed to have an opinion. Or if they did, they didn't dare voice it. The teacher's union swooped in here almost as soon as the shit hit the fan and told everybody that their duty was to stand behind a fellow teacher and show him a united front against these false accusations. They weren't supposed to talk to anyone about it, not the parents, not the press, and they were supposed to answer police questions only about things they personally knew."

"Wise under the circumstances."

"Sure. And what did that tell the parents? You have no idea how many upset parents came through that door to complain to me the teachers were implying the kids were lying—"

"Kids? What kids?"

"Well—the ones who said Matt molested them."

"I thought there was only one."

"Only one that went to trial—and what a little piece of work she turned out to be—but there were a few who started reporting things in the months after her. Anyway, it doesn't matter. The point is the union told the teachers to support Matt, which meant saying the charges were false, which meant saying the kids were lying. Or at least imagining things."

"Where did the school board stand on this?"

"Where it usually does, as far from the stink as possible. Don't want to interfere with the case, that was their line. Offer counselling to the families, keep Fraser away from kids, and let the courts do their thing."

"Also probably wise under the circumstances."

Her baleful look returned. "Easy for you to say, you see this kind of thing every day. But schools are supposed to be like families, and here we had the parents suspecting the teachers, and the teachers accusing the parents of lynching, and the board not supporting either the parents or the teachers."

"In other words, a mess."

"You got that right. After Matt was acquitted, the guys in power—I mean the parents, the board and the union—had two choices for the mess. Blame the six-year-old girl who started it all, or blame Matt Fraser. Some choice, eh? Especially when the lawyer who was heading up the parent group happened to be the little girl's stepfather."

"So Matt Fraser was history."

She nodded and went for her third mint. "Best all around, don't you think?"

Eight

Best all around, except for Matt Fraser, Green thought, as he switched the car's air conditioning on full and sat for a moment studying the school. The inscription "Duke of York Elementary School, 1924" was set in stone over the transom of the front door, and the overall effect was one of dignified decline. There was no hint of the pain and vitriol which had fomented inside.

Schools were supposed to be like families, the secretary had said. Green tried to envision Tony arriving home one day with a dark, bewildered tale about his favourite teacher. Or even his daughter Hannah, who emerged from his ex-wife's infrequent letters as little more than a disembodied scrap of rebellion. The mere thought of either of them in the clutches of a predator knotted his gut. Faced with the most primal and abhorrent violation of their child, what parent could be blamed for losing their head? And what teacher would fail to sympathize, no matter where their professional allegiance lay?

"Mike, what are you doing?" Barbara Devine demanded when he posed her those very questions back at the police station half an hour later. He had found her in her office eating a soggy hotdog with her stocking feet propped on the window ledge and an open policy binder balanced on her lap. She swung around to her desk and shoved her feet back into her high heels.

"The Fraser disappearance may become a homicide investigation," he replied blandly. "I'm gathering background."

"Oh, damn," she muttered, then dropped the half-eaten hot dog in the garbage and scrubbed the mustard from her hands with a napkin. "Why do you assume it goes back to this abuse case, rather than some new trouble he's got himself into?"

Green debated whether to tell her about Fraser's visit to Bleustein or the CAS, but decided against it. He didn't entirely trust her not to meddle. "Instinct," he said instead.

She eyed him for a long moment. A smudge of mustard on her upper lip detracted from the look of professional disinterest she affected. "Mike, you don't know sex crimes. Trust me, these guys don't change. Fraser has probably made a hundred new enemies by now, while you're busy barking up the wrong tree."

"Then enlighten me. I want to know why the investigation took so long and why things got so out-of-hand."

She sighed. "There was no way to handle that case without it getting messy, because everything had to be kept secret. You know the laws on sex crimes and offences against minors, Mike. We couldn't reveal who the victims were or what Fraser was alleged to have done to them. In fact, before we laid the charges, we couldn't even confirm that Fraser was under investigation, and we certainly couldn't solicit information or question classmates about other incidents."

"Even subtly?"

She folded her arms across her chest brusquely, a sure sign he was getting to her. "Investigating child abuse is not like any other criminal case, Green. You can't inquire subtly about it. I'd investigated dozens of allegations against teachers and other professionals, many of which had no substance whatsoever. Building a credible case is like dodging landmines in the dark. You have to protect the rights of the accused and the privacy of the children, but still uncover the facts in the case, all the while watching your back so the accused doesn't sue the pants off you if he gets off. You don't want a witch hunt; you don't want the man's reputation slandered or his name smeared, nor do you want the defence to be able to argue undue influence. So you keep as tight a lid on the information as you can."

She planted her elbows on the table and leaned forward. "The problem is, at the first hint of funny business, people go ballistic, imagining all sorts of horrors. Parents started phoning each other and questioning their children. Teachers went paranoid because they didn't know which children had complained or what the substance of the complaints was. They started questioning their own behaviour and wondering if they'd be the next to be accused."

She was on a roll now, the rawness of her feelings welling up through her words. Green could tell that ten years had not buried this case for her one iota. Devine might be trying to refashion herself as a corporate administrator, but beneath the tailored navy suit and the expensive blouse, her passion for the fight was with her still.

"And we couldn't do a damn thing to reassure anyone. Naturally, I told the principal to assure his staff that no ordinary behaviour, not even hugs or sitting the little ones on laps, would get them in trouble, but I couldn't tell them Fraser had made the little girl undress, he'd made her give him blow jobs, and he'd ejaculated between her thighs. Becky was graphic and clear on this, Mike. No matter what the teachers said and what the defence alleged—that Becky had been a behaviour problem all along, that she was a habitual liar and drama queen—no child makes those details up. And these child molesters are smart. They don't penetrate or leave marks, so there's no physical proof, and they pick the marginalized children whom no one will believe. Children who are already angry and upset, who crave the attention and whose new problems will be masked by the behaviour problems they already show. And that's exactly what happened. My worst nightmares came true in that case, Mike. Parents pumped their children, children embellished their stories, the defence tore their evidence apart on cross. And the creep walked."

"But you should have seen that coming," Green replied. "With no information or direction from us, hysteria would take over."

"I did see it coming!" she snapped. "But we couldn't handle things any differently. We couldn't just interview every little girl he'd had any substantial contact with over the last four years. That would have been a fishing expedition which would have biased the public's perception of the accused and endangered his right to a fair trial by undermining the presumption of innocence. Talk about handing Bleustein his defence on a silver platter. Not to mention he'd have accused us of manufacturing evidence."

"On any new cases that surfaced, possibly. But what about Rebecca Whelan herself? Surely with that graphic description, you had more than enough to proceed with her alone. If you'd charged him immediately, there would have been less time for the rumours to start and less time for her to get confused about her story."

Her face flamed, and he thought for an instant she would leap over the desk at him. "I didn't screw up this case, Green, if that's what you're implying! The girl wasn't stable. She kept changing her story of the events—the sequence, the times and places. Sometimes it was last week, sometimes last year, all normal enough for a little kid who doesn't understand time. But white, middle-aged, male judges don't always understand that. Twenty-six sexual abuse cases I had that year, Green, and twenty-six acquittals. I wanted this one to stick, for once. So I was trying to get other cases to back her up. Waiting for other parents to come forward with more complaints on their own. That took months!"

"Did you know about the kids he drove home late from school?"

Her eyes clouded, and she snorted at the memory. "Oh, yes. And that was an example of the parents being too overzealous. When they got wind of the rumours, they questioned their kids and asked them point blank 'Did Mr. Fraser do this, did he do that, did he give you candy, did he ever touch you?' By the time we got to them, the kids were telling me about every little pat on the shoulder. Only two cases sounded suspicious, but in the trial—"

Devine's phone rang, and her demeanour changed instantly from backroom cop to polished professional as she picked it up. She listened in silence for a moment, then her gaze flicked towards Green. A scowl marred her mask of calm.

"That won't be necessary, counsellor. It was Inspector Green, who is right here. Shall I put him on, or—?" She paused to listen, then glanced at her watch. "How about twenty minutes. He'll meet you in the lobby."

Green raised an eyebrow as she hung up, but he waited her out. Her scowl deepened. "Green, I don't need this crap. That was Quinton J. Patterson, of McKendry, Patterson and Coles. The little girl's stepfather. And he's on the warpath."

*   *   *

Quinton Patterson arrived five minutes early, suggesting that he had come directly from his law office, which was just up Elgin Street, opposite the main court house. Feeling perverse, Green kept him waiting ten minutes and endured two pages over the station's PA system while he refreshed his memory about the family background.

Rebecca Whelan's parents had separated when Rebecca was just a baby and her brother Billy was eight. Custody had been awarded to the mother after a bitter court dispute in which both parties had accused the other of being unfit, but the children continued to have regular weekend visits with their father up until at least the time of the trial.

On one of her many court appearances during the custody battle, Rebecca's mother had met Quinton Patterson, who was appearing in the same court on an unrelated matter, and they began an intense love affair which led to their marriage as soon the papers were finalized in her divorce. It was the first marriage for him, and the couple had no subsequent children of their own, but police reports at the time of Fraser's trial described Quinton Patterson as fiercely devoted to his stepchildren, although more so to little Becky than to his stepson, who'd been a surly ten when Quinton came on the scene. Although he'd only been a junior lawyer in his firm at the time, Barbara Devine had clearly felt the pressure of his legal sabre-rattling to lay a charge in this case.

So does the man come now as friend or foe, Green wondered as he made his way down to the lobby. Is he hoping I have new evidence or a fresh resolve to put Fraser away, or is he trying to put the lid back on the whole painful mess? As a lawyer, Patterson certainly knows about double jeopardy, which prevents our retrying the case in criminal court, but perhaps he's hoping for some new legal toehold by which he can go after Fraser and the teacher's union—indeed why not the whole school board and the police department—in a civil suit. Green's answer came the minute he laid eyes on the man striding back and forth across the marble foyer with a cellphone glued to his ear.

Quinton Patterson had a baby face he was trying very hard to counteract. He had soft, rosy cheeks, a mop of black curls and only the faintest shimmer of silver above his ears. Like Green, he looked barely thirty, but unlike Green, who enjoyed the camouflage that his youthful looks provided, Patterson had affected a corporate power dress and a haughty sneer in an attempt to bulk up his image. Today he was crisply dressed in a navy pinstripe suit, coordinated royal blue tie and polished Italian shoes, and his face was a dangerous shade of pink as he snapped orders into the phone. The man's not pleased with the latest developments, Green decided.

"Mr. Patterson," he began. Patterson held up a sharp finger to silence him and turned his back.

"He can try all he wants, that's our final offer!"

"I'm Mike Green." Green extended his hand.

"Wait a—" Patterson barked, then swung around to give Green an incredulous look. Green smiled inwardly. He hadn't bothered to put on his sports jacket, and his wrinkled shirt and scuffed shoes were clearly not what Patterson expected. "I'll call you back," he said into the phone and snapped it shut. Ignoring Green's outstretched hand, he started toward the elevator.

"Is your office on the third floor?"

Yet another subtle putdown, Green observed, for Patterson almost certainly knew that the third floor was reserved for the senior brass. Three putdowns in the space of ten seconds. No wonder Barbara Devine said she didn't need this crap.

"I've reserved one of the interview rooms," Green replied and pointedly headed toward the stairs, which had a fire escape decor that didn't quite match the imperial mood Patterson was striving for. Neither did the interview room, which was small, windowless and contained nothing but a table and three moulded plastic chairs. Green took one and gestured Patterson into another.

"What can I do for you, Mr. Patterson?"

Patterson inspected the seat before sitting down, then set his briefcase on the table and flipped it open. After extracting a yellow legal pad, he balanced a pair of reading glasses on the bridge of his nose. Glancing at his watch, he made a note on the blank pad.

"I understand you've been making inquiries into my daughter's sexual molestation case."

"Who told you that?" The question was not simple fencing. Green was genuinely interested in Patterson's connections.

"Is it true?"

"Who told you?"

Patterson jotted again on his legal pad, then peered at Green over the rims of his glasses. "Josh Bleustein."

Green had suspected as much, although he'd thought Bleustein and Patterson would be on opposite sides of this issue. Bleustein had defended the hated child molester and won. On top of that, Bleustein was the quintessential loud-mouth, brawling Jew, and Patterson was old-firm Rockcliffe Wasp. But the legal fraternity was full of strange bedfellows.

"What exactly did Bleustein tell you?" Green asked.

"That Matthew Fraser was probably dead, and I should be prepared for the police to come after me and my family."

"How collegial of Mr. Bleustein, given that he worked the other side of the fence."

"Josh never believed Fraser was innocent."

"Then you must despise him for being so good at his job."

Patterson had been scribbling industriously on his notepad, and now a faint flush spread up his neck. "I despise the education system for betraying the innocence of children, and the police department for acting like spineless sycophants."

"So what can I do for you, Mr. Patterson?"

"I want to protect the interests of my family. You'll forgive me if I haven't much faith in your department's ability to do that, nor in your investigative competence. My daughter's case is ancient history. The death of this man—if he is Fraser, and my sources tell me that's far from assured—has nothing whatever to do with us, and I'm here to tell you that I will regard any attempt to connect the two as police harassment."

"You may regard it however you wish, Mr. Patterson. I have a suspicious death to investigate, and I'm sure you know the law well enough to—"

"Don't patronize me, Green! Personally, I want to pin a medal on whoever killed him, but if it was going to be me or someone in Becky's case, we would have done it ten years ago, when it mattered! Not now, when it's all over and buried. And you know damn well that's true!"

"In my business, it doesn't pay to know damn well anything is true until I've looked into it. My team will be pursuing any and all lines of inquiry that we deem relevant."

"He's probably done it again, you know! Have you thought of that?"

Green inclined his head slightly. "Your daughter's case is one of several lines of inquiry."

Patterson scribbled furiously on his notepad, and after a moment he stopped and tapped his pencil rapidly on the page. He seemed to be calculating his next move.

"Very well," he snapped. "However, I want your agreement that if you have something to ask of my family, you will direct it to me. I will cooperate with you."

"Have you or your family had any contact with Mr. Fraser since the trial?"

Patterson sat with pen poised. "So do I have your agreement you'll go through me?"

The man's intensity vibrated through the small room. Green sensed that beneath the adversarial legal façade, Patterson was a father dealing with powerful emotions in the only way he knew how, by playing the game he knew best. Green softened his tone. "Of course not, and you couldn't have expected any other response. But I'm not insensitive to the pain in this case, sir. I've been in Major Crimes more than fifteen years, and I know how a crime like this leaves the victims feeling brutalized and betrayed. Those feelings never really go away; they just get paved over with a thin veneer that can easily be picked away. I can't deny this investigation will do that, but I'll try to be as sensitive as I can be. That much I can promise you."

Patterson sat suspended for a moment, then dropped his eyes and made a show of jotting more notes on his pad. The pen quivered in his hand and his tone, although brusque, was conciliatory.

"We haven't seen Mr. Fraser in over six years. After the trial, I kept track of his activities until he left town. It was my form of citizen's justice. I didn't want him to feel secure when our daughter would never feel secure again, so I sent him letters and made anonymous phone calls at night. I wanted him to know someone was watching him, so he'd better not go near any other child."

"Did the other members of your family know about this activity?"

Patterson set his jaw. "This was my decision, Inspector. My wife had been through hell with her first husband—in fact, he was still jerking her around and keeping the children on an emotional roller coaster. His reaction to the molestation was to blame her for not giving Becky enough attention. When Fraser walked away free, she was almost a candidate for the Rideau Psychiatric Hospital. The only thing that kept her going was that Becky needed her help. So I let her focus on Becky, while I took on Fraser."

Green heard the brittle edge to the man's tone and shifted his focus gently. "Can we talk about Becky? Did she recover?"

Patterson removed his glasses to examine a speck on the flawless glass. The tiny interview room was soundproof, and for a few seconds the hum of the air conditioning was the only sound to fill the room. "We had several really rough years, during which we got useless advice from every single professional in the city. Then finally she seemed to settle down. She never got over it, but at least now she keeps it in the corner of her life. That's why I insist—"

"So what's she up to now? She must be almost seventeen. Still in high school?"

"No." The man paused while he polished his glasses and perched them back on his nose. "School and Rebecca never did see eye to eye. Anne and I tried to put the awful experience behind us and cooperate with her teachers over the years, but Rebecca never could. She felt constantly in danger, and she was so angry deep down inside that she took it out on every teacher she's had since."

"When did she drop out?"

"Oh, about Grade One?" Patterson looked bleak for a moment and pushed up his glasses to pinch the bridge of his nose. When he replaced them, he was all business again. "I don't see how all this is relevant, Inspector. Rebecca's been through hell and back, but she's pulling out of it, and eventually she'll overcome it. But as far as her contact with Matthew Fraser goes, it ended the last time he stuck his—" He sat rigid, his eyes fixed on his notepad, but Green could almost see his rage battling for expression. "Please let her continue her recovery in peace."

I only hope I can, Green found himself thinking. For your sake and for hers. He steered the interview to less sensitive ground. "What about your wife and son? Billy, I believe it is. He's in his twenties by now, right? Either of them have any recent contact or interest in Mr. Fraser?"

"My wife wouldn't have the energy, and frankly I doubt Billy would have the interest." Patterson's expression hardened subtly, as if he'd remembered where he was. "You see, Rebecca wasn't the only casualty of that useless legal charade. While all of that was going on, Billy didn't get the attention he deserved. He was ten when I came on the scene. He'd spent years watching his father torment his mother, and then years dealing with his father's emotional blackmail. So at first Billy wanted no part of me. When the sexual allegations came to light, we expected him to understand Rebecca was our first priority. Instead, he started dabbling in goth culture and drugs, and before we noticed, he had a major cocaine addiction. He was out for nights on end, stealing from us and bringing dubious characters around, and in the end he went to live with his father. Broke his mother's heart."

"Are things better with Billy now?"

Patterson slapped his pen down on his notepad and peered at Green over his glasses. "You know, Inspector, I believe I've been more than forthcoming in my replies to your questions, but our private vicissitudes are not something I feel obliged to share further with you. At this point, I think if you want to know anything more about my stepson, you should ask him yourself."

Green made a mental note to do just that, before casually turning the page of his notebook. "I do appreciate your candour, Mr. Patterson. I have one last question of a less personal nature. Rebecca's natural father—do you know his reaction to the verdict and his current feelings towards Fraser?"

Quinton thrust his notepad away and sat back. No need to take notes on this topic, Green observed. "Steve Whelan is a chronic malcontent, and I don't imagine he's undergone a transformation for the better since I last saw him. If you bother to read the files, no doubt you'll find all the information you need. Steve wrote dozens of letters of complaint to the police chief and commission on your department's handling of the case, he filed numerous motions with the courts about our failure to protect her, I believe he wrote the school board, the teacher's union, the trustees and probably the Minister of Education in Queen's Park to complain about their cover-up on Fraser's behalf. The only person he never blamed was himself, for making her the confused, angry and vulnerable child whom Fraser found so easy to prey upon and whom the middle-aged, middle-class judge found so easy to disbelieve. Adults, Inspector, all banding together against a hyperactive, defiant and decidedly naughty little girl."

Green felt again the tug of pity. "What about now? Is her father still bitter?"

"Oh, undoubtedly. But I expect he's far too busy attending to the slights against himself to dedicate much effort to the suffering of others."

"Ever known him to be physically violent?"

Patterson considered the question in silence for a moment,

then pulled his notepad back and jotted down a few notes. "To those weaker than himself like Anne, yes. But when it comes to facing down another man, he wouldn't have the courage."

Perhaps not, Green thought after he'd thanked Quinton Patterson for his cooperation and escorted him out of the interview room. But Fraser was himself a meek man, crippled by fears and doubts. A beaten man, perhaps weak enough in Steve Whelan's eyes to be no threat at all.

Green returned to his own office with his curiosity piqued to learn more about both Steve Whelan and his son, who'd be a young man by now and capable of some revenge of his own. On speculation, Green ran a police computer search on both of them. The computer spat out a long list of police contacts with the father, but nearly all in his role as complainant, with a couple of harassment charges and one impaired driving. Nothing violent. If Steve had been mistreating his wife as Patterson claimed, the police had never been called. Not unusual in domestic cases, but hardly a confirmation of any hard-core violent tendencies on Steve Whelan's part.

The son's sheet painted a picture more pathetic than sinister. William Steven Whelan had a sealed Young Offender file and three pages of minor offences as an adult involving break and enters, drug dealing and disturbing the peace. He'd done some minor time in previous years but nothing in the past six months. Either he'd grown smarter, or he'd cleaned up his act. Some of his known associates were local players in organized crime, but it was a stretch to think that this petty criminal, whose antics seemed to do harm mainly to himself, would have the daring to commit murder any more than his father did.

Still, neither man could be ruled out. If Patterson was to believed, Billy had spent his formative years learning the art of violence from his father, and as an inadvertent, invisible, unacknowledged victim in this tragedy, he certainly had the motive. And Steve had a memory for wrongs that could rival an elephant's. It was worth checking both men out, to see what they'd been up to in recent weeks.

Green glanced at his watch. Past five o'clock. Rebecca's biological father lived in the eastern suburb of Orleans, which was the wrong end of the city for Green's drive home. But Billy lived on Woodridge Crescent in the west end. It was an area notorious for poorly planned, overcrowded public housing projects which, despite the proximity of the river and its waterfront parks, had driven real estate prices down and petty crime statistics up. Woodridge Crescent would only require a minor detour on his way home.

After the usual crawl along the Queensway, Green exited at the Bayshore Shopping Centre, pulled up to the curb outside a large low-rent apartment building and slapped a police sticker in his windshield. There was no answer when he buzzed Billy's number from the lobby, but he slipped in easily behind a bevy of Somali women negotiating the heavy doors with umbrellas, strollers and shopping bags in hand. It had begun to rain again, and they were all windblown and wet. He made his way up in the elevator to the eighth floor and down the long hall filled with the chatter of foreign languages and the pungent aromas of exotic foods. Number 821 was tucked into the end of the hall against the fire stairs, and there was no answer to his knock. He listened through the door but could detect no noise above the chatter of the French TV next door.

As he left, he intercepted a young woman letting herself into an apartment down the hall. She had a little girl in tow, both of them sporting matching raincoats and blond pony tails.

"Do you know your neighbour in 821, a young man named Billy Whelan?"

She edged away from him, shielding her child and shaking her head sharply. No, of course not, Green thought. This is not a building where you give information to total strangers. He debated whether showing his badge would improve his chances and decided it wouldn't.

"I'm a friend of his father's," he said instead. "His dad's worried about him."

She unlocked the door and shepherded her daughter inside. "Katie, honey, go watch television, okay? Mummy will be there in a moment."

"Is Billy in trouble?" the little girl asked. The woman pushed her again with a sharp look, then turned to Green. She shifted her gum to the other side of her mouth with exaggerated disinterest. She was trying to look hard, but there was a hint of anxiety in her face. "Why's his father worried?"

"Well, you know—Billy's had his ups and downs."

"Not that his dad ever noticed."

"Yeah, well Mr. Patterson's had his ups and his downs too."

"Oh, that dad," she exclaimed. "Now I know you're lying. His stepfather has no use for him, never sees him. Never even comes to any of his shows."

"What shows?"

The young woman shrugged. "A few gigs here and there. His band even had an opening spot at Barrymore's last month."

Green masked his surprise and thought fast. Barrymore's was a prestigious downtown club which featured live musicians and entertainers. Most of Canada's top bands had played the club at one time or another, and for Billy to have landed a spot there, he must be doing something more than racking up summary conviction offences. Green tried his friendliest smile. "So what's his band called? I'll try to catch a show."

That clammed her up faster than if he'd shown his badge.

She blew a huge pink bubble and shrugged her skinny shoulders. "Look, I haven't seen him, okay? Not in a few days."

"But you're a friend of his—"

"Was."

"Still, you obviously care." A slight exaggeration, given her emphatic use of the past tense, but he was anxious to keep the conversation going.

"I care if the cops are looking for him. If he's fucked up again." She gave him a long stony stare which told him he hadn't fooled her for an instant. "He was supposed to cash my cheque for me, days ago. Oh, screw it!" she muttered and closed the door.

Well, well, Green thought as he made his way back to the car. Someone else who's dropped out of sight. Although, of course, the girlfriend was simply speculating, and even if Billy had disappeared, it might not be for reasons connected to the case. Billy was a drug user with a habit of getting into trouble and an unexpected fistful of cash in his hands. The lure of the open road might have been irresistible. Tomorrow, in between the paperwork and the report Green was meant to be preparing on cross-jurisdictional collaboration in CID, perhaps there would be time to worry about where Billy had run off to.

As he pulled into the empty drive of the Dreaded Vinyl Cube, he frowned. Despite his detour, Sharon's car was not yet in the drive, and when he entered the house, it was deserted. His shout brought back nothing but an echo.

That's strange, he thought. Sharon had been acting a little oddly the last couple of nights. She had jumped whenever the phone rang, she'd stared into space during dinner and forgotten to tease him when he described his day at the conference. And now she was at least two hours later than she usually was.

Inside, he checked the phone for messages, of which there

were none, and headed upstairs to strip off his wet clothes. He was just beginning to worry in earnest when he heard a car door slam, and Tony's excited chatter filled the air. He reached the front door in time to see Sharon mounting the front steps with Tony and his bag in one hand, and in the other, towed along like a reluctant barge, was the biggest, ugliest dog he'd ever seen.

Nine

Sharon's day had crawled. Many times she had found her mind wandering from the mundane duties of her job to the unanswered questions of the Fraser case. Both yesterday's and today's lunch hour had come and gone without a call from Leslie Black, and as the afternoon ticked by, Sharon felt her hope fading. The clock on the wall above the nursing station read three thirty-five when she paused in her charting to rest her chin wearily in her hands. Leslie was not going to call. She must have lost the fight with her conscience.

It was probably just as well, Sharon thought. She didn't really need to be in the middle of this investigation, trapped by issues of confidentiality and forced to choose between loyalties in what was already a murky and personally repugnant case. Mike could build his own case without her help. He'd been doing it long before he met her and without the moral confusion she felt. The facts alone mattered to him, and once he'd laid them bare, then others could begin the task of sorting out right from wrong.

She pushed the case out of her thoughts with relief and picked up her pen to continue her charts. At that moment the phone rang and when she answered it, her heart sank.

"Sharon? It's Leslie. Can we meet when you get off?"

"Well, I've been thinking..."

"So have I." Leslie Black's voice was unusually furtive.

"Meet me in the library, back table, four o'clock."

It seemed ridiculously cloak and dagger, even for a potential violation of the privacy laws, but as Sharon made her way through the maze of corridors which connected one wing of the hospital to another, she felt excited in spite of herself. She arrived at the library less than one minute late and was surprised to see Leslie rise from the table at the back the instant she walked in. Leslie drifted slowly along the shelves towards the front, her face resolutely averted. As she drew near, Sharon opened her mouth to speak but was stopped by Leslie's very faint but unmistakable shake of the head.

"Go to the table at the back. Slowly!" Leslie whispered, and then she was out the door and gone.

Sharon suppressed a laugh, for Mata Hari tactics did not quite suit the shabby and virtually deserted atmosphere of the Rideau Psychiatric staff library. Life among the phobics must be rubbing off on you, Leslie, she thought, as she made her way towards the table Leslie had left.

The table top was cluttered with journals and open books, which Sharon perused curiously, noting that Leslie had been reading up on treatment efficacy studies for social phobia. For a few minutes, Sharon puzzled over the significance of Leslie's asking her to read these, before noticing the blank manila envelope sitting on the chair beside her. She picked it up and out slid the thick, well-worn file of Matthew Robertson Fraser.

Bingo. Without a qualm, surrounded by the camouflage of a half-dozen scientific journals, Sharon opened the file and began to read.

Matthew Fraser's connection to the Rideau Psychiatric Hospital spanned ten years and began innocuously enough with an outpatient appointment with a psychologist. His initial complaints had been anxiety, insomnia, inability to concentrate and occasional crying spells. Entirely understandable, the psychologist had postulated, given that the patient had recently come under investigation for sexual abuse and had been relieved of his teaching duties. The psychologist had seen him five times, provided supportive counselling, and suggested a mild anxiolytic which the psychiatric resident on staff had duly prescribed.

Some months later, Fraser was brought into Emergency by his father in a distraught state, unable to eat or sleep and contemplating suicide. At that time he was under the care of his family doctor, who had prescribed both stronger anti-anxiety medication and a sleeping pill. The emergency room psychiatrist in his wisdom had taken Fraser off both medications, prescribed the then new and highly touted Prozac, and sent him on his way. Prozac, Sharon thought drily, why not? Guaranteed to make you happy and forget all your troubles. Forget that you're on trial for abuse, forget that your career is irredeemably lost and forget that your friends have deserted you.

Curiously, there was no record of his having been seen in forensic psychiatry prior to the trial, which suggested that either the Crown had not been certain of the wisdom of a psychiatric evaluation, or they had thought they had a strong enough case without it.

Sharon flipped through the file in search of the Sexual Behaviours Assessment Leslie said he'd undergone three years earlier, but there was no trace of it. She found notes on Fraser's outpatient admission two years ago for severe anxiety and multiple phobias, at which time the consulting psychiatrist had prescribed an anti-depressant, and Emmerson-Jones had designed a treatment plan to desensitize Fraser gradually to the situations he feared. Sharon knew these were both sound treatments for his condition, but they left her wondering where in this list of symptoms and remedies was the man himself.

Where was the recognition that above all, he needed the chance simply to learn to cope with what he'd been through.

Almost against her will, she felt a tweak of sympathy. In a way, the tweak was comforting. She'd always considered herself a compassionate person who tried to see the salvageable in everyone who came into the ward, no matter how bizarre or unsympathetic their life story. But pedophiles were predators, and she always felt an unexpectedly hard kernel of condemnation in her core whenever she thought of them. It was comforting to know that even for one of them—for the human part of him—she could still feel sad.

She was about to close the file when she noticed a wad of folded papers shoved in among the therapy notes from long ago. There was nothing odd about this. In the hands of careless or harried clinicians, files often became jumbled and out of order. When she unfolded it, she discovered it was the sexual behaviour report she'd been looking for. Dated three years earlier, it detailed the results of Dr. Pelham's interviews, the psychological tests and the results of the laboratory studies of sexual arousal. The conclusions were as Leslie Black described. All three assessments suggested a man who experienced normal physical attraction to adult females and who displayed no sexual reaction either to children or to coercive sex. In short, not a typical profile of a sexual deviant at all.

Beyond that, however, the report said a good deal more. Matt Fraser was described as an anxious, depressed and overwhelmed man who could see no escape from the pressures of a hostile world. Although attracted to women, his sexual experience even before the accusation, which had occurred when he was twenty-six, had been minimal and rather unsuccessful. He'd had recurring problems with self-doubt and impotence and had a genuine fear of aggressive women.

In general, the laboratory studies proclaimed in brutally clinical language that his erectile responses, although normal in type, had been weaker than most men his age, from which Dr. Pelham had concluded chronic depression. This was confirmed by the fact that when informed that his sexual interests were normal, the patient had wept. Pelham had prescribed a course of yet another anti-depressant.

The assessment revealed another detail which Sharon found intriguing. Although she knew Fraser had a clear agenda for taking the tests, and that all his answers in both the interview and the questionnaires were probably slanted to make himself look good, a skilled clinician could usually catch a glimpse beneath the surface to the patient's deeper core. This psychologist had found Matt to be an intelligent but sensitive and hyper-vigilant man whose development might have been marred by an early trauma that left him forever anxious and on guard. The patient himself could articulate nothing, but the psychologist suspected some form of abuse.

Pure speculation right up there with reading tea leaves, Sharon thought, as she closed the file and slipped it back into the manila envelope. Still, it was intriguing. Although far from inevitable, habits of abuse could be passed on from one generation to the next, the victimized child becoming himself the abuser. Had Fraser been a victim, and if so, what had it done to him?

The library was nearly deserted, and Sharon glanced at her watch. It was nearly five o'clock, too late to track down Dr. Pelham, even if she could think of credible grounds on which to ask him to discuss the case with her. But on the shelves around her was a wealth of information about every kind of mental health question, and perhaps a little bedtime reading to expand her knowledge of sexual abuse was in order.

Fifteen minutes later, she walked out the glass entrance doors of the Administration Building with two books tucked under her arm. Rain lashed at her umbrella, and she hurried towards the parking lot with her head bowed and her thoughts already focussed far ahead on Tony and dinner. Suddenly, a figure jumped out of the bushes directly into her path and thrust out a bony hand to clutch her arm.

"Sharon Levy! Thank God!"

Instinctively, Sharon recoiled and knocked away the hand. A second figure emerged from the shadows, this one massive, dark and snarling.

"Modo! Down!" the woman cried, and Sharon recovered enough to take in the sight before her. A giant black and brown dog had settled on the wet ground and rested its massive head on its paws, but its eyes watched her every move. The thin, angular woman had retreated back into the cover of the trees, both hands clinging to a huge umbrella. Her eyes skittered over the parking lot nervously.

"Thank God, you're still here!" she exclaimed. "I was afraid I'd missed you."

Sharon suppressed the anger that had followed her fright, and she searched her memory warily. The hair colour was different and the face, even white with fear, was fuller. If Mike hadn't described her the other day, Sharon would never have remembered her. Excitement and curiosity tempered anger, and she forced a soothing smile.

"Janice Tanner, how are you?"

"I'm okay." Janice's words tumbled out in a rush. "No, I'm not. I think someone's following me!"

"Oh?" Sharon probed dubiously.

Janice forced a nervous laugh. "I know, you've heard that before. I used to see stalkers behind every tree. But this time it's

137

different. I've been getting better. Going to a group, taking the bus by myself, even taking walks in the park in the evening. But the last few days, there's been someone watching me."

"Do you know them?"

Janice shook her head vigorously.

"What do they look like?"

"I don't know, that's the thing. I never get a clear glimpse. First, on Monday there was a face outside my bedroom window. Then two days ago, someone tried to pick open my lock. But..." She gave another nervous laugh. "I have four locks, so they couldn't get in. Then yesterday, when I went to group, I'm sure someone followed me here. I heard footsteps behind me, and every time I stopped, they did."

"But you didn't see anyone?"

"They were real! I wanted to go to the police station to tell that husband of yours, but I'm—" She gulped. "I'm getting panic attacks again. I got as far as the bus stop, and I froze. Then I thought of you. And if I brought Modo, who could hurt me? I thought you could tell your husband they're after me too."

"Who?"

"The people who kidnapped Matt Fraser! Your husband is still investigating that, isn't he?"

Sharon hesitated. She should feign total ignorance and stay as far away as possible from Janice's irrational fears, while at the same time protecting the confidentiality of Mike's case. But the safe route had rarely been her first instinct.

"Yes, he's still investigating."

"He thinks Matt's—" Janice tightened her lips as if to prevent the dreaded word from escaping. "Dead, doesn't he?"

"I don't know. But why would the same people be after you? What's the connection?"

Janice backed further into the shadows. "I don't know!

Maybe they think I know something."

"Do you?"

"No! But they don't know that, right? I'm not safe, I can't go home because they know where I live—"

"Janice—" Sharon laid a calming hand on the woman's arm to draw her out of the bushes. The dog raised its head sharply. "You're okay now. The dog's here, I'm here. Let's go sit over there out of the rain and examine this calmly."

She led Janice to a bench by the entrance to the hospital, and when Janice had settled with her back to the brick wall and the dog pressed against her feet, some colour returned to her ashen face.

"You're right, I'm safe. I don't know what they want. I wish I did, then maybe I could shed some light on Matt's disappearance. But he told me so little, just that he was afraid of something from his past."

Sharon remembered the psychologist's report about a long-buried trauma. "Did he ever talk about his past? About any bad experiences or abuse in his childhood?"

Janice seemed to mull the idea over doubtfully. "A lot of us had bad experiences, and we'd talk about them sometimes. One man had been a relief worker in Bosnia, and another woman had her parents blown up in Tel Aviv. I...I was raped eight years ago. But Matt didn't talk, he just listened. Why, do you think his childhood is important?"

"It might be." Distant thunder rumbled on the horizon, and a fork of lightning split the western sky. The dog pressed itself closer against them, whining softly. Sharon felt its damp heat soak through her pant leg, and she leaned forward to shift the weight. Modo's anxious brown eyes followed her every move.

"So Matt never let anything slip?"

"Well, we knew there'd been trouble with the law—some

sort of false accusation—and that some people never accepted his innocence. Besides that..." Janice took a deep breath, and Sharon could see her struggling to focus on her memories through her fear. "I think he had an unhappy childhood. The few times we talked, I had the impression it was lonely, and that pretty well everyone had let him down in one way or another."

"Everyone? Did he mention anyone specific? Parents? Other family?"

"His mother, for sure. I remember him talking about Modo and how Modo was always there, through thick and thin. When he'd come home from group, she'd be there wagging her tail to say hi. And he said his biggest memory as a kid was coming home from school, and there'd be no one there. Just an empty house. And how scared that made him feel." Thunder cracked overhead, causing both Janice and the dog to jump. Janice clutched Sharon's arm, and her colour fled again. "I don't think I can go home. I can't—" She began to hyperventilate.

"Maybe you could stay with a friend for a few days."

"Sharon, I—I don't really have any friends."

"Not even a distant relative?"

Janice shook her head. Her eyes were glazing, and she began to sway. Rapidly, Sharon weighed her options. She didn't like to feed the woman's panic, but at this rate Janice was headed for an emergency admission to the Rideau Psychiatric. Sharon rose to her feet briskly.

"Okay, I know an excellent woman's shelter. You're not exactly fleeing a violent husband, but in a pinch, why not? They're friends of mine there."

"What about Modo? Would they take her?"

Sharon stopped in mid stride. The dog had risen at the sound of its name and timidly nuzzled Sharon's hand. Its nose felt like damp velvet.

"They don't allow pets, but how about the Humane Society? They can find a foster home for her."

Janice shook her head. "Matt got her from there when they were just about to put her down. They have far too many puppies, and a big dog like this, with her traumatic history, they'd likely have to put her down." Janice knelt down and pressed her face to Modo's. The dog licked her eagerly. "She really is a sweet, wonderful dog, and the fact that she still trusts humans is a miracle."

Then Janice looked up at Sharon, and the question in her eyes was as plain as day.

*   *   *

Green stared at Sharon in astonishment, convinced he must have heard wrong. While they both juggled busy work schedules, babysitters, temper tantrums and the running of the household, his wife had volunteered to take this hundred-pound monstrosity under their wing. "You've got to be kidding!"

They were all standing on the driveway in the drizzling rain. Sharon shifted Tony on her hip and held out the end of the leash impatiently. "It's only temporary, while Janice figures out what to do with her. Now either take the leash or take your son. Help a little!"

Gingerly, he took the end of the leash, but he didn't move. "We can't take a dog! We don't know anything about dogs!"

"We'll learn. We didn't know anything about babies either," she replied as she mounted the front steps towards the door. At the last minute she flashed him a grin. "It could be worse. I could have brought Janice home too."

She disappeared into the house, and Green turned to look at their acquisition with dismay. The name certainly suited.

Modo stood on the driveway, rain dripping from her ears and tail. Her back was hunched, her huge head bowed, and her eyes gazed up at him timidly. Her tail gave one faint wag before she sank down onto her belly.

"Oh, that's just great. Going on strike already!" He tugged on the leash. "Come on, Modo. Inside."

At the sound of her name, the dog's ears perked up, and she got to her feet. Encouraged, Green tried again. "Come on, Modo!"

Obediently the dog trotted behind him up the stairs into the house, where Green found Sharon in the kitchen, already setting up the baby gates.

"She's a traumatized dog," she said. "So we have to be very gentle with her. She has to feel accepted, so we can't shut her off by herself."

"And how are we supposed to know how to treat a traumatized dog?"

"I'm going to assume the same way as a child. With gentleness, patience, closeness and security. So for starters, why don't you take Tony and her to bond in the living room while I make dinner?"

He could see she was on a mission, and no amount of caution or logic would sway her. She spent her days caring and healing, whereas his days were filled with danger and distrust. It had been that very boundless compassion that had first attracted him to her, but sometimes it blinded her to the dark side. Modo looked harmless enough, but she was huge, and who knew what she was capable of? Tony would snap like a twig in her jaws.

With all the innocent curiosity of his age, Tony was already poking his fingers through the gate at her and chattering excitedly. Modo lay still, but she was watching.

"I'll take Tony," Green replied, scooping his son into his

arms. "You can do the bonding bit with the dog."

It was past nine by the time Green had finished the bath and story ritual and had tucked Tony into his crib. When he returned to the living room, he found Sharon sprawled on the living room sofa with her nose buried in a book. Her eyes were smudged with fatigue, but they lit up gratefully when he handed her a frosty bottle of Upper Canada Lager.

The dog had stretched herself out over Sharon's feet and acted as if she were never going to let her new mistress out of her sight. Green stepped over the dog to snuggle next to Sharon on the couch. Modo emitted a low growl.

Green nuzzled the soft curls at the nape of Sharon's neck. "*Oy*, Levy, what have you done?"

She laid the book down with a grin and took an appreciative sip of her beer. "I'll get Janice back under control tomorrow. Emmerson-Jones will have to get her meds increased."

"So you think this fear of being followed is all in her head?"

Sharon shrugged. "Janice is as suggestible as they come. She was stalked and brutally raped a few years ago, so she sees danger in every shadow."

Free association is a bizarre thing, Green reflected, as an idea popped into his head. Maybe it was just alcohol mixed with the exhaustion of a wild day, but he wondered why he hadn't made the connection earlier, for Janice had been one of Fraser's only confidantes. "Speaking of shadows, has she ever mentioned the name mistwalker?"

Sharon stopped with her beer bottle poised at her lips. "Your thought processes do the oddest things, Green. Explain."

He told her briefly about the empty folder in Fraser's computer, and she shook her head. "Sounds spooky. Like someone walking the edge. I don't think Janice would pick a creepy name like that. Bubbles would be more her style."

He sipped his beer in silence, troubled by the stray fact that fit nowhere. "Maybe mistwalker was not one of Fraser's friends, but the name he'd given the mystery person he was tracking. Maybe the folder was his repository for all the information he'd been collecting on them. In which case, either he'd wiped it all out before leaving his apartment, or someone else did."

"How is the trail of Matthew Fraser going, by the way?"

He told her about Fraser's frantic last days and the fire that ended his life. "I don't have MacPhail's autopsy results yet, but I don't think it was an accident. Either he killed himself, or someone else killed him. Something very peculiar is going on."

She lay in his arms without speaking for a moment, but he sensed she was wide awake. Finally, she drew back to look at him gravely. "In that case, I have something to tell you. This is absolutely confidential, Mike. Leslie and I could both be in deep shit if it ever came out. But if Fraser is dead, I think it's important you know, because it may have some bearing."

She described her phone conversation with Leslie Black, her visit to the library and her perusal of Fraser's file. Green didn't interrupt, but he puzzled over the conflicting opinions he'd heard about Fraser in the last couple of days.

"Honey, he had a tattoo of a little girl on his groin," he protested. "Even his lawyer and his sister—who's known him all his life—thought he was guilty. Now, on the basis of a bunch of tests and interviews years after the fact, these shrinks are saying he wasn't?"

"Well, they can't say that. What they did conclude was that he probably wasn't a true pedophile. Children didn't turn him on."

"But I've heard lots of court cases about those plesthmograph tests. Some guys can fake them."

Sharon tapped the book she'd been reading. "True, a man can try to suppress his natural response, shut his eyes or even substitute his own fantasies for the pictures. But—"

"So all that tells us is that Fraser may have been smart enough to dupe two professionals."

"But you said he was shy and retiring. Not the type to march into an expert psychiatrist's office, cocky enough to think he could dupe him. Besides, he had nothing to gain if he succeeded, and a lot to lose if he failed. He'd already been acquitted, and people had moved on. He never made the results public, never even told his therapists."

Green thought about the Child Abuse Register the CAS had mentioned. Fraser might have been trying to garner proof to get his name removed, but this testing had been done three years earlier, and Fraser had never told a soul. The whole damn thing didn't make sense.

"So why do you think he did it?" he asked.

"Maybe to satisfy himself," Sharon replied. "To have an objective, professional expert tell him he's sexually normal."

What guy needs a shrink to tell him what turns him on, Green wondered, and his skepticism must have shown, because she shook her head impatiently. "This is a very insecure man, Green, and especially after all he'd been through, he may have wondered if there was some dark secret deep within himself that even he didn't know about."

He chuckled and snuggled her into the crook of his arm. Sharon was usually the epitome of pragmatism, second only to Brian Sullivan in reeling Green's wild flights of fancy back to earth. "Freud hijacked your brain?"

She didn't laugh. Instead, she picked up the second book that lay at her side. "It's a long shot, I agree, but it's possible. Humour me and listen. The psychologist thought Fraser had

145

suffered some early trauma or abuse which he didn't remember. Now I know it's possible to fabricate or distort memories; people do it all the time, unconsciously and without devious motives—"

"Absolutely. Eyewitnesses drive us crazy with that. They colour the memory or fill in the gaps, or remember things as they think they should be. Memory is not an instant replay button." He grinned. "It's why we love forensics in court. Forensics is 'just the facts, ma'am'. Memory is a creative process."

"But on the flip side, it is possible to repress the memory of bad things that really did happen. If the trauma or abuse is too terrifying or painful and the child has no escape, they may escape mentally, by blocking out the experience or by taking themselves out of the situation in their mind. That's called dissociation. People in shock are in a partial dissociative state. They're there in body, but they've blocked out their feelings so they're not experiencing the whole pain."

"Partial dissociative state?" he said dubiously. "I've always called it numb."

"But to be numb, the mind has to block stuff out, or separate feelings and experiences into compartments in their head. Come on, Mike, you separate yourself into compartments all the time. You deal with a bloody murder all day, yet when you walk through our front door, you put it out of your mind."

"But that's a conscious effort, and I have to work hard at it. Every cop does."

"But it gets easier, doesn't it? And that numbness you bring on yourself when you face a tragic case, sometimes that creeps into your feelings at home here too. We call it being desensitized. But you have a healthy adult mind, and you have some control over your life. You can quit your job or take a transfer if you can't stand it, and you know that escape hatch is there."

Green sobered. How many times had he seen officers bail out for just that reason, because they could no longer keep the carnage at work from spilling into their personal lives? How many times had he seen them scavenge for that numbness at the bottom of a bottle?

Sharon's dark eyes glowed as her conviction grew. "But a child who's abused from an early age and who can't escape the relentless pain and fear—they can't do anything but dissociate or block out. It's a powerful survival tool, but it leaves them with few other skills for handling stress or facing problems, and it leaves them with huge holes in their memory. Even as adults, they may dissociate under stress and do things they have no memory of."

"Don't tell me you think Fraser abused this girl after all and had no memory of it!"

She rolled her eyes. "No, I think he was *afraid* that maybe he'd abused her and didn't remember it."

He opened his mouth to protest further, but she swatted him playfully. "Listen! You said he was obsessed with the case and had all these books on memory and trauma. He probably bought them to learn about the girl who accused him, but maybe when he read about the link between early abuse and dissociation, he began to fear that the deception lay not in the girl's mind but in his own."

In his twenty-odd years of policing, he'd encountered just about every twist the human mind was capable of. He'd interviewed men too drunk or high to remember bludgeoning their best friend to death the night before, psychotics who'd thought they were God's avenging angels, psychopaths who'd calmly fed their victims to their dogs before leaving for work. But this idea was perhaps the most convoluted ever. "So you're saying he was really innocent but didn't know it, so three years

147

ago, he went to the sex guru and learned that no matter how screwed up he was, little girls didn't turn him on?"

She ignored the disbelief in his tone. "It fits his psychiatric history perfectly, Mike! Let's say before all this started, he was just an eager young teacher who loved kids and wanted to go the extra mile for them. There was nothing perverted about him, he was just shy and nerdy, probably felt more comfortable around children."

He grew serious, listening closely to see how her bizarre theory matched up with the picture he'd uncovered in the past few days. "That was the general view of him among the other teachers," he acknowledged reluctantly.

"Okay, so for being such a nice guy, he gets accused of sexual abuse. He must have felt completely sandbagged. And to make matters worse, when he defends himself and wins, he discovers nobody believes his innocence, and they drop him like a leper. No wonder he ended up paranoid, suicidal and afraid to go out."

In spite of his skepticism, Green's interest was piqued, for in this crazy quilt of facts, a pattern was emerging. He took a slow, thoughtful sip of beer. "His friend Janice, his lawyer, his sister, even me... Everyone saw this guy as weak and overwhelmed. But now I'm not so sure. He's been trying to fight back. He fought to defend himself in court, even though it meant putting the child through hell. When everyone turned against him, he picked himself up and left town to start over. But even then, he was driven to understand the girl and why she did it. Unlike some of his more cynical fellow teachers, he didn't see six-year-olds as inherent liars."

Sharon's eyes danced, her fatigue quite gone. "So he started researching. And when he learned about the tricks the mind can play, he began to doubt himself. He gets himself evaluated and learns that he likely wasn't guilty."

The pattern grew clearer. Green sat forward excitedly. "That leads him to the logical next step. If he didn't molest the little girl, why did she accuse him?"

Sharon shrugged. "Maybe she misinterpreted what he did, or someone else blew it out of proportion. There's a lot of hysteria surrounding pedophilia these days."

"No, the investigating officer said the girl was very graphic. There was no physical penetration, but she described explicit acts of fondling."

"Could she have been mad at him and wanted to get him into trouble? She was a kid, and she might not have realized how far things would go."

Green mulled the idea over in his mind. It explained the girl's changing her story and ultimately recanting. "Well, apparently she was a problem child, so I guess that's possible. But Devine was adamant the abuse had really occurred. She said little children don't lie about such things. Nor can they make up the details she gave."

"Devine wouldn't be the first officer to get overinvested in a case, Green. Present company included."

He was too absorbed to be sidetracked. "But there was testimony from psychiatrists and experts. Not enough to get past reasonable doubt, but pretty convincing. They all thought she showed classic signs of abuse."

She gave him a long, knowing look over the top of her beer bottle. "I know what you're thinking. The obvious conclusion. Someone else molested her, and she pinned it on Fraser."

He pointed his finger at her. "Bingo. I bet that's exactly what Fraser concluded. And after three years of poring over documents and articles, I think he'd tracked down who."

He thought of the body lying on the mattress in the

rooming house, of the fire that had burned so hot and fierce around the bed that the charred remains had been almost impossible to identify. He jumped to his feet so abruptly that the dog cringed in fear. "I bet that fire was not an accident, not a suicide, not a nutcase who flipped out! Fraser may have been a little neurotic, but he knew reality from delusion, and someone found out. I think this was a goddamn, cold-blooded, premeditated murder!"

He reached for the phone, punched in Brian Sullivan's home number, then listened impatiently through four rings and the voice mail greeting. "Brian, meet me in my office first thing in the morning with the autopsy results on the rooming house victim. As of now, I want this officially upgraded to a homicide investigation."

When he hung up, Sharon was looking up at him with a bemused smile. "I've done it now, haven't I? I sense some long nights alone. Me, my son and our trusty new companion."

He smiled, stretched over the dog on the floor and nibbled her ear teasingly. When the dog lifted her head sharply, he chuckled. "I have a feeling she won't let me near you anyway."

Ten

After the stifling week, Friday dawned a glorious, cool, rain-washed blue. At nine o'clock, after a long battle through the rush hour, Green strode across the squad room towards his office, scanning the room for Sullivan. His mind was already in high gear, but he detected a curious hush in the air as detectives raised their heads to watch his progress. For a moment he wondered if the prime minister had been assassinated, or if Jules was on the warpath about some dismal bungling on his part. Jules had been furious at his skipping out on the conference Wednesday, and as punishment was threatening to assign him as coordinator of the interprovincial anti-gang initiative. Given that coordination and team work were such strengths of his.

But the atmosphere was more one of titillation than of tension, and his question was soon answered by the desk clerk, who waved a pink message slip at him.

"Inspector Green, this woman has called you three times. Ashley Pollack, from Vancouver. She was pretty angry that I wouldn't give her your home phone number."

Green glanced around the squad room. All the officers were too new to the squad to know about his ex-wife, but to judge from their open grins, someone had tipped them off. Sullivan was nowhere to be seen, but the prehistoric Constable Blake was doing his stint downstairs at the main desk. Meddling *putz*.

Green snatched the number and disappeared into his office, careful to shut the door. As he dialled, he felt a surge of anxiety. He hadn't spoken to Ashley in years. Her only communication had been through lawyers, and then only when there was bad news about Hannah, and she wanted him to solve it. Or rather, she wanted money to solve it. Three calls in the space of two hours signalled serious desperation, especially since it had been four a.m. in Vancouver when she'd placed her first call.

When her strident voice came on the line, the fifteen intervening years seemed to melt away, and a vivid image of teased blonde hair, sulky eyes and a querulous pout sprang to his mind. True to form, she wasted no time on niceties. "About time! Goddamn police force hasn't changed a bit. Easier to get information out of the CIA."

"I'll give you my home number—"

"Do that! Like it or not, Hannah is your responsibility too."

"What's wrong, Ashley?"

"Hannah's on her way to visit you."

Green sat down with a thud. Intelligent thought deserted him. "What do you mean?"

"I mean she left last night. I think she caught the red-eye out of Vancouver, so she should be there any minute."

Still no intelligent thought on the horizon. "You think? What the hell is going on!"

"I mean that's where she said she was going when she stormed out the door. She seems to believe life will be better with you. That you're her dad and it's time she got to know you. I tried to tell her you're a jerk, but she's got to see that for herself."

He ignored the classic ex-wife invective as he struggled to grasp the implications of the news. "But she doesn't know where I live. Where's she going to find me?"

"I told her to go straight to the police station. That'll be a nice bit of irony. Hannah hates cops, thanks to a few encounters with your buddies on this side of the mountains—the usual drugs, under-age drinking, panhandling with her friends on Hastings. So she's going to sashay into your station with a chip the size of a Douglas fir and boy, I'd love to be a fly on that wall."

"Okay, okay." Green's mind raced. "What should I do?"

Ashley laughed, a high pitched giggle that had once reminded him of bells, but now sounded like a witch's cackle. "If I had the answers, do you think she'd have gone off to see if the grass was greener with you? She'll be looking in the goddamn desert."

"Did she bring any clothes? Has she got any money?"

"Of course she does! You think I'd let her stomp out of here without a cent? I gave her two hundred dollars, plus she cleaned out Fred's wallet before she took off, just to make a point."

An intelligent thought finally drifted within grasp. He sensed the hurt beneath the anger and spoke more softly. "Okay, Ashley, I'll try to help. Do you want me to persuade her to go back home?"

There was silence on the phone, and when she spoke, some of the anger had gone. "No, Mike. I think this is something she has to do. And...if you can keep her just for a bit, maybe till school starts again, who knows, maybe it will help her. God knows, shrinks at a hundred plus an hour haven't."

Keep her till school starts! Two months? His astonishment bulldozed the fragile beginnings of common sense he'd been rallying, so he signed off as quickly as he could get a word in. Once he'd hung up, he glanced at his watch. Her overnight flight from Vancouver had almost certainly arrived in Ottawa. In fact, Hannah should be walking through the front doors of the station any second.

Ignoring the questioning looks, he barrelled out of his office and downstairs to intercept her before Constable Blake had a chance to meet her. But there was no teenage girl in the lobby, and a quick check outside in the street revealed no sign of her either. Reluctantly, Green approached Blake to inquire if she'd turned up and to alert him to her imminent arrival. He tried to sound as if his daughter came to visit all the time, and if the desk officer was at all intrigued or titillated, he kept his face carefully deadpan.

"What does she look like?" was all he asked.

Green hesitated, for he had no idea. The latest picture Ashley had deigned to send him was of Hannah as a chubby preteen, complete with braces and braids. "I'll get a full description of her clothes and current hair style from her mother if it matters, Blake, but I should think her name, Hannah Pollack, is sufficient. Just call me when she arrives."

He returned upstairs to phone the airlines and learned that most of the overnight flights from Vancouver, even those that puddle hopped through every provincial capital along the way, had arrived at least an hour earlier. Even allowing for her catching the cheapest shuttle into town, she should have arrived. But there were still some avenues to explore before calling Ashley back and whipping up some serious concern.

Green spent the next few minutes on the phone checking flight manifests with the police at Airport Security and determined that Hannah had indeed boarded the midnight flight from Vancouver, which had arrived in Ottawa at eight in the morning. However, no one at the Ottawa airport was able to confirm whether she'd disembarked.

Reluctantly he phoned Ashley back with this update, and she surprised him with impatience rather than worry.

"Welcome to life with Hannah, Mike. This has been my

life for almost ten years. She's never where I expect her to be, never when she's supposed to be, just like you. She pleases herself and never thinks what effect it might have on the rest of us. Or if she does, it's just 'oh well, too bad'."

"But she doesn't know Ottawa, and she has no friends or contacts here. Does she?"

"Doesn't matter. She'll find out where the kids hang out, and within hours she'll be settled right in."

"So you're saying she won't even call me?"

"Oh, she might. I've given up trying to predict what she'll do. All I know is, the more buttons of ours she can push, the better. She knows you're calling me, she knows we're at each other's throats—"

"We're not."

"But she hopes we are. She knows she's got us both good and worried, and when she's bored of the game, she'll probably turn up. Either there or back here."

"Good God, Ashley—"

"Don't 'Good God' me, Mike! She's your goddamn daughter with your goddamn genes, and I've done the best I can. No thanks to you!"

He calmed her down enough to obtain a description of Hannah and the clothes she was probably wearing. When he raised the topic of photos, scanners and emails, Ashley began to dither, but agreed to enlist her husband's help. She warned that it might take a while, because she would have to locate him at work, and he was often on the road.

While he waited for the photo to arrive, Green ran the description by the baggage personnel at the airport, but to no avail. He swallowed his pride and checked with Blake again. Nothing. Sitting at his desk twirling his pen, he felt helpless. He couldn't concentrate on the mundane details of his work, but he could do nothing more to find Hannah or to restore the equilibrium of his life that had suddenly spun off course. Hannah was here. She was visiting him. *Oy veh is mir.*

When his phone rang, he snatched it up hopefully, but Barbara Devine's voice snapped through the wires.

"Mike, what's going on now? Jules tells me you've opened a Major Case file on Matthew Fraser's death. Why?"

Matthew Fraser... Green collected his scattered thoughts and forced them to focus on the case. Last night, the Fraser investigation had been foremost in his thoughts. Now, when he could barely think, he had to find an intelligent way to tell Devine that she might have screwed up and missed the real villain in the case.

Devine must have interpreted his silence as stonewalling, because she announced that she was coming down. Green snatched up his notes on the Fraser file from the corner of his desk and headed out of his office, intercepting Devine just as she strode out of the elevator.

He gestured her back inside. "Let's go grab a coffee. I need to pick your brains about the case again."

"That'll cost you a lot more than a cup of coffee," she shot back. "At least a double scotch."

Upstairs in the police cafeteria, he chose a table by the window in the deserted room, hoping the blue, sun-lit sky and the spectacular view of the museum would soothe some of the storm clouds gathered around her. Her make-up was impeccable, but one wing of her lacquered ebony hair was askew, and her eyes shot daggers over the rim of her cup. He waited until she'd had her first hit of caffeine before he broached his theory.

Predictably, her response was outrage, for no investigator likes to be wrong. "That's utter nonsense, Mike. We considered doing those penile arousal tests before the trial. That is, the defence considered the tests, but the truth is they're unreliable. So these results prove nothing."

Already worried and frazzled, Green had neither time nor patience for bruised egos. He had a case to solve, and even more importantly, a daughter to find. He stirred his coffee slowly while he counted to five and mustered the limited tact at his disposal. He deliberately couched his theory in tentative terms, because until he had MacPhail's ruling on the cause of death, his conclusions, however compelling, were pure conjecture. "I think Matthew Fraser may have been murdered. I think he was innocent of the abuse, but figured out who really did it. So let's just play what if, okay? Let's look at what other men were around in Rebecca's life ten years ago."

"I can't believe you're going to put innocent people through all this again."

His tact began to desert him. "To flush out the guilty one? Yes." He held up his thumb. "Number One on my list. Quinton Patterson."

She stared him down across the table for a long, sullen moment. Finally she seemed to sag, and a flicker of worry pinched her brow. "You like to start small, don't you?"

"He had daily access. And aren't stepfathers and mother's boyfriends the most frequent perpetrators of sexual abuse against little girls? In fact, don't pedophiles often hook up with the mothers just to have access to their children?"

"Statistically, yes," she admitted without enthusiasm. She blew across her coffee to cool it. "That doesn't make all stepfathers bad guys."

Green put his finger on an inconsistency that had nagged him all along. "But Patterson was a good-looking and

157

promising young professional. He could have had the pick of the pack, yet he chose a vulnerable single mother saddled with two messed up children. Alcoholic on top of it, I understand."

Devine shook her head sharply. "The drinking came afterwards, when not only her daughter's but her son's life went off the rails. When I first met Anne Patterson, she was one of those women who turned heads without even trying. Anyway, vulnerable would have appealed to Quinton Patterson, giving him a chance to play white knight. In case you haven't noticed, he's a take-charge kind of guy."

Control freak is the term I'd use, Green thought, but she had a point. Quinton had come on the scene just as Anne was being hammered in court by her ex-husband, allowing Quinton to show off his dazzling legal skills.

Devine took a careful sip and wagged her finger. "I certainly wouldn't put him ahead of her biological father. Becky spent every second weekend with Steve Whelan, and he was a piece of work. Selfish and manipulative, used the kids to get back at their mother. I could see him telling Becky she owed it to him." She mimicked a wheedling male voice. "'Make Daddy feel good, honey. Mommy's so mean to Daddy, but Becky loves Daddy, doesn't she? Daddy's so lonely...that's my special girl.'"

Green grimaced. "I get the picture. But Steve Whelan took a strange stance; he never believed Fraser was guilty, and he accused Quinton flat out of blaming Fraser to deflect the guilt from himself. Said Quinton planted the idea in Becky's head. If Steve were guilty himself, why wouldn't he lie low and hope the spotlight stayed firmly on Fraser? Why invite scrutiny?"

Devine rolled her eyes. "How many times have criminals thought themselves invincible, Green? And how many times has their own sick agenda—in this case his hatred of Patterson—won out over common sense?"

Often, Green had to admit, but asked if at any time in the investigation the father had come under suspicion. She sat a few seconds in silence, her long wine-red nails clicking the tabletop as she thought. Her coffee sat forgotten at her elbow. "No," she replied finally, sounding faintly surprised. "At least not for sexual abuse, and I suppose that's the biggest point in his favour. As usually happens in nasty custody disputes, they both accused each other of every heinous crime under the sun, but that one never came up, even though the father was flinging all kinds of accusations at her—"

"Like what?"

"Oh, mainly that she was neglecting the children while she ran around with her new man. That Becky cried in her sleep when she came to visit him and didn't want to go back to her mother's—"

"And that didn't make you the least bit suspicious that all was not kosher with the respectable Quinton J. Patterson?"

She flushed, and her tapping fingernails came to an abrupt halt. "We had our man, Green. And to be honest, I didn't consider anything Steve Whelan said credible. He was insanely jealous, and he was trying to pry the kids from their mother."

Plus, Steve Whelan doesn't have the baby-faced charm and the fancy connections that Patterson has, does he? Green thought. An uncharitable thought, but probably true. The harmless young Fraser had presented a convenient scapegoat for a lot of people in this case.

Including his fellow teachers, Green realized with a jolt. It seemed a long shot, but as long as they were considering all the men in Rebecca's life who had access to her, it ought to be considered. "What about Ross Long? Any dirt stick to him?"

At first Devine looked baffled by the name, then incredulous. "Fraser's teacher friend? What the hell does he have to do with anything?"

"He was the only other male teacher in the school. But he was older and more of an authority figure, so maybe Becky was afraid to point the finger at him."

Devine waved the red fingernails in dismissal. "Straws, Green. Why not the school custodian? Maybe he sneaked her off behind the boiler."

"Becky would have squealed on the custodian way before she turned on a helpful young teacher whom all the kids liked."

Devine stared at the ceiling as if seeking patience from some celestial source. "There was never anything to implicate Ross Long. Normal guy with a wife, kids and a house in Barrhaven. How's that for squeaky clean?"

He cringed inwardly, but there was not the slightest glint of mockery in her eye. "Appearances can be deceiving," he replied, deadpan. "I'm still keeping him up there. Every bit as much access as Fraser, and with his years of experience, probably a lot more practised at keeping it under wraps. What did you dig up about the guy?"

She shrugged, her eyes bored. "Dead end guy stuck in a dead end job. He wasn't a very good teacher; he hadn't changed his methods in years, and he trotted out the same old yellowed lesson plans year after year. Didn't matter what the curriculum said. The kids found him boring, the parents tried to get rid of him or at least get their kid out of his class—"

"Oh?" he demanded sharply.

"Nothing sinister, Green. Just a waste of their year, and to this kind of parent, a less than scintillating year does irrevocable damage. In our day, we had some terrific teachers and some awful ones, and we just endured them, and it all balanced out in the end, right? But the Duke of York parents are from the 'flash cards in the cradle' school, who see a child's brain turning to mush every moment it goes unchallenged."

Green eyed Devine with curiosity. The woman was full of intriguing surprises. He would have pegged her as one of those "never waste an opportunity" types herself, whereas he had cherished those endless idle hours of childhood. Hours he could wander lazily down dead-end pathways in his mind, exploring, poking, pondering and maybe occasionally discovering something. He pictured himself being rushed through today's childhood, herded through minor league hockey and cub scouts towards some invisible goal and given no chance to linger along the way. He would have hated that childhood. Thank God his parents had had no energy for herding and no idea of the goal anyway. They were too busy putting one foot in front of the other, avoiding the demons in their memory and the yawning chasm in their hopes by never raising their head to look beyond the present. Just one more legacy of the Holocaust.

"Anyway," Devine added, breaking into his thoughts, "Ross Long had two daughters of his own who seemed perfectly well adjusted, and—" She frowned as if to catch an elusive memory. "I didn't write it down, but I'm pretty sure he had a woman on the side. Another teacher on staff, who'd been quietly transferred to another school a year earlier to avoid a scandal. The parents would have loved the ammunition to force his transfer. It's almost impossible to get rid of a teacher, just like a cop. The union's all over you like a dirty shirt, and there are a thousand contractual hoops the principal has to jump through to get someone's competence reviewed. But you can transfer them through quiet agreement."

Green sighed. He was not looking forward to Tony's encounter with the school system, not if his son was anything like himself. He thought of Hannah and longed to check on her, but not with Devine in earshot. He forced himself to get back to business.

"Consider this," he said, continuing to play devil's advocate. "Ross's little piece was out of reach, and everyone thought he was a real loser. Isn't that the profile? Guys feel inadequate and disrespected, so to boost their spirits, they pick on someone even more powerless and needy?"

"Millions of guys feel crappy and belittled, but they don't turn to kids! It's a long way to connect the dots."

"Which is exactly my point about Fraser himself. For my money, Long has as good a profile as Fraser."

"But the little girl didn't accuse Long. She accused Fraser."

Another point taken, he conceded, aware that he was only thinking with half his mind. The other half hovered somewhere out in the vast unknown between Vancouver airport and downtown Ottawa.

"Okay," he said briskly, anxious to get back to the search for Hannah. "That's three. Is there anyone else who should be on the list? Grandfathers, uncles, coaches or clergy who were close to Becky?"

She clicked her nails in thought, then slowly wrinkled up her nose. The effect was oddly endearing, once again out-of-character with the corporate image she strove to project. It occurred to him she might be a very different woman away from the office and out of her power suits.

After a moment's reflection, she shook her head, and Green reviewed the suspects grimly. Although Devine was reluctant to see any of them as likely culprits, her information gave them all plausible motives for Sullivan and his team to sink their teeth into.

"One last question," he said as Devine was crumpling her styrofoam cup and preparing to rise. "Any one of these guys could have done it. Besides Matt Fraser, who gets your vote?"

Her reluctance vanished in a flash. "No contest. Steve Whelan."

Eleven

When Green rushed back to his office, there was still no sign of Sullivan or Hannah. Likewise, Constable Blake at the front desk reported no sighting. When Green called up his email, however, there was a new one from Fred Pollack which wasted no words. "Photo attached." While Green waited impatiently for the photo to download, he put in a call to the staff sergeants in charge of the uniform patrols in the East and Central East districts. After a brief explanation of the situation, he asked them to distribute Hannah's description and photo to the street patrols, particularly in the downtown and airport areas as well as on the bus routes in between. He was just finishing the request when the photo began to fill his screen. Transfixed, he stopped to watch.

Hannah was sitting cross-legged on the floor with a cat in her lap, looking up at the camera with an insolent half smile. Her hair stood out in a halo of blue-tipped spikes around her tiny, heart-shaped face. Even with the silver studs in her eyebrow and the white gloss on her lips, she looked so much like his mother that he felt a sharp twinge of pain.

"Inspector Green?" came the staff sergeant's voice over the silent line.

"Yeah. Ah... I'll send the photo along with the email." He hoped his voice sounded neutral as he hastened to ring off. Five minutes later, he had the photo and description up on an electronic bulletin for all the patrols to see in their car computers and had printed two dozen copies for the bicycle patrols and for street canvassing. A quick glance out his office door revealed still no sign of Sullivan, so Green stuffed some of Hannah's photos into his briefcase and turned to do one final check of his email. In his long list of unread messages, the name Quinton Patterson in the sender column suddenly caught his eye. Sent at 3:07 a.m. the night before. The prick had evidently not slept well following their confrontation yesterday, Green thought. Now what? More legal browbeating?

Curious, he clicked on the message and was surprised when a long, unlawyerly note filled his screen.

Dear Mr. Green, it began.

It's three o'clock in the goddamn morning, and thanks to you sleep has disappeared out the door. Sleep has been a fickle, fair-weather friend of mine for years, and even when she came, she used to bring nasty companions. You ever had nightmares? It got so I hated her to come and used to sit awake blasting the TV so I could get through till morning.

Three o'clock is the darkest, lowest hour of the night, and now here I am again, staring into the dark and remembering all those other three o'clocks from years ago. Evil creeps in at the small hours of the morning, detective. Evil memories, evil thoughts, evil wishes. Tonight, thanks to you, it's visiting our house again.

We all have our tricks to keep it away. My mother is passed out on her bed in front of the TV, my stepfather has been shut up in his study scribbling down legal precedents to keep you out of our lives. Like all the words and pieces of paper and all the laws in the world are going to make a difference. Like they ever have. Quinton thinks the law is a shield. I know it's more often a knife in the back.

I don't know you or why you're doing this, but I overheard Quinton on the phone saying you were going to open my whole case up again. I don't want it opened. I don't want your idea of justice. I don't want the memories or the nightmares or the knockdown fights that put my family at each other's throats over me. If you think you're helping, you're wrong. Or maybe like all the others, you just don't give a fuck. So what will it be, detective?

Rebecca Whelan

Green reread the email three times, fighting a swirl of very unprofessional feelings. Up until that moment, Rebecca Whelan had been an abstraction, a little girl whose allegation had set in motion a cascade of events that had ended, quite possibly, in the death of an innocent man. It had been the dead man's cause that Green had been pursuing, lured into the quest by the unanswered tragedy of his death.

Quinton Patterson had tried to warn him about the impact of his inquiry on the living, so had Barbara Devine and even the CAS worker. But Green had thought—arrogantly he realized now with a sick feeling in his gut—that exposing the lie, unearthing the truth, and nailing the guilty man would be cathartic for all involved. Including Rebecca Whelan, the little girl who had never seen justice done in the first place.

The Rebecca Whelan in his thoughts had been the bewildered six-year-old blindsided by a conspiracy of teachers and crushed by an anachronistic legal system run by a cabal of wilfully ignorant old men. Yet here before him was the real Rebecca Whelan, who had learned in her own way to take care of herself, who had overcome the nightmares and made it to morning, metaphorically as well as literally. Tough and jaded though she was, she had nonetheless placed her peace of mind in Green's hands and challenged him not to destroy it a second time. A challenge made all the more poignant by her underlying suspicion that he would probably fail her.

Do I have any choice? he asked himself as he considered the situation. If Fraser's death turned out to be a suicide or accident, as others had concluded before he started turning over rocks, then perhaps the whole sorry tale could be allowed to slip into obscurity. He and Sullivan wouldn't need to resurrect the painful events of years ago, even if they had indirectly driven Fraser over the brink.

But if, as Green feared, Fraser had been murdered in a calculated move to silence him, then Green would have no choice. This investigation wasn't about the events of ten years ago. It was about the brutal death four days ago of a man whose own clash with injustice had been almost as compelling as hers. Because if Matthew Fraser had been innocent, then it was her lie that had brought it all down on him in the first place. Could Green turn a blind eye to Fraser's death just to avoid reawakening the demons in the lives of Rebecca and her family?

He heard footsteps outside his office and looked up just as Brian Sullivan filled his doorway. The big man's face was alive with excitement.

"Well, buddy, your instincts are as sharp as ever."

Green's heart sank. The one time he was hoping they were wrong. "Where have you been?" he asked peevishly. "I expected you hours ago."

"Yeah, well, you weren't here, so I went ahead with some leads. I've already talked to MacPhail and the Fire Department. And it's dynamite."

Green eyed Rebecca's email out of the corner of his eye. "Okay, shoot," he sighed.

Sullivan eyed him curiously then sank into the guest chair

and propped his huge feet on Green's desk. He flipped open his duty book with a dramatic flourish. "Well, the PM's interesting. So interesting that MacPhail phoned me at six o'clock this morning before he'd even gone for his morning jog. How that guy drinks all night and then gets up at dawn for a run is beyond me."

"Sweats the booze out of his system, he says. What did he have to say?"

Instead, Sullivan turned to another page with a smile. "I also got a preliminary report from the fire investigation guys. Looks like gasoline was present on the mattress and the floor around the bed, which produced a rapid, hot, localized burn. Now what does that tell you?"

Sullivan was teasing him, but for once their Socratic game held no appeal. Green could only think of a teenage girl lying awake at three in the morning, hanging onto the slim and fading hope that she'd be left in peace. When he didn't respond, Sullivan narrowed his eyes thoughtfully and answered his own question. "You and I were right, Mike. He didn't set himself on fire accidentally. MacPhail says the guy was dead as a doornail before the fire even hit. Not a trace of soot in his lungs."

Fuck, Green thought. Not even a chance for reasonable doubt. "What did he die of?"

"MacPhail couldn't find any physical cause. No signs of smothering or asphyxiation. Looks like he just stopped breathing. We're waiting on the tox results, but no matter the cause, it looks like someone killed him and set the fire to cover it up. So we're going to have to go through his old case with a fine-toothed comb."

"Well, I've been thinking..." Green began, but even to himself the idea sounded lame. "We shouldn't overlook the residents of the rooming house. It might be a simple case of a robbery gone bad. His briefcase was missing, so somebody might have thought it was full of drug money."

"We've done a routine canvass, and there's no evidence of that. Nobody even knew he was there." Sullivan frowned and slapped his notebook shut. "Okay Mike, what the hell's going on? Last night you were hot to trot on this case; now you're acting like you want it to disappear."

"I don't. Well... I've got a problem." Green swivelled his computer monitor around so that Sullivan could see the email. Once Sullivan had read it, he frowned, and a wary skepticism replaced his initial dismay.

"It could be legit, I suppose," he muttered eventually.

"What do you mean? You don't think Rebecca Whelan sent it?"

"Well, there is that. It's obviously sent from Quinton Patterson's email account."

The possibility that the note was forged had not occurred to Green, and he pondered it with surprise. In yesterday's visit, Patterson had certainly been determined to keep a lid on the investigation and to prevent Green from talking to Rebecca himself. Had Patterson decided that an emotional appeal from a victimized girl would have more weight than his own legal posturing? If so, he had been right, and the thought angered Green.

Yet from his brief meeting with Patterson, Green sensed that the man knew no other rules than those of the courtroom. Rationalism, power plays and bluffs would be his weapons of choice, not the raw poignancy of emotion. Whoever had written that email had dredged it from deep in their soul.

Green shook his head. "It doesn't feel like Patterson. It feels like someone who's lived it."

Sullivan raised a baffled eyebrow. "Even if it is, what difference does it make? Jesus, Mike, we've been stirring up hornets' nests all our lives. Murder does that. And I'll tell you something else." He leaned forward to tap the computer screen. "That may be what she's trying to avoid. She doesn't want you opening up the case, because she doesn't want us uncovering the truth."

Green contemplated the idea in silence. He knew he was only thinking with half his wits, but Sullivan's theory had a ring of plausibility. Patterson was not the only one who wanted the truth to stay buried. If Rebecca had originally lied about Fraser's guilt to deflect suspicion from the real culprit, she might still be protecting that person.

"So you're saying this whole email could be a manipulation?"

Sullivan nodded. "Yup. To get under your skin. By the looks of you, you've fallen for it hook, line and sinker, which isn't like you."

"This feels so real, Brian. She's just a sixteen-year-old kid."

"Right at the height of her manipulative powers. Come on, Mike! Your bullshit sensors should be ringing loud and clear!"

They would be, Green realized, if his brain wasn't clogged with images of another sixteen-year-old kid, who in her own impetuous way was also trying to come to grips with a past that had failed her. And perhaps blundering naïvely into the clutches of some greasy pimp on the prowl at the airport. Fuck, sixteen was so young!

His preoccupation must have been written on his face, for Sullivan's eyes narrowed thoughtfully. "I heard Ashley called this morning."

Green hesitated. It was useless to pretend, because Sullivan could read him like a book. Better to come clean and get Sullivan's lecture over with. Sullivan never seemed to screw up his own family life, no matter what the demands of his job. He had a wonderfully maternal wife whom he'd loved since he was sixteen and three talented, well adjusted kids. Green and Sharon were still trying to navigate successfully through Tony's toddlerhood, and Hannah... Well, the therapy bills were testimony enough even before this latest imbroglio.

Green took a deep breath to fortify himself, then filled Sullivan in about Hannah as quickly as he could. To his surprise, after some initial exclamations of astonishment, Sullivan laughed.

"Christ, if she's anything like you, you're in real trouble."

Green scowled. "You know teenage girls. Be a help."

"You haven't seen the girl in how long?"

"Since she was three months old. I did try to visit her once, but Ashley said it would just confuse her, because when she was younger, she thought Fred was her real father. And so I..." He shrugged. "You remember. I just thought it would be better for her. I paid the support—Ashley never had a complaint about me on that score—but for the rest..."

"So you never showed any interest in her. No phone calls, no birthday cards?"

"Ashley cut me out."

"Bullshit."

Green quelled his protest and counted slowly to ten. How many times had he reproached himself for that very failing? How many times had he thought of her with a rush of yearning and guilt, only to take the easy way out? The truth was, he'd been angry, hurt and ultimately afraid, and hadn't known how to fit into her life. So he'd simply bowed out.

In the silence that fell between them, Sullivan seemed to soften. "Okay," he said, "so she's taken the first step. That probably took a lot of courage."

"To hear Ashley talk, it just took a rebellious impulse."

"Yeah. Well, I remember Ashley. Insight never was her strong suit."

Green eyed him with surprise. In the early years of their friendship, when Green's first marriage had been teetering on the brink, Sullivan had never implied that any of the shortcomings lay with Ashley. Only with Green and his inability to make others a priority.

Green smiled now with some relief. "No, but she does know Hannah a lot better than me."

"Which is my point. Your daughter has taken a leap into the unknown. She might be just taking her time coming in for a landing."

"Meaning?"

"I think she's wandering around out there screwing up the courage to come meet you."

Green digested that thought with dawning surprise. It made sense. If they'd been dealing with anyone else, he probably would have thought of it himself. Today was a beautiful, sunny day with clear blue skies and a whisper of a breeze. A day to be outside, soaking up summer. He felt his insides unknot for just an instant before a second thought struck him.

"Shit," he muttered.

"What?"

"I've given her name and picture to the beat cops."

Sullivan rolled his eyes. "Oh, that will go over well."

"I was worried."

"Right. So you sent the cavalry out after her like some common criminal. What a first impression that will make!"

"You think I should call them off?"

"I would."

Green picked up his phone, reached the staff sergeant and within minutes had rescinded his order. But not before the staff sergeant told him they'd already had some luck.

"One of my units stopped a girl fitting the description on the corner of Sparks and Elgin. Tried to talk to her, but she ran into an office building and never came out. Probably went out the back. You sure you want the search called off?"

Green digested this news with dismay. "How did she seem? Afraid?"

"Afraid?" The NCO chuckled. "Try furious. She's not going to come in voluntarily, that's for sure. But if you want, we can—"

"No," Green said hastily. "Just pull the order, and I'll let you know if I need further action taken."

When he hung up, he felt Sullivan's pensive gaze upon him. He drummed his fingers on the desk and tried to gather his thoughts. "Well, she's here, that much we know. Not lost or scared, just roaming around taking her own sweet time deciding to come see me."

"Just as I told you."

"So now what? I just wait?"

Sullivan nodded. "And try not to bite her head off when she shows up."

Green expelled his breath in a rush. "Can't promise that. I don't know what it will feel like to see her—my own flesh and blood but still a total stranger." He shook off his anxiety with an effort and leaned forward with what he hoped was a business-like air. "Okay, so maybe I'm a bit sappy on the subject of teenage girls. You're right, we have a case to solve. A murder, whether Rebecca Whelan likes it or not. And I already have a pretty good working theory."

Briefly, he filled Sullivan in on his discussions with Sharon and Devine. The big man looked as skeptical as Green had been on hearing the psychological test results suggesting Fraser was not an abuser. "But a guy who has a little girl tattooed next to his dick has got to have some pretty interesting fantasies on the go, Mike."

Privately, Green agreed that the tattoo was a big hole in his theory, but then nothing was straightforward in this case. It was like grappling with shape shifters in the dark, and today he hadn't the patience for the fight. "Yeah, but he's the one who ended up dead, so somebody didn't like whatever he was up to." He flipped open his notebook to his conversation with Barbara Devine and tossed the book across the desk. "I want you to start with background checks on each of these guys, and be alert for any other close friends and family Devine and company might have overlooked."

Sullivan looked up from his notes with surprise. "You think Devine was sloppy? The Sexual Assault guys are usually first rate."

"I think Devine was..." Green searched for the right word to capture the passion and frustration she'd radiated. "Determined," he finally settled on. "But when I pushed her, she fingered the biological father, Steve Whelan, as the most likely suspect. I haven't met the man, but she knows the players better than us, so start with him. Try to make inquiries discreetly if possible so we don't tip them off that we're suspicious. Unfortunately, Quinton Patterson knows that we'll be sniffing around the old abuse case because Fraser's dead. But Patterson thinks I consider it a revenge killing. Nobody has any idea I think Fraser might have been killed by the man who actually perpetrated the abuse."

Sullivan nodded toward the computer. "Except Rebecca there. If she was lying to protect someone ten years ago, it was probably one of these guys. No wonder she's trying to shut you down." He jotted a few final notes, shut his notebook and hauled his feet off the desk. "What about you? What are you going to do about Hannah?"

Green mulled over the chaos of his morning thoughtfully. He could waste time running around the Byward Market waving Hannah's picture, but in truth he'd already done all he could to find her. The next move was up to her. Meanwhile, Rebecca's email troubled him. He knew his objectivity was nil and his instincts were shot, but something about it drew him like a magnet. Perhaps it was just teenage girls and the mysterious whims that drove them. He reached for his own notebook.

"I'll take your advice and wait. Meanwhile, I need a crash course in the sixteen-year-old female mind. Perhaps it's time I meet the young lady who started it all and see for myself what she's up to."

Twelve

As befitted a junior partner in the law firm of McKendry, Patterson and Coles, Quinton Patterson lived on one of the avenues in the Glebe, in a stone house with a steeply pitched roof, a carved oak door and leaded windows that overlooked a sweep of rose beds in full bloom. As Green walked up the fieldstone path, he eyed the house with a new appreciation. In the past six months, he had gained a whole new understanding of the rigours of home ownership. Old houses didn't simply mature into the perfect picture of charm; someone worked very hard at them.

It was nearly noon, but the June air was still fresh, and an easterly breeze rustled the grand old trees that arched their canopy over the street. As was his habit, he had not called in advance. Families almost always circled the wagons, so he was counting on the first moments of confusion and fear, as well as the absence of Quinton himself, to catch a glimpse of the truth. But just as he raised his hand to press the bell, he caught a twitch of movement in the drapes on the second floor and knew that he'd been spotted. No one answered his first ring, which sent a piano chime echoing into the depths of the house, and only after he'd leaned extra long on the bell the second time did the door drift open a crack. Two haggard blue eyes peered out at him from behind a clump of blonde hair, and a whiff of scotch wafted through the crack. The woman's face was sallow and marred by purplish pouches below her eyes, but her high cheekbones and long limbs still hinted at the elegance which had turned Quinton Patterson's head fourteen years ago. Green held up his badge and introduced himself.

"Mrs. Patterson? May I come in and have a word with you and your daughter?"

The haggard blue eyes revealed no surprise, leading Green to suspect she'd expected him to show up some time. She propped herself against the door frame and shook her head cautiously, as if too rapid a movement would throw her off balance.

"My daughter's not here."

"Where might I find her?"

"My husband's not here either." She thrust her head forward through the crack in the door to cast a surreptitious glance up the street. Not a soul was in sight. Nothing stirred but a pair of squabbling squirrels chasing each other Tarzan-style through the overhanging boughs.

"I've already had a word with your husband. I just have a few questions for your daughter. Where is she?"

"At work. She'll probably be back this evening." Anne Patterson made an attempt at a friendly smile. "But you know how teenagers are. Sometimes there's no telling."

So I've discovered, Green thought ruefully, but didn't return her smile. "Perhaps I can catch her at work. Where is that?"

"Oh..." She flicked a limp wrist up the street. "Some shop on Bank Street. I can never keep track."

"I'm sure this is a difficult time for all of you," he continued chattily. "I imagine your husband told you Matthew Fraser has disappeared and is presumed dead."

Now the blue eyes registered shock, and she clutched the door frame. Her jaw dropped, but no words came forth. Only a faint squeak. So Quinton hasn't told her, Green thought with a surge of excitement. Was he afraid of sending his wife deeper into the boozy swamp in which she lived, or had he a more sinister reason? Green pressed his advantage.

"It looks as if someone set him on fire. I'm new to the case, and I'm trying to acquaint myself with the background and the people involved. Could we speak inside for a moment?"

She found her voice at last and threw it at him. "No! I mean... I don't know anything! I—I haven't heard about that man in years."

Tires screeched around the corner, and she broke off, sagging with relief. Green turned to see a silver Audi swoop into the driveway. Quinton Patterson leaped out, whipped the door shut and strode up the drive, purple with rage.

"I thought I told you to go through me!"

Green thought fast. So Anne Patterson's two-minute delay in answering the door had not just been slow reflexes. Hubbie had not told her about Fraser's death but had clearly warned her about unwanted visits from the police.

Green was tempted to squelch the man, but chose not to, for challenge was a battlefield Quinton understood and loved. "Mr. Patterson," he said amiably, "we've been discussing teenage girls, and how you never know what they're up to."

Quinton shot a glance at his wife, who started to shake her head. The movement made her teeter.

"I do need a word with Rebecca, and I can find her the hard way, through intensive sweeps of the teen hang-outs, or I can make our little chat much more private and discreet."

Quinton edged around Green so that he was next to his wife. The better to shut her up, Green suspected. "Our daughter has nothing useful to tell you."

"Entirely possible, Mr. Patterson. But I *will* question her."

"My God!" Anne cried. "You think she killed that man?"

"Anne, honey, go inside. I'll handle the detective."

"But that doesn't make any sense!"

"Anne!" Quinton cracked the word like a whip. "Go inside."

Anne shifted her bloodshot eyes from the detective to her husband, and her astonishment mingled with something new. Apprehension, even fear. Like the look in Modo's eyes last night in the driveway, Green thought, when he'd taken her leash. Dutifully, Anne withdrew inside, and Quinton slammed the door shut. He whipped off his sunglasses and skewered Green with his finger.

"Don't you ever try to pull a fast one on me again, Green. You piss me off, and the gloves are off. I'll make you sorry you ever picked up this file."

Green worked at keeping his face deadpan and his voice flat. "Your threat against an officer of the law is duly noted, Mr. Patterson. Now, because parents often act under the irrational influence of emotion where their children are concerned, I'll give you one last suggestion. Produce your daughter, or her whereabouts, in my office by two o'clock this afternoon, or I'll institute standard police measures to locate her."

With that, he turned and walked down the drive, aware of the utter silence in his wake. He would have loved one last glimpse of Patterson's face, but the game would not allow it.

As soon as Green rounded the corner onto Percy Street, he pulled his Corolla over to the curb and stopped while he still had a view of the Patterson house through the trees. He was glad he'd taken his own car, which bore no resemblance to even the deepest undercover police car and so wouldn't give Patterson a moment's pause.

Keeping one eye on the house, he dialled the station and spoke to the desk sergeant and to the major crimes clerk, who both reported no sign of Hannah. The same news from airport security. Green sighed and drummed his fingers on the steering wheel. He ought to phone Sharon to warn her about their unexpected houseguest and to see if her feminine intuition had any light to shed on Hannah's behaviour. But just as he was dialling the phone number of the Rideau Psychiatric Hospital, the silver Audi roared out of the Patterson drive. Hastily he shoved the Corolla into gear and was about to take up pursuit when Quinton Patterson came flying out the front door, his silk tie flapping, shouting at the top of his lungs.

"Anne! Get back here!"

But Anne was already halfway up the block, lurching dangerously from curb to curb and slewing to a semi-stop at the corner. Quinton clutched his head as he watched, then, swearing loud enough to be heard by Green, he stomped back into the house and slammed the door.

Green's mind raced as he eased his own car forward. This was a nice mess. The woman was drunk enough to be a menace, and she was heading up Fourth Avenue past two elementary schools on her way towards the popular shop-lined thoroughfare of Bank Street. Yet she was probably going to tip off her daughter, and in the process would lead Green straight to the girl. Which had been his hope, although he'd expected Quinton to do the leading.

But Green didn't hesitate long. When Anne jumped the curb and breezed within a hair's breadth of the tree outside the school, Green called for back-up and gunned his own car down the street. She wove ahead of him, straddling the whole street and making it impossible to pass. A red light at Bank Street loomed ahead. He didn't know how to stop her. If he honked, she might panic and run the light. If he simply trailed her, he was powerless to prevent her from mowing down those in her way. Ahead, he knew somewhere in the distance a patrol car would be responding to his radio call, but it might be too late.

Then, miraculously, her brake lights lit up, and he realized she was actually slowing for the light. He jerked his wheel and jumped the curb to cut her off, but before he could get around her, she suddenly floored the accelerator, and all the horsepower of the German performance engine leaped into service, hurtling the car out into the traffic with a shriek of rubber.

Horns blared, tires squealed, and everyone shouted at once. But Anne, hunkered down behind the wheel, seemed oblivious as she veered around the corner and gunned up Bank Street. Praying for safety, he followed. He heard the wail of a siren, and over the rooftops of the streaming traffic, he could make out the approaching flash of red. She would soon be cornered, he realized with relief as he followed her wobbly path. But at the next block, she suddenly swerved into a parking space, jerked to a stop and leaped out into his path as if to cross the street. He slammed on his brakes and watched in horror as her figure loomed in his windshield. At the last minute she turned in surprise, her eyes locked his with a terrified dawning of recognition, and she bolted across the street.

Straight into the path of the speeding police car.

The crunch was sickening, and in the swirl of movement that followed, Green made out the blur of red lights as a massive white missile hurtled toward him. He had time to think "Fuck, I'm dead" before the missile hit, and the explosion rocked his car. A huge whoosh of air and heat flattened him against the seat, and in this marshmallow cocoon he felt himself careening sideways, ricocheting against cars and curbs and street poles before crashing to a stop through a store front window. In the aftermath, something thudded on the roof of his car, and a thousand shards of glass rained onto the hood.

"Fuck, I'm alive" was his next thought as the airbag slowly deflated and he fought to uncover his face. Around him bedlam erupted.

"Sir, are you all right?" Anxious eyes peered at him through his shattered windshield. It was a young police officer, her face ashen, her hair in disarray and her eyes huge with shock. I don't have the least idea, he thought to himself, for he hadn't yet reconnected with his body. But that didn't matter now. Anne Patterson had been hit, and it was she they should be attending to.

"I'm a police officer, and I'm fine. Check the woman!"

She nodded hastily and withdrew. Through the gaping hole in his windshield, he surveyed the street. Bystanders stood in hushed knots, eyes glued to the drama, and the pavement was littered with glass, blood and streaks of black. The police cruiser that had hit him had spun around and come to rest wedged against what had once been the Corolla's trunk. The cruiser had a broken windshield, a crushed grill and a smear of blood across its hood. Near the opposite curb he could see a small group on their knees, murmuring urgently, and although he couldn't see her, he knew Anne was there. He struggled to open his door but couldn't budge it. Miraculously, his radio functioned, allowing him to call for the Duty Inspector and Traffic Investigations. He had no idea whether he sounded coherent.

More sirens screamed up the street, among them the deep, commanding blast of a fire truck. Soon paramedics and uniformed officers were swarming over the scene, trying to attend to the traffic jam, the witnesses and the wounded. As the ranking officer on the scene, no matter that he knew nothing about emergency response, crowd control or traffic investigations, he knew he was supposed to be in charge until the Duty Inspector arrived.

He also knew the fallout would be messy, and that every "T" needed to be crossed. A police car responding to a radio dispatch had struck a civilian and endangered numerous other lives on a crowded downtown street. The media would be arriving any second, eager for blood, of which there looked to be plenty.

He yanked at his door and flung his shoulder against it, but to no avail. Black spots laced his sight, and pain stabbed his head. Gingerly, he pressed his fingers to his left temple. They came away bloody.

"That's quite a gash, sir," came a voice through the window, and he looked up to see a young paramedic peering inside, his eyes scanning the interior rapidly. "Pain anywhere else, sir?"

Green didn't dare shake his head. "I'm fine. I'm Detective Inspector Green of the Ottawa Police. How's the victim?"

The young paramedic hesitated. "Can you wiggle your fingers and toes, sir?"

"How's the victim?"

"They're working on her."

"Help me get out of here."

"I have to wait till my boss checks—"

"I'm fine! Now get a couple of firemen and a crowbar."

The loss of temper cost him, and he leaned back, fighting pain until the reinforcements arrived. Car metal screeched, and more glass shattered as they pried open the door. Green felt an irrational twinge of sorrow,. The Corolla had served him well but far too briefly. Two paramedics took his arms and drew him out. As he straightened, the street spun and his legs jellied, but he forced himself to stand tall. Red lights strobed the scene, and distant horns honked as the traffic backed up. Ahead, in the middle of the street, more paramedics worked on Anne, surrounded by a crowd in a grave and quiet ring.

Even the uniformed police were hushed as they moved through the crowd taking statements.

The hush told him all he needed to know.

Suddenly through the drama, Green heard shouting and the thud of racing footsteps. They drew nearer and the crowd parted as a man shoved his way through. The angry shouting rose to panic.

"Out of my way! What's happened? Where's—"

Quinton Patterson stopped short at the sight of his wife's crumpled body. He stared, sweaty, purple and panting for breath, then raised his eyes to beseech the crowd. His eyes locked Green's.

"*You!* You fucking son of a bitch!" He lunged forward, and before anyone could stop him, he slammed Green backwards against his mangled car.

*   *   *

Following his meeting with Green, Brian Sullivan spent several hours combing through files and court records to get his own overview of the case. By the time he'd finished, he was convinced of two things. Rebecca had truly been molested, and the entire school staff had ganged up on her. In their testimony, the little girl had been demonized as a trouble-maker, a liar and a manipulator desperate for attention at any cost. Reading this and piecing together the girl's pathetic family portrait from the testimony of her family, he felt himself grow taut with anger. Not all children had white-picket-fence childhoods, but in the years before the molestation occurred, no one—not the courts, nor her teachers, nor her mother—seemed to care. Except perhaps her father. Steve Whelan had been cast as a bitter outsider, striking back at his wife's newfound happiness by accusing her new husband of being the abuser. No one had taken him seriously. Barbara Devine had dismissed him as a chronic malcontent who manipulated the truth to serve his own ends. But from the man's own statements, Sullivan had the sense he really loved the girl. Perhaps beneath the avalanche of petty letters and tedious complaints, there was a kernel of truth in what he alleged.

At least it was a place to start.

From the reports in the police files, Sullivan had visualized Steve Whelan as a ferret-like man with small, shifty eyes, tight lips and a thin, coiled body. But the man he found on his hands and knees in the flower bed outside his suburban Orleans townhouse was rotund, with a bald, sunburnt dome and sagging jowls. When he straightened up to watch Sullivan approach, worry lines carved deep across his brow. His shoulders stooped, as if worn down by life.

But when Sullivan introduced himself, he stiffened in alarm. "What's happened?"

"I just have a few questions, sir."

"About who? Becky? Billy? Has something happened to them?"

"No, I'm conducting some inquiries related to your daughter's old abuse case."

"Why?"

"There have been some new developments."

"What developments?"

Patiently, Sullivan gestured towards the door. "This may take a few minutes. Perhaps we could sit down."

Whelan didn't budge. The worry lines grew hard. "What developments?"

"At the time of the trial, you always maintained that Fraser was innocent. Why was that?"

Whelan's eyes narrowed shrewdly. "You've found proof. You know that poisonous snake Patterson did it."

"Why were you so convinced Quinton Patterson was the perpetrator?"

"If you'd read the file, Sullivan, if that bitch lady detective hadn't been so hot to trot over the curly-haired wunderkind with the thousand dollar suit, if any of you guys had listened to a word I said, you'd know why."

"I wasn't there at the time, Mr. Whelan. So cut me some slack, okay?"

Whelan seemed to deflate. He peered out across the lawn of his modest townhouse as if trying to draw strength. "I don't know if I want to go there again. Christ, I beat my head against that brick wall for years trying to get you cops and your fancy judges to see my side of things. Spent my last fucking dime on lawyers, who probably pocketed it and went off to buy a round for their buddy Patterson at some overpriced Elgin Street pub. Not the fairest system in the world, eh, when a poor working man has to go up against the likes of Quinton J. Was anyone listening?"

"I'm listening, Mr. Whelan."

"I wrote letters, you know. Since I been on disability, I've been taking courses. I knew my rights. I knew who to write to."

"I've read the letters, but I need specifics. Did you have any proof?"

Instead of answering, Whelan cast him a sidelong glance and turned to make his way over to the front stoop. He eased himself down with a groan.

"Sullivan. You from up the Valley?"

Sullivan nodded. "Near Eganville."

Whelan permitted himself a grim smile. "Thought so. I was

at school with your brother Joe. Detective Sergeant, eh? Joe always said you were the smart one. What's he up to anyway?"

Sullivan kept his expression carefully neutral, but inwardly he was surprised. He'd always thought no one in his big, noisy Ottawa Valley farm family had ever noticed him, which suited him fine. It didn't pay to draw attention to yourself in the Sullivan house. It paid to keep your head down, out of reach of the flying fists and drunken diatribes of Sullivan Senior. Escaping the farm had been the second best move Brian had ever made. Marrying Mary had been the best.

Glad for the icebreaker, Sullivan joined Whelan on the stoop. "Joe's still up on the farm. Doesn't work it much any more, of course, leases most of the land to a big dairy operation that moved in nearby, but he keeps a few head. Does odd jobs, landscaping, snow removal." In between drunken binges, he thought but didn't add. "When did you come down to the city?"

"1978. Me and Annie were just kids fresh out of high school. I came down to work in construction, helped build most of Orleans here—" He stretched his hand to encompass the winding sprawl of suburban homes. "Before my back gave out. Now of course, sometimes I can hardly walk. Quinton J. makes in an afternoon what I get in a week from disability."

Sullivan waited. He could have posed his question again, but he sensed that the man was working his way around to it. For a moment, Whelan stared at his hands, picking bits of dirt from under his chipped nails.

"You got kids?" Whelan asked.

"Three."

"Girl?"

"My oldest. She's fifteen."

Whelan nodded. "Bad age. That's when my son really started to hit the skids—he was living with me at the time, and he'd just go on these black rampages. Couldn't reach him, couldn't talk to him. He'd spend hours up in his room listening to heavy rock and playing creepy games on the internet. He'd been a good kid, you know, smart in school, wrote poetry. He'd taken care of his mother when she had her breakdowns, taken care of Becky since the day she was born. She was his little sister, and what happened to her, it nearly killed him."

Sullivan nodded. How often over the years had he seen children forced into the protector role before they were even out of primary school? Forced to call 911 when Daddy took to Mommy with a knife. Forced to get meals and shepherd all the siblings to school while their parents slept it off. His own sister Pat had done that for him, and now she was on her third husband, still looking for someone who'd take proper care of her.

"Yeah, that's rough on a young lad," he said. "Lot of responsibility. How's he doing now?"

Whelan shrugged. "Up and down. Had a pretty bad coke habit for a while, thought I was going to lose him, but he has his music now. He gets a lot of stuff out in his music, you know? So I'm hoping... Just like with Becky. She's starting to come out the other side." He raised his head to give Sullivan a grim look. "A father knows his kids, see. You know something's wrong. She'd always been a handful, my Becky. Lots of spunk, lots of sass. You say black, she'd say white. But she was a beautiful little girl, the picture of her mother in those days. Loved life. Till Quinton J. came along. That's when I seen the change, way before she ever had Mr. Fraser as a teacher. She'd come to visit me, she'd cry, she didn't want to go back home. She started destroying things, locking the bathroom."

Whelan paused, focussing intently on a piece of dirt beneath his thumb. His hands shook. "That's when I started trying to go for custody. But that's not proof, eh? My lawyer said I'd need a psychological assessment of her, but I didn't have that kind of money. And even after the charges were laid, I told the CAS what I'd noticed, and they said that was normal in divorce. Said she was trying to get her daddy back, showing signs of stress and mixed loyalties they called it, and they said my custody battle only made it worse."

He stopped picking and flexed his hands to form fists. His voice was so quiet, Sullivan wasn't sure he'd heard. "She knew, though."

"What?"

"Anne knew. That's why she asked the psychologist to change her story. The school psychologist who Becky told in the first place."

Sullivan frowned. "That wasn't in the file."

"It wouldn't be, would it? Didn't look good for the prosecution's case. But that bitch detective knew, because the psychologist told her. And when the Crown wouldn't drop the charges like Anne asked, Becky changed her story."

Sullivan had a sinking feeling. It was just a whiff of rot, but he had a sense that if he poked a little deeper into the police investigation, the stench might get much worse. He grasped at straws.

"She didn't recant, though," he pointed out. "Just got confused about dates, how far he went..."

"Yeah. Not enough to reopen the investigation, just enough to bring down the Crown's case in court. Carefully coached by Anne, I'm sure. And probably, if you could find the strings, by that legal genius Quinton J. himself."

"But if Anne knew it wasn't Fraser, if she knew it was her new husband, why...? We're talking about her own daughter. Surely—"

"Are you kidding me? Patterson was her meal ticket. Annie was always a looker, but she was getting up to thirty, and time was running out. He was a jackpot beyond her wildest dreams."

Ten minutes later, Sullivan was back on the Queensway, heading west towards the station. With a sense of dread, he mulled over the implications of Whelan's story. If there had been a deliberate miscarriage of justice and a deliberate cover-up of crucial testimony by Barbara Devine that involved the very heart of Ottawa's powerful old legal fraternity, Sullivan knew he was looking at the end of his career. He wouldn't be fired, not even disciplined, but he could kiss his promotions good-bye, he could kiss the esteem and easy camaraderie of his fellow officers good-bye, and probably even kiss his job in Major Crimes good-bye. It would be back to ticketing speeders and rounding up drunks in the Byward Market in the dead of night.

Goddamn Green and his nose for trouble, Sullivan thought. Now what?

Before he'd even begun to formulate an answer, he heard his call sign over the radio. He responded, and as he listened, all fury at Green vanished from his mind.

*   *   *

Adam Jules' face was the first thing Green saw when he came to. He was aware first of pain, then the acrid smell of bleach and alcohol and the discordant bleat of voices and machines. He opened his eyes, swimming up through layers of dense fog that blanketed all light and sound. Slowly, as scraps of fog lifted, Jules' face came into focus. Lips tight, eyes narrow with apprehension, he loomed over Green's bed.

"Adam?" Green wasn't sure he should move anything. Nothing felt as if it would respond anyway.

Something like relief flickered in Jules' eyes. "How do you feel?"

"What happened?"

Jules' eyes grew hooded. "You've had quite the day. You don't remember?"

Green cast his thoughts back. What day? His confusion must have shown, for Jules' lips drew even tighter. "The accident on Bank Street. Witnesses say you drove the woman to it."

Green shut his eyes against the bright light, hoping it would help, but his mind felt like molasses. Thoughts would not take shape, and he couldn't find anything in his memory. Jules was bent close, hissing urgent words in his ear.

"Michael, I'm supposed to get the doctor now. But you have to tell me what happened, or how can I protect you?"

Green's head felt jackhammered, and nausea spun him in circles. Speech was a great effort. "I don't know, I can't remember."

The curtain drew back, and a swarm of white coats bustled in, poking instruments at him and peering dubiously at clipboards. One of them, a young woman half Jules' age, shooed him outside then returned to wave a pen officiously around in front of Green's eyes. Fighting pain, nausea and the faint budding of fear, Green ventured a smile.

"So am I dying?"

"Nope," the woman replied without looking up from her clipboard, then walked out of the room.

Time drifted. People appeared and disappeared. Police officers who wanted his statement, nurses, doctors and technicians who poked and measured and extracted things for reasons that escaped him. An official-sounding doctor finally came to speak to him, but Green understood nothing of his monotone pronouncement other than the word concussion.

Concussion. Concussions had destroyed countless NHL

hockey careers and reduced heavyweight boxers to drooling idiots. Concussions scrambled the brain, disconnected the precious circuitry he so prided himself on. He lay alone in his little cubicle, abandoned for those more gravely ill than himself, left to his own elliptical and reverberating thoughts, and working himself into a first-class panic.

Then Sharon walked in. Finally. Calm, practical, experienced Sharon, still dressed from work and breathing heavily from the rush.

"Poor you!" she exclaimed, planting a careful kiss on his cheek. She was trying for her nurse's cheerfulness, but the darkness in her eyes betrayed her. "Your face will be all colours by tomorrow, but you'll be all right."

He tried to sound coherent as he explained about the concussion. "I want to go home, but they want to keep me overnight for observation."

"I know. It took some talking, but I've sprung you. I told them I was an experienced nurse."

"You haven't done real nursing in years."

She made as if to swat him, but stopped herself. "I lied. But it's good to see your critical faculties are still intact. Anyway, I've brought you fresh clothes, so as soon as the doctor signs you out, we'll get out of here. I phoned your father, by the way, so he wouldn't have a coronary when he sees the news."

Green pictured Sid, sitting alone in his senior citizen's apartment where the TV was a constant background companion. A widowed Holocaust survivor, Sid had placed his only child at the centre of his world. "He's not going to relax until he hears my voice."

"Tomorrow, honey. The sitter's going to keep Tony all night so you can rest. However, that crazy dog is still at home and desperately in need of a pee by now, I suspect."

It was nearly midnight by the time they were able to get away, and Green was exhausted. Throughout the long ride, he floated and chased fragments of thought that made no sense. Whenever he dozed, Sharon prodded him awake.

"Sorry, honey, doctor's orders. Talk to me about today."

"I don't remember anything after following Anne Patterson up Bank Street. Do they say I killed her?"

"No. And she's not dead," Sharon added hastily. "She was in surgery most of the morning with bruises, lacerations, and some head trauma, but she's stable."

"Is she going to be all right?"

"She hasn't come out of the anaesthetic yet, so they can't say for sure. But from what the officers told me, she was really drunk, and she just ran in front of the police car. Like her mind was a million miles away."

Probably was, he thought, gazing through the darkness of the corn field. I know that feeling. That you've lost your anchor and have no idea what's coming next.

Thirteen

Green's first conscious thought the next morning was "What the hell am I doing on the living room couch", closely followed by "What the bloody hell has exploded in my head?" He risked turning his head to survey his surroundings. Early morning sunshine slanted through the living room window and cast oblongs of sharp light on the carpet. Sharon was curled up fast asleep in the armchair, and Modo was stretched out in a pool of sun at her feet. Understanding dawned on him as he remembered the concussion and the long, bewildering wait in the hospital. Nervously he tested his memory, but found it still stopped short of the actual impact. Deciding a shot of caffeine might help, he tried to sit up and nearly cried aloud. Every muscle in his body felt pummelled. After a few cautious stretches, he slipped gingerly off the couch and limped into the kitchen. Modo seemed to fight conflicting loyalties but finally followed him in. The coffee grinder woke Sharon, who arrived with her make-shift nursing kit to check him over.

"I feel two hundred per cent better," he protested.

"Yes, and in fifteen minutes you're going to crash." She shone a flashlight into his eyes and asked him to track her finger. "This is not something to fool with, honey. You ignore a concussion, and that scrambled eggs feeling could be permanent."

He wanted to prove his own invincibility, but the fifteen

minutes had barely elapsed before he found himself flagging. His tongue tripped on words, and his limbs grew heavy. Humbled, he cradled his second cup of French roast in his palms and went back to the sofa.

"You made the headlines," Sharon remarked, settling into the armchair with her coffee and the paper. "Lots of gory photos of the police cruiser and your poor little car."

He reached for the paper, hoping the photo would jumpstart his brain, but all he could make out was the front hood of the mangled Corolla. "Fuck," he muttered. "The insurance probably won't pay a damn cent for that accident. Personal car used in the line of duty. Damn..." He rested his head wearily against the cushions, picturing the money swirling down the drain. "I'd better call Dad before he sees that picture. Can you bring me the phone?"

When Sid Green heard his voice, there was silence on the phone. Then a whispered. "Thanks to God. *Nu*, Mishkeleh, you don't look where you are going?"

"It couldn't be helped, Dad, but I'm okay. Everyone is okay."

"That woman you hit. She's not okay, and they said on the news her husband is a big lawyer."

Through the blankness of his memory, Green felt a stab of worry. What if he had hit Anne? What if his own recklessness had been responsible for permanent damage? "Don't worry, nobody's going to charge me," he said, praying he was right. "It was an unlucky accident. And Dad? If reporters come bugging you, don't talk to them, okay? Let me handle it."

With a few more reassurances, he disconnected, handed the phone back to Sharon and slumped back in the pillows. Worry gnawed at him. "Any news on Anne Patterson in the paper?"

"Her name's being withheld at the request of the family—"

"Which means Quinton Patterson. As always, trying to do

damage control. Nothing in there about him suing me?"

Sharon paused to scrutinize the article. "Not as of last night. Apparently, they hadn't located all the family. Sounds as if the daughter hasn't turned up yet."

"Yeah, that's who I was trying to find—" His eyes flew open, and he sat up abruptly as a memory came back. "My God, Hannah! Bring me the phone again."

"What?" Sharon looked at him in alarm. He shook his head as if to reassure her that he hadn't lost his faculties and dialled the station. No, said the clerk in Major Crimes, Hannah had never shown up or contacted them yesterday. Green ordered the clerk to put out a new bulletin for everyone to be on the look-out for her. As he hung up, he caught Sharon's expression, which had changed from alarm to astonishment.

"Hannah is in Ottawa? Your Hannah?"

He held up a soothing hand. "Long story. She has apparently decided to check out her roots." He dialled another number and waited impatiently through five rings before Ashley's breathless voice snapped through the line.

"Mike? She there?"

Call display, Green realized, old enough to be disconcerted. "Not yet. Has she been in touch with you?"

Ashley launched into a tirade about his callous and cavalier attitude and berated him for letting her stew for almost twenty-four hours without so much as a phone call. He held the phone away and massaged his temple, choosing to endure rather than defend himself.

"Something came up," was all he said.

"Oh, it did, did it? Well, I'm glad to hear some things never change. I hope your new wife appreciates her position on Officer Green's list of priorities."

"I promise to update you every hour. I have to go now, but

don't worry, I have the whole police force looking for her. We'll find her."

He extricated himself with relief and turned to Sharon, aware of the throbbing in his temple and the coffee churning in his gut. By the time he had finished explaining Hannah's story, fatigue was steamrolling over him. He prayed that Sharon's experience with the vagaries of human behaviour would save the day.

"Should I be worried?"

When she shook her head, he wanted to kiss her, but hadn't the strength to leave the couch. "She's sixteen, Mike. Lots of kids travel all over at that age, and she sounds like she's nobody's fool."

"Maybe not, but she's still a middle class kid from the Vancouver suburbs, and if I know Ashley, she's been pampered to death."

"Overprotective parents didn't stop you any."

True, he thought. As Holocaust survivors, his parents had come by their paranoia honestly, but during his childhood this had not prevented him from breaching the walls of their fear to run wild and free through the rough inner city streets of Lowertown, clashing with the French Canadian youth who controlled the turf. But the memory of himself as a kid brought no reassurance. Teenagers could get themselves in such messes.

He set his coffee aside and leaned back into the pillows. "What should I do? I've already got the uniforms keeping an eye out."

"You could try hiring a sky writer to say 'Hannah, call your father.'"

He didn't rise to her laughter. "Some Jewish mother you make."

"I'm serious, Mike. Hard as it is, you have to wait. She's circling the landing strip, gathering the courage and getting the lay of the land. She took off on a whim, and now she's probably wondering what happens next. She'll turn up once she's figured out what to do."

"Can you be home? Stay by the phone?"

She eyed him knowingly. "Yes, I'm staying home with you, remember? Monitoring your concussion."

He contemplated the current chaos of his situation; Anne Patterson unconscious, Quinton out for his blood, Rebecca Whelan a giant unknown, and his own daughter on the lam in unfamiliar waters. To say nothing of the mystery arsonist who was trying to obliterate all evidence of a past crime.

And worst of all, a dizzying fatigue that made every word an effort. He couldn't even think which problem to attack first, let alone how, and all he really wanted to do was crawl back under the covers.

Fortunately, at that moment, a familiar old Chevrolet pulled into the drive, and Brian Sullivan climbed out.

*   *   *

Sullivan hadn't slept well. He'd lain awake in his darkened room, staring at the ceiling and listening to the whir of the air conditioner and the muffled cheep of crickets outside his closed window, chasing futile worries through weary loops in his mind. Green was going to be a wipe-out, perhaps for days, unable to remember things and subject to bouts of fatigue and nausea which would sap him of his usual vim and acuity. It left Sullivan all alone to confront Quinton Patterson and the possible scandal brewing within the force.

Saturday was supposed to be a short shift, and he hoped to spend the afternoon with his boys at the antique air show out at Uplands Military Base. At barely six a.m., as the sun was just skimming the rooftops across the street, he slipped out of the house and headed down to the station for one more peek at Fraser's file. Perhaps he had missed something yesterday. Perhaps the report on the psychologist's visit to Barbara Devine was somewhere in Devine's notes, and he had simply missed it. It was a huge file, with pages of witness statements, reports and interview transcripts. Surely somewhere in Devine's official records or court briefings there would be a reference to Anne Whelan asking the psychologist to change her story.

There was nothing. There were several neatly prepared official witness statements signed by the psychologist attesting to her initial conversation with Rebecca, as well as photocopies of her rough case notes in which key parts had been highlighted in yellow. Sullivan peered at the highlighted sections closely, trying to decipher them.

Becky very active today, wiggly in seat, trouble sitting still. Says she has go peepee, hurts down there. Touching her panties. How? 'not supposed to tell.' Q (n.a.) Q 'Mr. Fraser' (looks frightened) Q 'wouldn't let me go.' Report CAS' The next notation was made at 2:10 p.m. the same day. *Report made Jocelyn Marquis, CAS intake, referred to case worker, will be in contact.* The next notation was at 2:30. *Principal R. S. informed, impressed on him need for confidentiality.*

Neither the psychologist's case notes nor her formal statement contained any direct statement implicating Matthew Fraser. She was very careful to report that Becky had made a series of comments about needing to urinate, about her crotch hurting and about Mr. Fraser, but that the connection between the ideas was unclear. Although the psychologist had refrained from asking more questions in order not to compromise the CAS investigation, she felt Becky's agitated behaviour and her reference to keeping a secret provided reasonable grounds to suspect abuse.

Sullivan flipped through subsequent witness statements and numerous transcripts of interviews, but as he had feared, there was no report in the file to the effect that only days after the initial disclosure, Rebecca's mother had approached the psychologist and asked her to change her story. And even more damning, the psychologist had not been called to testify for either the prosecution or the defence. The Crown had apparently thought that the testimony of the CAS social worker and that of the investigating police officer were more probative than that of the psychologist, who had already indicated in her statement that the connection between the pain and Fraser was very unclear.

Which should have been music to the defence lawyer's ears, so why Josh Bleustein had not called her, Sullivan didn't even like to guess. It certainly lent credibility to Steve Whelan's supposition that Quinton Patterson and Becky's mother had carefully orchestrated the evidence to throw the trial without shifting the spotlight to anyone else in the family.

The question was—had Barbara Devine been party to that orchestration? And did he even want to know? He could forget he'd ever heard the story, but if in fact Anne was covering up for her new husband, then he might very well be Matthew Fraser's killer. And scandal or not, fellow police officer or nor, Sullivan couldn't turn a blind eye to that.

The simplest way to check the story's veracity was to ask the psychologist, but doing so might open up a Pandora's box which no one, not even Green, could shut again if a cover-up were revealed. Sullivan stared morosely into space. Before he did anything irreversible, he needed to meet Anne Patterson herself and probe a little into her past, to judge for himself the type of woman she was.

When he pulled onto the grounds of the Ottawa General Hospital, he spotted a cluster of people on the front lawn and a white van with a local TV station's logo parked at the curb. With intuition honed from years on the job, he recognized trouble. He parked his unmarked Taurus behind the van, and as he climbed out, his instincts were confirmed. In the centre of the cluster, flanked by the local news reporter and facing the camera resolutely was Quinton Patterson, looking suitably outraged and distraught. He had taken the time to comb his dark curls and throw on a clean shirt, but his eyes were bloodshot and his face dark with stubble.

"I can't tell you all the details, but I also can't keep silent any longer," he was saying. "My wife may never recover. Ten years ago, the justice system failed her, the police failed her, and the man who destroyed our world walked free. How do you reconcile yourself, when the guilty walk free and the innocent are condemned to an eternal hell? How do you reconcile yourself, when the people you trusted betray you and the system you believed in deserts you? The answer..." He paused with a look of infinite sadness, and the ring of people hung on the silence.

"The answer is you can't. My wife couldn't. She needed help. She needed compassion and support and someone to erase the pain. I failed to. I know that, and I'll live with that forever. But at least I tried, and maybe in time with our children slowly healing, I would have succeeded. But this case wouldn't let her rest, and the police, after their bungling had messed it up in the first place, wouldn't let her rest. Wouldn't let her forget or let me take the brunt of their intrusion."

Patterson leaned forward, his gaze skewering the camera. "Yesterday an Ottawa Police Inspector Michael Green turned up on our doorstep—on our own private doorstep, for God's sake!—to catch my wife off guard, and told her things I'd been shielding her from. And then, not content to let her escape down the street, he chased her, called in the troops as if she was a common criminal, and spooked her so badly she ran right in front of them. I hold Inspector Green personally responsible for the accident, and if my wife dies, I'll hold him personally responsible for her death. Yes, I hit him. I'd just seen my wife's mangled body. Yes, I knocked him out. And I'd do it again."

Sullivan listened with disgust. The camera had never wavered, and the reporter had not said a single word. She was clearly a rookie and no match for the slick and practised legal orator. She had simply given Patterson his soap box and allowed him to do what he did best—sell a case to the jury. To the jury sitting in every living room in the city, who would now declare Green guilty, no matter what the facts might say. No matter that Patterson's wife was nowhere near death and had been pissed to the gills behind the wheel of her car.

At the end of his summation, Patterson turned to leave and the reporter suddenly came to life. "Mr. Patterson, what case are you talking about?"

He shook his head and continued to walk towards the hospital entrance. The reporter scrambled after him. "Was it a criminal case?"

He ignored her, and the cameraman swung his camera off his shoulder, ready to pack it up. Sullivan hung back unobtrusively, waiting for the crowd of onlookers to disperse. Suddenly he heard footsteps and a frantic cry.

"Dad! Dad!"

He turned to see a young woman about his own daughter's age hurrying across the lawn from the street, tottering awkwardly on her platform shoes. Her dreadlocks shone green in the sunlight, and her black-rimmed eyes looked sepulchral. Sensing a story, the cameraman hoisted his camera back onto his shoulder and flipped it on. Patterson whirled on him.

"Turn that thing off!"

The cameraman pointed his camera away as if in acquiescence, but Sullivan could see it was still on. More importantly, it was now pointing towards the approaching girl. She was red-faced from the unaccustomed burst of exertion, and she panted as she lumbered up.

"What happened? Did Mom do it on purpose? Did that goddamn cop...?"

Patterson's lips were tight, and Sullivan recognized that glacial "where-have-you-been" glare that fathers reserve for teenage daughters, but then the man forced the glare into a smile as he pulled the girl into his arms. He spoke very quietly in her ear, and Sullivan drifted across the lawn casually so that he could see the girl's response. Instead of fear or worry, her initial panic gave way to disgust, even contempt, as she thrust him away.

"Oh, that's rich! Drunken cow runs right in front of a cop car."

Patterson yanked her roughly away from the listening media, fortunately in Sullivan's direction. Patterson tried to keep his voice low, but it shook with outrage.

"She was rushing to warn you!"

"More like shut me up," Rebecca countered.

"Don't you even care, you little—" He stopped himself. Gripping her by the elbow, he began to march her toward the hospital. "We're not having this conversation here. You're going to come upstairs to see your mother. And don't you ever call her a drunken cow in my earshot again!"

Rebecca wrenched herself free of his grip. "Oh, sorry. Forgot the rules. I'm the one who poured the booze down her throat."

"All your life, things have been about you!" Patterson snapped. "But just this once, your mother comes first! You're going to hold her hand and tell her you love her. So help me God, you're going to help me pull her out of this!"

Sullivan had fallen into step several yards behind them and

followed them through the glass entrance doors and across the marble foyer to the elevators. They both seemed oblivious to his presence among the crowds milling to and fro. Rebecca stared straight ahead and gave her stepfather the deep freeze while they waited for the elevator, but Sullivan recognized the unique mixture of defiance and panic that characterized a teenager out of her depth. Rebecca Whelan was scared to death for her mother but damned if she would let her stepfather know it. Patterson broke the deep freeze first.

"Where's your brother?"

She shrugged, a slight "do I know, do I care" lifting of the shoulders.

"He should be here too. If ever your mother needed you two, it's now."

"Yeah, that should keep her in a coma forever."

"Does he even know?"

"That would be your job, Dad. He doesn't talk to me, remember?"

The elevator finally arrived, and the crowd pushed in, jostling to punch in their floors. Sullivan eased in with the flow and stationed himself in the corner. Rebecca glanced at her stepfather, and in that unguarded moment, Sullivan could see how much her defiance was costing her. Unshed tears glistened in her eyes, and she turned her attention to her black fingernails.

"Steve might know where he is," she muttered finally.

"I spoke to your father last night," Patterson replied. "Apparently your brother has skipped out on his rent and on some debt he owes his girlfriend." He sighed as if the tale had a familiar ring. "Any idea where he might have gone?"

"On the road? Wasn't he trying to get a tour together?"

Sullivan made a quick mental note to check the whereabouts of Rebecca Whelan's brother, then glanced up just as the elevator slid open. When Rebecca and her stepfather disembarked, he hung back and followed at a discreet distance. He saw them stop to talk briefly at the nursing station, saw the nurse shake her head, then watched them make their way through a door down the hall. He approached the same nurse, but her face fell at the sight of his badge.

"I'm sorry, sir. We're under strict instructions not to discuss her case with anyone, not even the police, without going through her husband."

Sullivan was not surprised. From what little he'd seen of him, the man was a control freak. He gestured to a small row of plastic chairs and said he'd wait there if one of the nurses would be kind enough to tell Mr. Patterson of his arrival.

He'd barely settled into a chair and opened his duty book when the door burst open and Patterson strode out. On his heels, despite his sharp words of discouragement, was Rebecca. His eyes raked the waiting room angrily, then narrowed with confusion when Sullivan rose to greet him.

"I was expecting Inspector Green."

"I'm Detective Sergeant Sullivan. I'll be handling the investigation."

"What investigation?"

"Please sit down, Mr. Patterson. It won't take long."

Patterson didn't move. Hovering just behind his shoulder, Rebecca glared out from under her green mop. "What investigation? My wife's accident?" Patterson repeated.

"To ensure objectivity, all incidents involving the police, including your wife's accident, will be handled by the Special Investigation Unit. I'm assigned to the assault on Inspector Green."

"Assault? That's ridiculous. I was in a state of shock due, I might point out, to the extreme provocation of that same officer. No judge in his right mind would find me culpable."

"We're not at the stage of charges yet, Mr. Patterson. I'm still investigating, but are you prepared to give me a statement as to your recollection of the incident?"

"Certainly not while I'm standing vigil—"

"Don't even try, Dad," Rebecca chimed in. "He'll twist it and turn it, until pretty soon he's making you say things you never meant to say, and claiming you said things you never did."

Sullivan eyed her sharply, wondering if she was referring to her own attempt to change her story. The whiff of rot that he'd detected yesterday floated by again, but he steered carefully away.

"How is your wife, sir?"

"Not well," he replied curtly. "She's in extreme pain."

"Is she conscious? Able to speak?"

"Under no circumstances would I permit you to speak to her even if she were. She's had a severely traumatic experience."

"I won't be disturbing her, I assure you, sir. I asked out of concern."

"Right. Concern for just how much trouble I can make for the Ottawa Police, isn't that correct, Sergeant?"

"Sir, as you're aware, Inspector Green was investigating the death of Matthew Fraser—"

"He *what!*" Rebecca barged in, her black-rimmed eyes suddenly huge with shock. Too late, Sullivan realized no one had told her. All the bravado and armour in the world could not hide the raw horror that raced across her face. "How did you—"

But before she could react further, Patterson caught her arm. "Rebecca, that's what your mother was rushing to tell you."

Emotions warred across the girl's face so quickly that Sullivan had no time to interpret them before she wrestled her veil of sullen bravado back into place. "What happened to him?"

"We don't know yet." Sullivan thought quickly. Patterson

looked close to apoplexy and about to leap to her rescue, but perhaps some useful tidbits could be gleaned from the few words she let escape before he silenced her. "Have you seen or heard from Mr. Fraser in recent weeks, Miss Whelan?"

"Why would you think I'd seen him?"

Her mask hadn't slipped. Chilly piece of work, Sullivan thought, looking for a way to unsettle her again. "Because he was trying to prove—"

"That's enough." Patterson gripped his stepdaughter firmly by the elbow. "We don't have time for idle police speculation. Come on, honey, let's go find your brother. Your mother's asking for him, remember?"

*   *   *

As Sharon ushered Brian Sullivan into the living room, Green struggled to a sitting position and hoped he looked better than he felt. Sullivan was dressed in jeans, golf shirt and his trademark mirrored sunglasses, and the lines of worry across his brow eased at the sight of Green.

"I can't stay long, but I wanted to see how you were doing—" He spotted Modo, who was planted in the middle of the living room, her massive head lowered and her dark eyes watchful. "Holy Mother of God! What's that?"

"That's Sharon's latest charity case," Green replied. "Meet Quasimodo."

As Green explained, Sullivan folded his bulk into the armchair and tried to get the dog's attention, but to no avail. Modo returned to her guard post at Sharon's feet.

Sullivan smiled at Green grimly. "You look a hell of a lot better than yesterday, buddy. But I hope you're going to take a few days off."

"Two weeks, the doctor said," Sharon interjected.

Green snorted. "That means one week, and I'll take two days. But tell me what's up? How's Anne Patterson?"

"Conscious, I think. Patterson's pissed."

"Oh, I know. I read the news just now, saw him laying the curse on me."

"Jules is concerned he's going to sue."

Green probed his bandaged temple gingerly. "Just let him try, I'll bury him."

Sullivan didn't smile. "All the same, Jules wants you to keep out of his way. Patterson can be a persuasive sonofabitch."

Green's temper flared. "Why didn't Jules just pick up the phone? Why send you?"

"He didn't send me, Mike. For Christ's sake, can't a guy come to see how you are?" The dusky red had returned to Sullivan's face, and his gaze was evasive.

Green eyed him sharply. "Okay. But you're here for another reason too. Something's not right."

"Nothing I can't handle."

"What?"

Sullivan cast Sharon a questioning glance before returning to Green. "You sure you're up to this now? It can wait, I was planning to take my boys to the air show anyway."

Green didn't say anything, just leaned back and waited. He knew he had to look healthy for Sullivan to unburden his worries, and he hoped his act would be good enough. Sullivan looked tired, and the crease of worry over his brow ran deeper than usual. A moment of silence ensued before Sullivan sighed, fished out his notebook, and began to speak. Over the next fifteen minutes, he filled Green in on his visit to Steve Whelan and to the hospital. Green listened, pressing his fingers to his temple and willing his scrambled brain to put things together.

"So, bottom line," he observed, when Sullivan finished, "is that, even after all this time, the disgruntled ex is still fingering his arch rival Quinton Patterson as the molester, and saying the loving mother covered for him."

"Yeah, to protect her new wealth and status."

"At the expense of her daughter?" Green frowned. "Seems a bit of a stretch."

"A stretch? You're obviously not yourself. You love stretches."

Green pondered the observation wryly, unsure why he was reluctant to admit the obvious. Only the day before, he'd been arguing the case for Patterson's guilt with Barbara Devine, and the intervening events had not improved the man's image one bit. Even Rebecca's email appeal made sense in this context, for exposing Patterson would slice through the very core of the family bonds. Patterson had certainly tried every way he could to keep Green from his wife and stepdaughter. He'd been obnoxious and threatening, and to top it off, Green had him to thank for his scrambled brains. Patterson was desperate to protect something. But was it his wife and stepdaughter, as he claimed? Or was it his own ass? It would be a long, hard fall from the carpeted halls of McKendry, Patterson and Coles to a cell in Kingston Pen.

Yet despite all Green's years dealing with human depravity, he found himself hoping that Patterson's concern was above board. The man had undertaken the task of loving someone else's angry, rebellious daughter and had tried to stick by her through all these heart-wrenching years. Few men would do as much, he reflected with a twinge of guilt.

"Brian, you saw father and stepdaughter together. How did they strike you? Close? Loving?"

Sullivan grunted. "This kid is not into loving, not so's you can tell. Prickly as a cactus. But I didn't get a creepy feeling.

And she calls him Dad, for what it's worth. Calls her real father Steve." Sullivan flipped through his notes, as if trying to recreate his impressions. "In fact, I'd say she was more angry at her mother than her father. Almost like her mother was the one causing all the grief in the family."

Which she would have, in the girl's distorted perception, if all those years ago she had sold her daughter's innocence for a plush and pampered lifestyle in the Glebe. But before he could voice that observation, Sullivan's cellphone rang. It was the clerk in Major Crimes. Green listened as Sullivan asked a few clipped questions, jotted down a number and rang off, immediately punching in another number. As he waited, he glanced across at Green.

"Speevak, the forensic ondontologist. He's got some results for us. I—" He broke off as a voice crackled over the line. Sullivan introduced himself, then listened. The conversation was brief, and as Green waited, he saw a look of dawning astonishment pass over Sullivan's face. When he'd rung off, Sullivan raised his head.

"This absolutely takes the cake! The crispy critter? It's not Fraser. The fucking teeth don't match!" He chuckled wryly. "I wouldn't like to be in the Police Chief's shoes when Quinton J. Patterson learns this."

*   *   *

Sullivan was barely out the door before Green crashed on the sofa with relief. For once he was grateful for being an invalid. Let Jules and the Force's legal beagles handle the fall-out from Patterson's wrath. Let Sullivan go back to his tattoo search, and let the Fraser file revert to a simple missing persons. Important, but not a homicide. He sensed there was something definitely off-kilter about this whole case, but right now he couldn't think of it through the incoherent mush his brain had become. He was dimly aware of Sharon pulling the cover up over him, touching her lips softly to his brow and whispering, "Sleep, love. I'll go get Tony and pick up a few groceries."

At least he thought that's what she'd said. Beyond that, he was aware of nothing until the phone rang, dragging him from a deep, cobwebbed sleep that robbed him of all sense of time and place. When Sharon didn't pick up, he staggered off the sofa and found the phone by its fourth ring, praying it was Hannah.

At first he was greeted by silence, followed by a brusque, wary "Sharon Levy, please."

He mustered enough authority to reply in kind, indicating that she was out and could he take a message.

"Damn," came the most unprofessional reply, followed by "Sorry...uh...are you her husband, the police officer?"

Suddenly the voice sounded much younger and more insecure. Green felt his hopes surge. "Hannah?"

"No," the young woman replied. "This is Safe Haven calling, about your wife's friend."

Green pawed through the cobwebs. Safe Haven? Sharon's friend? Finally, as if from eons ago, he remembered, and felt a twinge of concern. "Janice Tanner? What's wrong?"

"We're not sure. She's disappeared."

Fifteen minutes later, Green was sitting in the back of a cab on his way downtown, trying to organize his thoughts. He knew he shouldn't be going anywhere, shouldn't even be out of bed, but fortunately adrenaline kept the fatigue and headaches at bay. His sense of uneasiness had returned stronger than ever. It didn't make sense that people kept disappearing in this case. First Fraser, then Hannah and now Janice. He felt as if events were unravelling before his eyes.

Safe Haven was a deliberately unobtrusive house in a mixed neighbourhood of retail businesses and low cost housing. He'd been there often over the years to investigate threats and to interview victims, so a couple of the staff knew him by sight. By the time he arrived, the director herself had come in from home. Pamela Pascale was a briskly efficient woman who acted as if there was very little human depravity she had not seen. She raised an eyebrow briefly at his bandaged head then bustled into the sitting room as if bruises were second nature to her. Perhaps they were.

"We wouldn't have called you normally, Inspector, because women come and go here all the time. But Janice hardly ever left her room. Came down once or twice to get something in the kitchen but then beat it back upstairs like a scared rabbit. Any time the front doorbell rang, she jumped. So I was very surprised when she left, and when I heard about the phone call, I was even more surprised. We were hoping it was your wife."

"What phone call?"

"One of the mothers took it early this morning. Janice apparently talked for only a minute or two, then without saying good-bye to us, without even going upstairs for her things, she disappeared out the door."

"Perhaps she's planning to come back."

Pamela nodded. "That's why we waited. But Sharon said she was being stalked, and she was certainly fearful enough. It got us concerned."

A very subtle pain was beginning to pulsate behind Green's left eye. He shut his eyes, hoping to ease it while he thought. The simplest explanation was that Sharon herself had called, but a quick phone call home went unanswered, as did a call to Sharon's cellphone. He scowled. Where was she? She'd taken the day off so she could hover, yet she'd been out now for well over an hour. How long could a few groceries take?

He looked at the trim, no-nonsense woman waiting expectantly in the silence, and forced himself back on track. The next step was obviously to interview the mother who took the call. Pamela summoned the young woman, whose barely concealed insolence suggested that her previous encounters with police officers had not been gratifying. But she was clear on her facts and willing enough to share them.

"Can't say if it was a man or woman. Could have been a man with one of those faggy voices, or could have been a woman who smokes two packs a day. Sounded kind of like they were trying to fake it, you know?"

"Did they ask for Janice Tanner by name? As Janice? Ms. Tanner?"

"As Janice Tanner. 'May I speak to Janice Tanner, please? I believe she checked in two days ago.'"

The mystery caller was well informed, Green thought, as well as reasonably educated, from the sound of it. "What could you overhear from this end of the conversation?"

The young woman shrugged. "She didn't seem scared. Seemed happy to hear from the person, almost like she knew them. It was a quick conversation, and mostly she listened. 'Are you sure?' she asked, and 'Of course I will. I always will.' Then 'Sure, where?' And she hung up. Grabbed her bag and went out."

"Did she seem upset? Excited?"

"Both, but excited, more like."

Green pondered the bits of conversation the young woman had overheard. It sounded very much as if someone had asked for her help, and without question she had offered it. Without fear or sober second thought. There were not too many people for whom Janice Tanner would desert her safe haven and leap to the rescue. Green could think of only one.

Fourteen

It was the middle of the Saturday day shift by the time Sullivan arrived back at the station from Green's house in Barrhaven. His first duty was to phone Matthew Fraser's sister and let her know that her brother was not the poor man who had died in the fire. She sounded relieved but querulous.

"What happens now? Inspector Green's accident was in all the papers, linking the burn victim to the old abuse case. Does this mean my brother's disappearance just gets dropped? He's still gone, you know."

He reassured her that Matthew Fraser would still be an active missing persons file, then rang off, anxious to get on with his own investigation. The burn victim was a John Doe again, and Sullivan was back to trying to trace his identity through missing persons reports and through the fragment of tattoo on the man's groin.

In the autopsy, MacPhail had estimated the victim to be five feet seven inches tall and a hundred and forty pounds and had surmised from the condition of his liver that he was headed down the road to chronic alcoholism. The odontologist had observed that although the victim's teeth had been atrocious, suggesting that he lacked either the finances or the will to make dental care a priority, the amount of wear on the teeth showed that he was relatively young. Probably in his twenties. At least ten years younger than Fraser.

Armed with these descriptors and the Shirley Temple tattoo, Sullivan searched the missing persons database and spent the next couple of hours tracking down every hit he made. In the end, he'd turned up nothing. A couple of families were faxing dental records for comparison, but he was not hopeful. One family lived in Sault Ste. Marie and their son, a world adventurer, had been missing for fourteen months. Another man had disappeared from work about the same time as several thousand dollars had gone missing from his company's payroll.

By two o'clock, Sullivan's eyes were burning from staring at the computer screen, and he was ready to call it a day. Outside, the glorious, blue-sky afternoon was perfect for the air show. Savouring the idea of a Harvey's hamburger and an ice cold coke with his sons, he logged off the computer and headed out the door. On his way down toward the parking garage, he passed near the Ident labs and caught the sound of murmuring from within.

The Ident guys never seemed to see the light of day. When not down on their hands and knees at crime scenes, they were holed up in their labs, fiddling with chemicals and swabs and powders, teasing out the microscopic pieces of physical evidence that would nail the guilty to the wall. They were the only guys he knew who had orgasms over a fingerprint whorl and threatened bodily harm if you breathed on their scene. But they could also be a godsend.

Looking for a bit of banter to lighten his day, Sullivan poked his head into the lab and saw his friend Lyle Cunningham perched on a stool, peering at his computer. His latest new trainee was glued excitedly to his side. Cunningham glanced up in surprise at the intrusion.

"Hey, Brian! Just the man I was thinking of. Come look what I've done to your tattoo. MacPhail lifted it right off the body, and we've stretched it and photographed it, taken out the burnt bits. Come take a look. I think it will be much easier to trace now."

Curious, Sullivan stepped into the room, recoiling from the smell of chemicals, which the Ident officers never seemed to notice. Cunningham had the tattoo blown up on the screen and Sullivan could see quite clearly now that it had once been a fine multicoloured specimen in black, gold and skin tones. Not a little girl at all, but the head of a woman with snakes coiling about her head.

"Medusa," Cunningham said. "Cute. Our tough guy has culture."

"Medusa?" Sullivan asked dubiously.

"Yeah, she was a temptress from Greek mythology. Anyone who so much as looked at her died."

Sullivan grunted. "Says something about our guy's experience with women, eh? And his level of education. Let's see if we can get a hit."

Cunningham called up the local police database and entered the new descriptors of the tattoo, trying Medusa, woman's head and Greek myth. Three men came up. One had a picture of his girlfriend, another was sixty-two years old, but the third was a hit on all counts. White male, height five foot-seven, weight one-forty, age twenty-four years. Name—

"Holy shit!" Sullivan exclaimed.

*   *   *

When Green arrived back home from the shelter, Sharon's Cavalier was in the driveway, and she was in the living room, wearing a path in the carpet. She flung her arms around him, gave him a hug and a playful swat before dragging him to the sofa.

"A note would have been nice," she exclaimed. "Something like 'I'm not on my way to Emergency'."

He was about to launch into an explanation about Janice's disappearance, but Sharon held up her hand. Her chocolate eyes danced, and she seemed unusually ebullient even for her. In a flash, she disappeared into the kitchen and reappeared with the cordless phone.

"A zillion messages. I was just starting to listen to them, and there's one you won't want to miss."

It was a nurse in the ER at the Ottawa General Hospital, following up on Green's treatment. "Post-concussion symptoms can be tricky, so please give me a call to let me know how you're doing today. The number's 555-0204."

Green gave Sharon an impatient look, but she waved him on. "Listen!"

"Oh—and also a young woman was here a few minutes ago asking for your home phone number. I told her we don't divulge personal information pertaining to patients. She said she was your daughter, but the media's been playing all kinds of tricks, so I told her nothing. Hope that was the right move."

Green disconnected and dialled the hospital with shaking hands. Fortunately, the emergency room nurse had just returned from an exam room and was writing up a chart.

"She was in about noon, I'd say, asking about you," the nurse said. "She didn't look like the press, I admit, but you can't be too careful. She's gone now."

"If she shows up anywhere in the hospital, please give her this number. It's very important. Make sure everyone knows."

Her voice chilled. "We're not an answering service, you know."

Green quelled his agitation. At least Hannah was alive and well and was finally trying to make contact. Her approach showed some resourcefulness too. He thanked the woman and prepared to hang up when his brain belatedly tuned in.

"Did she give any indication where she was going?"

"Well, she was inquiring about the woman who was hurt by the police car. Asking where she was. She may have gone up to her floor."

Green jotted down the number, thanked the woman hastily and dialled again. A bored nasal voice announced the surgical floor. When Green introduced himself, the voice dropped an octave.

"We can't give out any medical information to the police."

"Certainly not, this is a personal call." In his most frazzled fatherly tone, Green explained his predicament and the woman seemed to thaw.

"Blue hair, you say?" Her voice faded as she turned from the phone. "Chantal, didn't you say there was a blue-haired girl here earlier today, to go with the green-haired one? Yeah, when was that?"

An unintelligible conversation ensued against a backdrop of PA pages and electronic beeps. When someone finally took the phone, it was another woman. Probably Chantal, Green deduced.

"A teenage girl was here a couple of hours ago. In fact, she did say she was your daughter."

"How did she seem?"

"Okay. A bit unkempt, I'd say. Worried about this patient."

"Anne Patterson?"

"Yes, she wanted to know if she was going to be all right."

"What did you tell her?"

"Well, we couldn't tell her anything, of course. But the patient's husband and her daughter were here, so I steered her to them."

Green winced. In the mood Patterson was in, God knows

how he'd react to Hannah. At the very least he'd fill her mind with enough angry invective against her father to scare her away for hours. On a more sinister level, perhaps he'd unleash on her the rage he felt for Green.

"What did they do? Put her in her place?"

There was silence over the phone, and Green could hear his own heartbeat. He hoped Chantal was merely trying to remember.

"No, I don't think so. Actually I think they went off together. I heard them talking about food."

When Green hung up, Sharon was looking at him expectantly. "Well," he said. "The good news is she's in town and still in one piece. The bad news is she's hooked up with a man who hates my guts." He glanced at his watch. "They were going to get some food. Maybe they went to the hospital cafeteria or one of the little restaurants in the vicinity. If we hurry—"

He rose from the sofa and was heading for the door when she blocked his path. "You're going nowhere, Mike. You're absolutely grey."

"I'll catch a nap in the car."

She started to shake her head, but he faced her down. "Sharon, this is not your call."

She stared up at him unblinking, and the seconds ticked by before she nodded. "Fine, I'll go. I'll take Tony, and you get some rest!"

After she'd left, Green stumbled back into the living room and collapsed on the sofa, his head throbbing. Modo had been watching Sharon through the front window, and now she came over to rest her muzzle on his chest. Her large amber eyes gazed at him, full of concern. Absently he reached down and stroked her silky ears, drawing a strange comfort from her warmth. He knew he ought to call the station, and even

Ashley, about Hannah, but he hadn't the strength. He closed his eyes to gather it.

He was yanked awake some time later by a loud volley of barking, through which he could hear the very faint but incessant ringing of the bell. Before he could mobilize himself from the sofa, the front door swung open and Sullivan strode in.

"Geez, Green, you've got to move out of Barrhaven. This forty-minute drive is killing me!"

Green frowned out the window into the street. The afternoon sun was still high in the sky, and there was no sign of Sharon's car.

"What time is it?"

"Three o'clock. I've been trying to call, but I kept getting the answering machine, and I knew you had to be home." Sullivan pocketed his mirrored sunglasses, and without them Green could see the frank relief in his eyes. "You've been sleeping, I'm glad to see."

"Three o'clock! Fuck!" Green propelled himself off the sofa in search of the phone.

"I've got some unbelievable news, buddy," Sullivan began, following him into the kitchen and opening Green's fridge to fish out a coke.

Green found the phone, held up his finger to forestall Sullivan, and punched in Sharon's cellphone number. It rang seven times before he gave up. Sharon and her cellphone had only a passing acquaintanceship. Even when she actually remembered to take it, she rarely remembered to turn it on. Self-preservation, she called her lapses. She had so little time to herself that she didn't want to be on constant call.

He dialled the station, where he was assured of an answer, although not the one he wanted to hear. No one had seen or heard from Hannah, and now that she knew her father was home on sick leave, she was unlikely to turn up at the station in search of him. "But she doesn't know where I live," he shouted at the hapless clerk, "so for God's sake keep an eye out."

He hung up and rested his head in his hands, feeling defeated. It was three o'clock, and Hannah had last been spotted at noon, presumably heading off for lunch with Quinton and Rebecca. So far, Sharon's search had not been successful. Surely she would have called otherwise. If Green wanted to find Hannah, there was only one option left.

"Fuck," he muttered, head in hands. "Fuck, fuck, fuck."

"The kid will show up, Mike. So will Sharon. I'm telling you it takes forever to get anywhere from out here."

"Tell me about it. But she should have called."

Sullivan pointed to the phone. "Maybe she did. You've been sleeping through all my calls."

Feeling sheepish, Green accessed his messages and left them to run on speaker phone. He felt like an old woman, running in futile, agitated circles. Sullivan eyed him thoughtfully, then reached for the fridge again. "When was the last time you had anything to eat?"

Green couldn't remember but suspected it was breakfast. While messages droned in the background, Sullivan rummaged in the fridge and produced a container of what looked like Singapore fried vermicelli.

"Any idea how old this is?"

Green cast his mind back but couldn't recall Chinese take-out for several weeks. On the tape, Mary Sullivan was enthusing about the Highland Park house. "Too old," he replied. "I'll settle for some soup."

Sullivan pointed to the phone. "Mary says that's a beauty, by the way. And if you like, I can help you fix it up." He heated two cans of vegetable soup with the finesse of a short-order cook and rummaged through cupboards for bowls, leaving Green to picture himself as a handyman, elbow deep in buckets of plaster. He was about to decline Sullivan's offer graciously when the tape announced the next message, which stopped both of them in their tracks.

"Sharon? Inspector Green?" came a breathy voice Green recognized. Janice Tanner! She sounded excited. "Oh, damn. I just wanted to say I think things are working out. I'm off to meet Matthew Fraser. He's okay, but he needs me to do something for him. I'll be in touch when I know more."

The message clicked off, and Green stopped the machine, needing time to think. Sullivan served the soup and sat down, looked perplexed and oddly uneasy.

"Well, at least that's one worry off our plates," Green said.

"Not necessarily. I don't know what this means, but you'll never guess who my crispy critter is."

"Who?"

"Billy Whelan."

Green stared at him, dumbfounded. For a full minute, neither man said anything while they processed the implications. Their soup sat on the table, forgotten. Eventually Green picked up his spoon and began to stir the steaming liquid absently. "Okay, let's get the picture here. Matthew Fraser rented the room in Vanier—we know that because the building manager ID'd him—but six days later Billy Whelan, brother of Rebecca Whelan, ends up dead in it?"

"Correct."

"Jesus. Any other tidbits of information up your sleeve?"

Sullivan shook his head. "I've got the standard lines of inquiry going. Known associates, recent movements. Charbonneau is also trying to track down the parlour where Billy got his tattoo, and Gibbs is doing research on the Greek myth about Medusa."

Green arched his eyebrow. "Gibbs is researching Medusa? What the hell does she have to do with anything?"

"You know who she is?"

"Vaguely. She was this beautiful young woman whose hair was turned into snakes, and her eyes were so deadly that men turned to stone if she even looked at them. Perseus lopped off her head by using his shield as a mirror."

Sullivan laughed. "There you go. See, that master's degree came in handy after all. With my simple farm country education, I thought the guy just didn't like women."

"But why—?"

"It was Medusa, not Shirley Temple, that Billy Whelan had tattooed on his groin."

"Whoa!" Green said. "I'd say he had a run-in with a pretty deadly dame."

"That's why I'm trying to track down the tattoo parlour. He's been arrested by us six times, first when he was a young offender, but he only got that tattoo last year. I'm hoping he told the tattoo guy something about its significance to him."

Green blew on his soup and ventured a sip, which scalded his tongue. "I don't see what relevance that would have, though. We might learn about his less than charmed love life, but his death—his murder—that's got to be connected somehow to Matthew Fraser."

"I'm not assuming anything, just using standard operating procedure."

"But what the hell else could it be?" Green asked. "It's too damn big a coincidence not to be connected."

"Probably. But besides the deadly girlfriend angle, according to our drug guys, Billy Whelan was a cocaine street dealer. A two-bit bad guy, belonged to one of the local puppet clubs the Quebec Hells Angels are courting to run their street action. He'd probably never make the cut—not tough enough—but the word is he's been trying to get out of the business. Maybe he pissed somebody off. Torching the joint is one of the ways they've been known to eliminate liabilities."

"Cement shoes are still the method of choice," Green countered. "No messy body or crime scene for us to sink our teeth into. By all means, put somebody on it, but my money's still on the Fraser connection. Get Billy's picture over to that Iraqi building manager to see if he can put him in the rooming house or with Fraser."

Sullivan nodded impatiently as he slurped his soup. "Already covered. Watts is on his way over there right now. And I'm just on my way over to search Whelan's apartment and interview his neighbours."

Green remembered a small detail he'd forgotten in all the intervening hoopla. "Check the girl down the hall in 817. I think she was his girlfriend, and she says he stole a bunch of money from her. Sounded like he was about to skip town."

"Maybe she's the Medusa. Did she look like the vindictive type?"

Green shook his head. "She knew I was a cop. If she'd killed him, she'd never have told me a thing."

"Still, if he was taking off, it's another sign he might have pissed off some nasty people."

Green returned to his soup and sipped in silence as he pondered the bits of disconnected fact. With Janice Tanner suddenly blundering into the picture, he felt a nagging sense of urgency. The heat and sustenance of the soup spread through him, but his thoughts still felt sluggish. Nothing seemed to fit. Billy Whelan had taken his sister's abuse hard. He had slipped into alcohol and drug use and tangled himself up in gang crime.

But his father said before the abuse, Billy had been a model son who'd taken care of his mother and sister all the time he was growing up. The abuse had spun his life off course. Perhaps he'd been consumed with rage or guilt that his little sister had been violated, and over the years he'd nursed a personal vendetta against the man he believed was at the root of it.

But how did this vendetta lead to his charred remains in a rooming house in Vanier?

Sullivan was devoting his attention to his soup and sopping up the dregs with a slice of bread. He seemed to be respecting Green's need to think, perhaps awaiting the wild flight into fancy that he'd come to expect.

"Okay," Green said eventually. "Let me run with this a moment. Humour me. We know—at least we thought—Fraser was trying to track down Rebecca's abuser, and he checked out of his apartment and into the rooming house under a false name because he thought he was being followed. So let's suppose he was being followed, but not for the reasons he believed. Rebecca's and Billy's lives have both been a mess since the trial, and Billy's had plenty of time to look for someone to blame. He fixes on Fraser. Fraser ruined his sister's life, ruined his life, and is walking around free. So Billy tracks him down, starts following him, and on the day Fraser disappears, he follows him to his apartment. Maybe he even knocks on the door, tries to get in, which is why Fraser freaked out and left in the middle of dinner. But Billy still manages to follow him to the rooming house, and…" Green stopped at the blank wall ahead of him. He'd been on a roll, but now things didn't seem to fit.

"And?" Sullivan prompted, ever the pragmatist. "There's a gap of six days in your chronology. Did Billy wait six days before confronting Fraser?"

Green's thoughts started to roll again. "He may have been

trying to gather the courage, or figure out exactly what to do. We do know in the interim he took his girlfriend's cheque and made plans to get out of town. And we know the two guys clashed—"

"You suspect, Green. We don't know a fucking thing."

"We've got one guy out to avenge his sister's abuse, and the other guy paranoid as hell that someone's after him. Recipe for a clash."

"So you're thinking Billy tracked Fraser to the rooming house with revenge on his mind, but Fraser turned the tables on him? Killed him in the panic of the moment?"

About to agree, Green stopped in mid-thought. Panic of the moment...something about that image didn't fit the facts. Billy's body had been laid out peacefully on the bed, with none of the disarray one would expect from an act of panic. Green groped slowly ahead into the confusion. If Billy's death hadn't been an act of self-defence but rather a carefully planned execution, Green had to throw out all his assumptions and start from scratch.

"What if..." he began, reluctantly standing his theory on its head. "What if Devine and Patterson and Billy were right? What if Matthew Fraser really was the abuser? First he thought he'd outsmart or outrun Rebecca's brother, so he holed up in the rooming house, where he had six days to contemplate the trap he was in. Enough time to realize he'd reached the end of the road and to plan a trap to lure Billy to his death."

"Lure?" Sullivan repeated dubiously.

"Yes!" Green's confidence grew as the theory took on shape and credibility. All the evidence in the rooming house pointed to advance planning, from the use of gasoline to the total lack of physical evidence. "This was not a clash. There was no violence in that room. Billy was dead as a doornail from something he'd ingested before the fire began. I'm guessing Fraser exploited his weakness for alcohol to slip him something lethal in his drink. And when Billy was dead, he laid him on the bed, wiped the room clean of his presence, set the fire, and slipped away. Probably intending the fire to obliterate the body's identity entirely, so that the death would be passed over as just one more unlucky drunk."

Sullivan grinned with a mixture of wry admiration and skepticism. "He didn't count on you and me."

"And the tattoo of Medusa."

Sullivan seemed to be weighing the theory dubiously. "But if you're right, you know what you're saying, eh? He's not the mild-mannered school teacher out to clear his name. He's just committed a carefully planned, cold-blooded murder."

Green nodded. "And Janice Tanner, agoraphobic extraordinaire, is walking into the heart of danger itself. We need to find this guy."

Sullivan reached for his cellphone. "I'll put out an APB. His particulars are downtown on file."

While Sullivan dialled downtown, Green replayed his phone messages in search of Janice's. What had the woman said? He listened again. *'He's okay, but he needs me to do something for him.'* She sounded happy, excited, thrilled to be indispensable to the man of her dreams. *'He needs me to do something.'* Damn! Even from afar, this man was still pulling the strings and manipulating this poor woman into doing his dirty work for him.

What could it be that Fraser himself could not do, and why not? Because he was afraid of being caught? Afraid to emerge from hiding long enough to do something—maybe procure something—for himself. As Sullivan spoke to the sergeant downtown, Green's thoughts raced. The briefcase! It was a longshot, a wild stab in the dark, but that damn briefcase had disappeared somewhere between Fraser's trip to the CAS and his stay at the rooming house. It had never been found. What if Fraser himself had hidden it for safekeeping in some obscure place until he needed it at a later date? Like now, in order to obliterate all records that might tie him to Billy's death.

Green combed through his recollections of Janice Tanner's conversation with him. What had she mentioned about Fraser's favourite haunts? Dow's Lake, where he walked his dog. And the Lemieux Island Bridge, where he had his secret beach away from the crowds. Green reached out and grabbed Sullivan's arm just as he was about to hang up. "Tell them to put three patrol teams out." Catching Sullivan's incredulous look, he waved in irritation. "Tell them Jules himself approved it. He wants a lid on this, doesn't he? So put one team to watch Fraser's apartment, in case Janice goes there to get what he wants. And one to search the remote corners of Dow's Lake. They're looking for a middle-aged red-haired woman, who's to be detained at once. Gently."

"I've already told them that."

"They're also looking for a briefcase, so look in small spaces protected from rain."

Sullivan was all business now. No arguments, no second-guessing. "Third place?"

"The third place is some hidden beach along the Ottawa River near the Lemieux Island Bridge. The guys will have to hunt. And fast, while there's still light."

As Sullivan relayed the information, Green scoured the plan for gaps. There were dozens, but he could think of no other paths to pursue. The story had come full circle, back to Janice Tanner. They had to find this guy. The poor woman had come to Green for help, and now that very generosity of spirit was leading her straight towards possible death.

Fifteen

"Mike, you're on bed rest. You can't put in a sixteen-hour day!"

Sharon had arrived home from her fruitless search for Hannah just as Sullivan was relaying final instructions and Green was easing his sports jacket over his aching shoulders. He had taken two strong painkillers, but the effect hadn't kicked in yet and his body was screaming in protest. He had paused long enough to listen to her brief summary of her search—no sightings of blue or green hair—before explaining his mission.

"I have to do this, honey. I owe it to Patterson to tell him myself that I was mistaken about the body in the rooming house. His wife was nearly killed because of my mistake. Worse, it's her son and not Matthew Fraser who died in that fire, and eventually he's going to have to tell her." He bent gingerly to tie his shoes. "And on top of that, Hannah's with him."

"At least take Sullivan with you in case you faint."

He shook his head. How could he explain that this was his responsibility, and his alone? Women believed in team work and mutual support. Men knew that sometimes honour demanded that they go it alone.

On the drive into town, he rested his head against the back seat of the taxi and pondered the paradox of Matthew Fraser. Devine had thought from the beginning that he was a chameleon, a master manipulator who lulled people into a

229

false sense of trust, who played the wronged and traumatized so convincingly that over half the staff at the Rideau Psychiatric Hospital had been duped by him. A mild-mannered young man who had lured a wild, needy little girl into repeated acts of sexual gratification, then lured her angry, street-hardened brother to his unwitting death. Green clenched his fists at the thought of how close he himself had come to falling for the victim act. He wanted to lay his hands on the man, get him under the interrogation lights, to see for himself the colour of his spots.

Patterson's silver Audi shone in the afternoon sun when the taxi pulled into the drive, but there was no answer when Green rang the bell. He hesitated, hating the mission he'd come to fulfill, then reluctantly pressed the bell again. This time Patterson himself opened the door, dressed in shorts and a tank top soaked with sweat. His cellphone was wedged between his shoulder and ear, and his hands fumbled with his wallet. At the sight of Green, his jaw dropped and the cellphone clattered to the floor. Rage purpled his face, and he slammed the door without a word.

Patiently Green rang again. And again. Finally, Patterson opened the door and eyed him coldly. "Do I have to call a Justice of the Peace for an injunction?"

"I have important news for you."

Patterson didn't reply. Merely stood in the centre of the doorway, his feet apart and shoulders squared. His dark hair was glued in sweaty locks to his brow, and his face was flushed with exertion. Working off the tension, Green suspected and decided to cut the preamble.

"We have a probable identification of the body in the Vanier fire. Not Matthew Fraser as I'd believed, but unfortunately your stepson Billy Whelan."

Patterson's face turned ashen beneath the sheen of sweat. Involuntarily, he gripped the door jamb for support. "Good God."

"I'm truly sorry, Mr. Patterson. We'll need the name of his dentist to confirm the ID. Can we go inside?"

Patterson didn't budge. Instead, he took two deep breaths and slowly drew himself up. "The dentist's name is John Carson. Now you've got what you need, Green, so get the hell off my porch."

"I know it's a difficult time, but I'd like to ask you some questions about your stepson. About his habits, his associates—"

"Send your sergeant. I'll speak to him." Patterson moved to close the door.

Green felt profoundly weary. He had to concentrate to stay upright. "I'm trying to help here, Mr. Patterson. To identify your stepdaughter's abuser and—"

"No one has asked you to!"

"Like you, I'm an officer of the court. It's my duty to investigate when I suspect a crime has been committed. Your stepson's death—"

"By all means, investigate! You'll find his life a sorry mess. Nothing but wasted chances, stupid choices and bad friends. One of whom no doubt had an account to settle. Billy dealt in cocaine, Inspector, but even that he wasn't very good at. Too much time spent writing pathetic drug poems and singing in deadbeat clubs. The fool thought he was going to rival Kurt Cobain someday. Well, now he has."

Beneath the bitter invective, Green could hear the ragged edge to Patterson's voice. He held up a conciliatory hand. "Mr. Patterson, I am sorry for your loss and for the way events transpired yesterday. I hope your wife—"

"Fuck the apology, Green. You'll be seeing me in court."

Bewildered parent or not, Patterson obviously needed the fight. Green leaned on the doorframe, his body sagging as he struggled to muster a response. "I'm not sure you'll want to do that, Quinton. I don't remember everything about yesterday, but there were witnesses. Your wife was very drunk, and she drove by two schools on her way—"

Patterson turned livid, and Green took a step backward, expecting the door to slam in his face. But Patterson merely jabbed an accusatory finger at his chest. "We'll see whose actions really endangered those children!"

A soft thud emanated from within, and Patterson glanced over his shoulder in alarm. Green shoved his toe in the doorway before Patterson could swing it shut.

"If that's your stepdaughter, I have a few questions for her."

"With her mother injured and now her brother dead? Not on your life."

"She doesn't know about her brother yet."

"And that makes it acceptable in your eyes? When you've finished dragging her through all her ancient history, you expect me to drop the bomb of her brother's death on her?"

"Were they close?"

"Becky doesn't make it easy for the people who love her. One by one she's turned on all of us. But Billy was her rock, and God knows how she'll react."

"Quinton." Green sensed his patience fraying. "Just let me in to talk to her."

"She's not here."

"But I heard someone—"

Patterson shoved Green back, stepped out the door and closed it behind him. Outside on the stone porch, he folded his arms across his chest like a brick wall.

"Not that it's any of your damn business, Green, but my

wife is inside with a nurse. Thanks to you, she was too frightened to stay in the hospital. Any other misperceptions you'd like me to clear up?"

Green controlled his temper with an effort. He didn't need a pissing contest with this man; he needed to locate Hannah. To extract her from the maelstrom of this toxic family. He hadn't seen her in sixteen years, and it hit him full force how much he wanted her first impression of him to be happy. He forced himself to sound humble.

"I'm glad your wife's home. I don't mean to be difficult, but I'm trying to find my daughter, and I understand she was with you."

A smirk stole into the corners of Patterson's mouth. Still he stared Green down for a moment longer, as if enjoying his discomfort. "To hear your daughter talk, she shares my exalted opinion of you. She and Becky had quite the contest cataloguing your flaws."

Green's heart sank. Until now, Hannah would have known him only through the distorted lens of her mother's views, which paled next to the rancour Rebecca had expressed in her email.

"Where is she, Quinton?"

"I have no intention of telling you, even if I knew. Let's just say I wouldn't count on seeing her any time soon."

"Patterson, where the hell is she!"

"Anywhere? Everywhere?" Patterson's smirk broadened. "When Becky gets in these out-of-control moods, she likes to move around, stay unpredictable. They're wherever she can find—or buy—the wildest ride, I imagine."

Green fought the fear that rose in his throat. Hannah had survived Hastings Street. She'd survived drug busts and loitering sweeps in downtown Vancouver. Surely she knew how to survive Ottawa. Trying to look casual, he took out his card and scribbled his phone number on the back. "If you see them, could you please give this to my daughter?"

Patterson took the card and flipped it over in his fingers with disdain. For a moment, Green feared he was going to toss it to the ground, but instead he shrugged. "Welcome to the world of heartbreak, Inspector."

*   *   *

An hour later, Green lay prostrate on his living room sofa, hazy from the pain killers but unable to rest. A bowl of chicken soup sat half-eaten on the coffee table at his side, and the familiar chatter of Tony and Sharon in the kitchen washed over him. His body was limp with fatigue, but his mind spun in unrelenting loops.

Rationally, he tried to reassure himself that Hannah and Rebecca were simply two teenage girls out on the town, in no danger from Matthew Fraser. Why should they be? If Matthew Fraser hadn't sought revenge on Rebecca ten years ago when she'd pointed the finger at him, why would he now?

Because she'd ruined his life, Green countered with a sick feeling. And because something had happened to tip the fragile equilibrium that had existed since the trial, something that had plunged Fraser into crisis and driven him to increasingly desperate ends. Green felt as if he were grappling with disparate pieces of the picture that tumbled into new patterns every time he looked at them.

He had no idea what Billy had been up to when he'd met his death at Fraser's hand, but Billy and Rebecca were brother and sister. What if she'd been in on it too? What if Fraser, in his paranoid panic, decided she was a threat too? Where were they, where was Janice Tanner, and why the hell didn't Brian call!

Abandoning his attempt at rest, Green dragged himself upstairs to his computer. Instead of cursing his impotence, he'd try a little detective work of his own, to see what kind of man this Billy Whelan was.

Once he'd connected to the internet, he did a Google search of William and Billy Whelan, garnering over eight hundred hits which were predominantly Irish in flavour. He tried various music keywords to narrow the search and scrolled through a number of hits related to fiddle music and Irish Ceilidhs before his eye caught a rock band named Eros and The River Styx. It was a long shot, but a guy with a Medusa tattooed on his groin might be into Greek mythology.

He clicked on the link and found himself looking at a skeletal figure cloaked in black and silhouetted against a murky river. "Cross if you Dare" pulsed below in blood red letters. Intrigued, Green clicked to enter and waited as images of fire, snakes and darkness began to unfold on the screen. "You have entered the realm of Eros and The River Styx" announced a new banner in jagged black font. In the centre of the screen, a three-headed dog snarled out at him with red eyes and dripping fangs. Behind the creature, mists swirled over a river. The effect would have been laughable had Green been in a laughing mood, but if this was Billy Whelan's rock band, Green was not reassured by his taste for destruction and death.

A choice of links popped up on the sidebar. Green chose "Who are we", and the picture changed to a group of decidedly twenty-first century punks complete with spiky hair, chains and black leather jackets. They posed with guitars in a semi-circle around a slender young man clutching a microphone in outstretched hands. His face was shadowed by a mane of black hair that fell loose below his shoulders, but

Green could almost feel the sombre intensity of his stare. Unlike his back-up musicians, he was dressed from head to toe in stark black; hardly the colour of choice for the God of Love.

Below the picture was the caption describing the band's formation and listing the band's earthly names. Green counted across and discovered with surprise that Billy Whelan was Eros, the band's headliner. He read the brief bio.

Eros and The River Styx grew out of the random jamming of a group of unemployed, messed up friends with not enough money in their pockets, too much time on their hands, and a message to share. "We want to build bridges," said Billy Whelan, the lead singer and creative inspiration for the band, who writes all the music and lyrics himself. "Beneath the differences in creed, colour and dress, people across the world have the same fears and hopes. They might express it in different ways, but they want to love, to belong and to matter. At its end, life is about good and evil, love and death."

Now there's a profound message, Green reflected wryly, echoed throughout history by every new generation trying to make sense of the mess they inherit. A second link on the sidebar read "Catch our sound." Green switched on the computer's speakers and leaned back to listen. The page filled with a picture of an empty highway fading into darkness. "Destination", the caption read. "Music and Lyrics by Eros."

A solitary drum began a low, gentle beat which was echoed in the next bar by the bass guitar. On top of the rhythm an electric guitar began to dance an exuberant solo, melding with the drum beat to create a strangely hypnotic pulse. After a few bars, a breathless, gravelly tenor joined the guitar.

You race the road of life's allures,
Wings on your feet, April wind in your hair,

Silk at your fingertips and laughter in your ears,
Through life's blinding highs and golden lights,
You race the road.

Abruptly the drum beat thundered, and the bass guitar began to drive. The voice turned urgent, angry, filled with despair.

Dark temp-ta-tion
Velvet hammers pound
Des-per-a-tion
Clawing hungers hound
De-gra-da-tion
Cast upon the ground
De-so-la-tion
Blackness all around

Green listened with increasing respect. The recording was amateurish and the sound tinny, but the talent shone through. Talent snuffed out before it ever had a chance to soar. As the last bleak strains of the chorus died away, the door opened behind him and Sharon came in to slip her arms around his neck. He braced himself for a lecture, but instead she kissed the top of his head. "What's that?"

"Rebecca Whelan's brother had a band," he replied. "They were heavy into Greek mythology."

"He was talented."

"Yes, he was." Regret stole over him as he looked at the desolate picture on the screen before him. At the empty road stretching into the misty night. Had that been a metaphor for Billy Whelan's life? Green pondered the sudden plunge from joy to despair in the song. The meaning of dark temptation and clawing hunger. Cocaine? Or something else.

Sharon leaned over his shoulder to tap the murky picture on the screen. "Jeeze, Mike, I wonder if he was the mistwalker. You were thinking mistwalker was a confidante or a friend of Fraser's, but what if it's a code name that Fraser gave to Billy, because of this picture?"

He swung around to look at her with excitement. Barely had her insight melded with his than his own vague idea crystallized, and a further piece of the puzzle tumbled into place. *Eros!*

Before he could speak, a thunderous barking erupted downstairs, followed by the loud insistent ringing of the bell. The moment Sharon opened the door, Brian Sullivan strode in with a glint of triumph in his eye.

"We've been idiots, Mike! The truth has been staring us in the face!"

* * *

An hour earlier, Brian Sullivan had stepped into Billy Whelan's apartment, shut the door and turned to absorb first impressions. Sparse, poor and none too clean; a place to sleep rather than a home. The off-white walls bore the stains of decades of grimy fingers, covered at intervals by pencil sketches on rough newsprint scotchtaped in place. The sketches were of animals—horses galloping with manes streaming, huskies straining eagerly in the traces, spaniels racing nose to the ground. For a moment Sullivan stood in front of the horse sketch, which was so keenly drawn that even the whites of the creature's eyes conveyed the wild joy of running. The man might not have amounted to much else, but he could sure use a pencil.

Apart from the art, the one-room studio contained nothing but a shabby brown sofa bed, a TV propped on an upturned plastic crate, a coffee table, and against one wall a dresser and a stack of books on a homemade shelf. Sullivan poked through the books. Poetry, fantasy novels, computer manuals and three big tomes on deities and mythology. On top of the dresser sat a high-end mini sound system and a pile of CDs. Sullivan recognized some of the hard-edged bands which his daughter Lizzie normally turned her nose up at, along with an entire collection of Nirvana. There's a hero to emulate, he reflected drily, if you're into drug popping and suicide.

The kitchen held the bare minimum of cooking utensils and the cheap, simple food of the poor—rice, pasta, canned tuna and a bag of slightly mouldy potatoes. Buried behind winter coats at the back of the closet, he discovered a laptop computer and an assortment of expensive musical equipment, including an electric guitar. Sullivan was trying to buy Lizzie a guitar for her birthday, and he knew this one was twice the price of what he had in mind. Probably stolen, and now hidden from Billy's creepier friends to prevent a repeat.

Crusted dishes emitted a rancid smell in the kitchen sink, and stained jockey shorts and T-shirts littered the floor. Sullivan did a quick search which turned up no cache of drugs or telltale accounts book. If Billy still had criminal connections, there was no evidence of it so far. But hidden under the stack of books on the makeshift shelf, he finally found a day book and three well-worn notebooks filled with poetry. A cursory examination of the day book revealed that Billy's appointments had been pretty sparse in the months before his death, but most were in initials or shorthand. Which could mean anything, but to Sullivan's suspicious cop mind, it suggested codes. The initials of buyers, perhaps?

He slipped the agenda book into an evidence bag for the drug squad, and as an afterthought put the poetry notebooks into a second bag for Green, who, with his university degrees, might be able to read something into the symbolism. For himself, Sullivan preferred the tangible fruits of old-fashioned evidence and real live witnesses.

He slipped back out the door, hoping to have more luck with the alleged girlfriend next door. But as he approached, he could hear a child crying even through the cinder block walls. It sounded like a full-blown preschooler's temper tantrum, and he hesitated before he knocked, wondering if he should come back later. Tiffany Brown was unlikely to be in much of a mood to answer his questions even if she could hear them, and he needed all the answers he could get. As he stood outside her door debating what to do, he heard shrill swearing within, and the crying stopped abruptly. He gave the neighbour an extra minute to restore her calm, then knocked.

Tiffany Brown was not surprised to see him nor to learn that Billy Whelan was dead.

"Does that mean I never get my cheque back?" she demanded. Black mascara smudged her cheeks, and her hair hung in straw-like clumps over her eyes. But beneath the make-up, she looked barely older than Lizzie, and her halter top hung over a flat, bony chest. In the background, her little girl sat on the floor, engrossed in TV and eating a box of Oreos.

He steered adroitly around the question and inquired about any known enemies or conflicts involving Billy. She shrugged.

"He dreamed big, but he was such a loser. Probably wouldn't have the nerve to hurt a fly. But he's done time, and he did deal some when he needed the cash. He wasn't big time, but he might have made enemies."

"Anyone in particular?"

She blew a clump of hair out of her eyes and clucked with impatience. Behind her, a kettle began to whistle on the stove, but she ignored it.

"Well, there was this one guy creeped me right out. Showed up on my doorstep about a month ago, asking questions about Billy. Like was he a friend of mine, what was he like, did he ever have any visitors in his apartment? The guy seemed especially interested in my little girl. Gave me the creeps the way he kept looking at her."

"Can you describe this man?"

"Yeah, like...mid-thirties, ordinary looking, dressed like a total geek. Brown hair long in the back like ten years ago. When I told Billy about it, he said it was probably some undercover cop."

Sullivan studied his notes, careful to conceal his excitement. Tiffany had just given the perfect description of Matthew Fraser.

"But he was interested in your little girl, you say?"

"Yeah, well, like in how Billy treated her. Which was creepy, because that's the reason I broke up with Billy. He was no good in bed with me, couldn't hardly get it up most of the time, but he'd wrestle with Katie, tickling like, and he'd get these humongous hard-ons. Freaked me right out."

Sixteen

"I knew it!" Green crowed before Sullivan had even finished his story. "It's so obvious! How the fuck did everyone miss it!"

"Well, after all, he was only fourteen–"

"Fourteen is plenty old enough, if you remember. My God, all the signs are there! Who else would she lie for?"

"Yeah, but we weren't the only ones to miss it, Mike. Everyone much closer to the case—Barb Devine and the CAS, the family..."

The two men had the living room to themselves, and Green was sitting bolt upright on the sofa. Pain and adrenaline pulsed through him, scattering his thoughts. Sharon had barricaded Tony and the dog in the kitchen with her while she cleaned up dinner, and Tony's incessant chatter washed over Green unheard as his thoughts slowly began to coalesce.

Green marvelled at how blind they'd all been to forget that children could be not only the victims but the perpetrators of evil, and that brotherly protectiveness and love could so easily transform into sex and domination. The abuse could have been going on for years, beginning as the barely pubescent curiosity of a ten-year-old and progressing slowly to physical exploration and experimentation, and finally to full-blown sexual acts. Beginning so innocuously that perhaps at first neither of them had thought anything wrong, until Billy's

242

adolescent urges coerced her into acts she found scary, disgusting or even painful enough to speak out. Since there had been no vaginal penetration, Billy may even have convinced himself that his little fondlings were harmless.

Yet now in hindsight, how clearly everything fit! Matthew Fraser had been wrongly accused from the start, a hapless target who was safer to finger than her own brother, and once Fraser had pulled himself together years later, he began his quest to find out who the guilty party was. He'd done research, analyzed court and newspaper records, and as his suspicions grew, he'd done his own questioning of Billy's neighbours. When Tiffany tipped Billy off that Fraser was nosing around, Billy began to follow him, perhaps to frighten him or simply to find out what he knew. Fraser had compiled his case, tried to take it to his lawyer and, when that failed, to the CAS.

But especially now that his band's success was finally within reach, Billy would have been desperate to prevent anyone from derailing his life's dream. Somehow he must have intercepted Fraser outside the CAS and panicked him into flight. Fearing that no one was going to believe him and that Billy was on to him, Fraser had tried to go into hiding. But Billy tracked him down to the rooming house, and in that final confrontation, with his back to the wall and desperate to protect himself, Fraser had killed him.

Which meant they were still looking for a killer, but at least not the cold-blooded manipulator Green had feared him to be.

"I wonder what difference this makes to the safety of Janice Tanner," Green mused. "Matthew Fraser may not be quite the bad guy we thought he was, but this still proves he's capable of murder when he's desperate. And after his last experience with the justice system, he's not likely to surrender to us without a fight. No one's been on this guy's side. No one. I have a very

243

bad feeling about what this guy's capable of when he has nowhere left to turn."

Sullivan fidgeted uneasily with his notebook, looking at war with himself, as if he had something to tell him, but didn't want to.

"What?" Green felt a twinge of alarm. "Is there news about Anne Patterson?"

Sullivan shook his head. "No, it's not that. I'm not sure it matters, but back in the original investigation, Anne may have tried to get the abuse charges dropped, but Devine—"

He stopped as his radio crackled faintly as his side. He turned it up to respond to his own call sign. A voice blasted over the radio, shrill with excitement, but the message was clear. The caller was part of the team conducting the search in the Lemieux Island vicinity. They had combed through all the underbrush and the abandoned house, and they'd just started along the water's edge.

Sullivan broke through the travel commentary impatiently. "Any sign of the Tanner woman or the briefcase?"

"No, but—but we found a body, sir!"

"What?"

The officer was breathless, his young voice cracking. "We found a fucking body, half sunk just fifteen feet off the shore!"

*   *   *

Sullivan barrelled down Woodroffe Avenue through the cornfields with his red light flashing while Green hunkered down in the passenger seat, coordinating with the sergeant on the scene and calling in the police units that would be needed. The Ottawa-Gatineau area straddled the confluence of three large rivers and one canal, so recovering bodies was a well-established routine. Most of these were accidental drownings due to boating and snowmobile mishaps which often occurred many miles upstream, but the bodies were swept down by the strong current. The occasional one was a suicide leap from one of the city's bridges. Only very rarely was it a case of foul play. Spring was the busiest time, as bodies began to warm up and rise to the surface. The section of the Ottawa River where this body had been found was deceptively fast moving, catching many a swimmer or kayaker by surprise. Green knew there was a good chance it had no relation to the Fraser case, but a knot of worry formed in his gut nonetheless.

Sullivan's efficient driving delivered them to the entrance of the Lemieux Island Bridge in just over half an hour, but the scene was already beginning to look like a carnival. Four cruisers with flashing lights blocked the entrance to the bridge, and yellow tape cordoned off the entire copse of woods on the east side of the bridge. There was no sign yet of the boats and divers of the Underwater Search and Recovery Unit, but the Forensic Identification van was parked on the bridge in a line of official vehicles that included the black coroner's van. Sullivan parked his Taurus behind the others, and the two of them climbed out.

Green scanned the surroundings to get his bearings and to form an initial impression of the terrain. The broad Ottawa River lay ahead of him, its shoreline meandering among a series of small islands, but its centre rushing deep and fast under the bridge. Along the water's edge, sandwiched between the Parkway and the river, was a thin swath of parkland with overhanging trees and the occasional beach along the rocky shore. The sun blazed off the river, elongating the shadows of the police officers poking around in the tall grass. Crowds of joggers, cyclists and strollers on the bike path along the river had stopped to watch the drama, craning their necks past the yellow tape.

At the Lemieux Island Bridge, the riverbank curved out to form a peninsula covered with thick woods. Near the tip of the peninsula, jarringly out of place in this wooded setting, were the crumbling remains of an old stone house, beside which the shoreline disappeared into a thick clump of trees. It was in the trees, invisible from the Parkway or the bridge, that all the activity seemed to be focussed. Green could hear the murmur of voices and the crackle of radios through the bush. Could it be Fraser's secret beach? he wondered, as the knot of worry tightened.

The uniformed officer who'd discovered the body was waiting for them at the curb, trying to look professional, despite the unusual brightness of his eyes and the green cast to his skin. He seemed doubly flustered to be dealing with an inspector, and he flitted from word to word as he pointed down the slope past the stone house.

"My partner was keeping surveillance, sir, and I was working my way along the shore looking for the briefcase. There's a fairly worn footpath along there, and at one point it dips down to this tiny beach. Really nothing more than a place for a couple of lovers, and there was some evidence of that, sir. So I stood on it to look around. Actually I was looking downstream towards the skyline. It's amazing, you can see all the skyscrapers and the Supreme Court and the Peace Tower up on the bluff, hardly a kilometre away, and here's this little piece of private paradise—"

"Officer," Sullivan nudged.

"Sorry sir. That's what I was thinking, and that's when I saw this thing bobbing in the water about fifteen feet out. Well, not really bobbing, but big and puffy just under the surface. I thought it was a dead fish, but it was awful huge, so I stepped out in the water a ways, and that's when I realized it was the body of a man."

"Man? You're sure?"

"Oh, no. I mean, you can't tell what it was. It's sort of green and red marble. That's when I called my sergeant, and Sergeant Sullivan too, because it was his operation, and my partner and I secured the scene. The Ident team is down there now, taking videos. And the coroner's there too."

"Who's the Ident in charge?"

"Sergeant Cunningham. He said not to let anyone near till he's processed the scene."

Green was familiar with Cunningham's new obsession with scene contamination. He turned to Sullivan with a grimace. "A green and red floater. I'm not in a big hurry to have a look anyway."

Sullivan chuckled. "Even the coroner's probably reluctant to look at this one. Sounds like it's been in the water a while. The good news is, it probably has nothing to do with our case."

Green stood in the road looking around. Despite the constant stream of cars on the Parkway, the bridge itself would normally have very little traffic, since it led nowhere but to the water purification plant on Lemieux Island, which sat in the middle of the Ottawa River. The bridge and island were closed to public access after eight in the evening, so at night the entire area would be virtually deserted. Certainly much more deserted than any of the other brightly lit and overcrowded bridges in the city. It must have been this very solitude, mere minutes from his home and from the spectacular downtown skyline, that Fraser found so soothing.

Green's eyes were drawn back to the stone structure at the water's edge, which looked like the remains of an old stone homestead blackened by fire. It was surrounded by an eight-foot chain link fence, and shrubs flourished in its gutted core.

"What the hell is that?"

"The old Hintonburg pump house," Sullivan said. "Remember the fire about ten or fifteen years ago?"

"And the city just left it there?" Green demanded incredulously, although he suspected that the heritage building's fate was trussed up in a thousand miles of inter-governmental red tape which might paralyze the authorities for decades to come. His curiosity was piqued, for it looked as if the crumbling stone harboured dozens of crannies where a briefcase could be hidden. He turned back to the constable. "Did you search it?"

"Well, no sir." The constable looked nervous. "It has barbed wire all around it."

"As soon as Ident gives us the all clear, search it," Green snapped. He began to stroll out onto the bridge, feeling the blaze of the evening sun on his face and the wind off the water in his hair. Soon the bridge reached open water, and the rush of the current filled his ears. He leaned over the edge, careful not to touch the railing, and stared down at the deep water which raced beneath him. His gaze followed the current as it roiled on downstream toward the bluff of Parliament Hill. Then he glanced towards the shore, which angled into a small bay where the coroner and the Ident team were clustered thigh deep in the water. Further downstream in the bay, he saw the flashing red of the Underwater Search and Recovery Unit van as it backed up close to the water. He imagined the men swarming out of the back and preparing their gear while they awaited the signal from the coroner and Ident. The diving suits, dinghies and nets would all be in readiness.

Green's eyes tracked the path of the current from the bridge to the small bay. Most of the water flowed straight downstream, but at the edges of the current, small eddies became sidetracked and drifted lazily into the bay. His pulse quickened. It was theoretically possible for someone to jump off the bridge expecting the current to sweep his body far downstream and thus delay its discovery for weeks, only to have it drift into the bay and surface several days later exactly where the Ident team was standing. Could it possibly be Fraser? Had he come to his favourite refuge for solace, only to realize that his future was over? That with the murder of Billy Whelan he had crossed the line from victim to villain, and that all hope of redemption and restitution was lost?

Green carefully scanned the bridge railing. It was slightly rusty and worn with the scratches of normal wear and tear, but he could detect nothing suspicious to the naked eye. He called Cunningham on his radio. "Lyle, it's Mike Green. I'm going to call another Ident team in to look at this bridge. It's possible our floater jumped from here."

To his surprise, the Ident officer gave him no argument, but sounded oddly excited as he signed off. A few minutes later, Green saw him leave the water and clamber up the slope to his van. Green and Sullivan walked back along the bridge to greet him.

"So what's the word?" Green asked.

"It's an adult male, but the body's too bloated to make any ID or even to guess at the size till we get it into the autopsy room."

"Any guess on how long it's been there?"

"Well, it's beginning to float, so it's got to be at least a week, but not more than two. Not too much skeletonization yet, although the fishies have been nibbling."

"So the coroner's figuring one to two weeks?" Green felt relief. Whatever the tragic story of this body, it couldn't be Fraser.

Cunningham grinned. "Dr. Lee took the call, because

nobody figured it was a suspicious death. But you know how much he hates floaters. He hasn't taken too close a look yet, and he's handing the PM over to MacPhail tomorrow."

"MacPhail?" The fact that the autopsy would be conducted by the forensic specialist rather than a regular pathologist meant something was amiss. "So you're saying this might be a suspicious death?"

"Might be?" Cunningham laughed, obviously enjoying his role in the drama. "Judging from the shoes the guy's wearing, I'd say so. Standard mob-issue cement."

Green stared at him. "He's wearing cement shoes?"

"Yeah. Nice new cinder block tied to his ankles. Although whoever did the job didn't have enough experience to do it right. Didn't know you need a hell of a lot more cement to keep a body under water once it starts to decompose. This guy's been bouncing along, dragging his anchor about a foot off the ground." He shook his head in mock disgust. "Christ, you just can't get good help any more." He held out a computer disk. "So he's all yours, guys. And here's a little photo album to get you started."

"I think Cunningham's been working in Ident too long," Sullivan remarked drily as they watched Cunningham walk back down to the shore.

Green barely heard him as he tried to absorb the latest twist. The man had not jumped off the bridge, he'd been thrown! Right near the very spot where Fraser liked to hang out. But where the fuck did this body fit in the Fraser story? If at all.

"Get the guys in Criminal Intelligence to check into recent enforcer activity," he said. "Especially any new kids on the block. This killer didn't know how to throw a body off a bridge very well either. An all-round incompetent bad guy."

As Green said the words, a picture came to mind of one of life's losers, who couldn't even make a success as a criminal, a Hell's Angels wannabe who'd hung around on the periphery hoping to make an impression. And who had himself ended up dead barely a week later. Billy Whelan. Yet that didn't make any sense! Why would Billy Whelan choose this particular spot to throw someone off? And equally to the point, why would he be killing anyone when he was rumoured to be trying to get out of the business so that he could move on to loftier dreams? There were probably a dozen other puppet club amateurs eager to prove their mettle to the kingpins from Montreal. Any one of them might have decided to bump off the competition. Perhaps they chose this location for the same reason Fraser loved it. Because of its seclusion.

Green watched absently as the young constable and his partner clipped the chain-link fence and began to search the stone house for the briefcase. Briefcases, dead bodies, favourite haunts... There were just too many damn coincidences.

"When the divers get the body out, I want to look at it," he said suddenly.

Sullivan swung on him, cellphone already to his ear. His mirrored sunglasses revealed nothing but above them his brows shot up. "Why?"

"Because it's one coincidence too many," he replied briskly. He hoped he sounded more convincing than he felt, for after less than an hour on his feet, he was already exhausted, and he wasn't at all sure he could manage the long night that lay ahead of them. Earlier, he'd had to lie through his teeth to Adam Jules about his health before Jules consented to his playing even a partial role in the recovery of this body, and he only hoped Jules would not show up to see for himself how Green was managing.

While Sullivan discussed the case with the Criminal

Intelligence Unit, Green sat down on the curb and watched with weary curiosity as the two uniformed constables blundered around inside the shell of the old stone house. They emerged a few moments later, shaking their heads. Green frowned to himself. The house itself was too obvious. Fraser was an intelligent, methodical man. He would have approached the question of concealment logically. He would have looked for a place most people wouldn't even know existed, a place where the briefcase would be protected from the rain and from the dampness of the earth. If the building had once been a pump house, presumably it had a cavity underground to house the pump and the pipes which ran from the river. This underground chamber might have remained untouched by the fire and would have had some means of access from either outside or inside the house. A hidden door, perhaps, or a hatch barely discernible on the floor.

Green scrambled down the embankment through the thick grass. Already the sun was sinking low in the western sky, shooting flames of colour across the river but plunging the stone ruins into deep shadow. He stepped through the hole in the chain link fence and began to pick his way through the tall grass and scrub that surrounded the walls. He could see that long ago the house must have been breathtaking. Built of rough-cut grey limestone, it perched on the shoreline with the remnants of its front porch facing directly down the river to the majestic Gothic spires of Parliament Hill.

First he inched his way around the exterior foundation, probing for signs of a hatch or a depression in the ground which might be stairs. Nothing. He stepped through the crumbling doorway into the interior, ducking under charred beams where the ceiling had fallen in and skirting the young trees that were taking root within. Perhaps I'm wrong, he thought. What do I know about pump houses?

He stood stock still in the centre and surveyed the interior inch by inch, using his policeman's eye to detect the least sign of something that didn't fit. Finally, almost lost in the deep shadows of the back wall, he saw something. A very faint line, like a path worn through the grass to a point near the wall. The grass was flattened. Not trampled by the young officers who had thrashed around in here, but eroded more subtly by repeated footsteps over time. Where the path reached the barbed wire fence, a small opening had been cut in the wire close to the ground.

Conscious of the rapidly failing light, he hurried over to inspect the base of the stone wall. The ground felt solid beneath his feet. No cellar or hidden chamber under there, he thought, but something about the stones in the wall looked odd. The joints were ragged and poorly aligned. He pushed a stone and felt it shift. He flinched, suddenly fearful that the entire wall and the remaining roof timbers would crash down on him. But nothing happened. He pushed again, and dislodged the stone enough to see there was a cavity behind. Probably at one time a storage bin of some kind.

Excited, he pulled harder until he yanked the entire stone out. Hoping there were no furry, sharp toothed creatures who would object to his intrusion, he pulled on nitrile gloves and slipped his hand cautiously into the hole to grope around. Almost immediately his fingers struck something soft and smooth. He explored its contours. Flat and square-edged, just like a briefcase!

Casting caution aside, he plunged both hands inside and struggled until he was able to lift the object up and draw it out through the hole. A battered, well-worn, brown leather briefcase, secured with a small lock.

Green carried it outside and scrambled up the hillside, his fatigue forgotten. Settling in the back seat of the Taurus, he broke open the case. As Bleustein had said, it was crammed with notes, clippings and articles, all meticulously highlighted in yellow and covered in scribbled notes. Pedophilia, incest, family systems theory, the pact of silence...all of which would take hours to sift through. In a separate pouch he found a sheaf of printed emails, most sent over the past two months between someone called "seeker" and the other "mistwalker". He frowned in surprise. Had Fraser actually been communicating with Billy? He scanned the emails excitedly. The messages were cryptic and full of code words, but rather than containing threats and warnings, they suggested collusion on a secret quest.

Gf found...3 girls...JP 606...M can't know!

It looked as if Fraser had been communicating with mistwalker about the success of his search. But if Billy was mistwalker, that didn't make any sense unless Fraser hadn't known until too late that Billy was the very villain he was after. That would certainly explain his sudden panic and his flight into hiding, Green thought excitedly, flipping through the pages for more clues. At the bottom of one of the emails was a note in the same scribbled hand. *She's friend, not foe. Remember that.*

The door jerked open, and Sullivan stuck his head in. "There you are! They've just taken the body out. They're waiting for you."

Green started and returned to the present with reluctance. His mind reeled. He knew the contents of the briefcase were crucial to the Fraser case, but to even know what case they were dealing with, he had to look at the body.

He gestured to the pages he had strewn over the back seat. "Take a look at that stuff while I'm gone, will you? See if it tells us anything." Then he took a deep breath, steadied himself against the side of the car and set off down the bike path toward the bay.

The huge, discoloured mound of flesh was splayed on a yellow plastic sheet beside the recovery van. Water oozed from its various wounds and orifices. Cunningham and the reluctant coroner were bent over examining it minutely, holding masks to their faces. Cunningham's new sidekick was fifty feet away, sitting on the ground with his head in his hands. Green sympathized; no doubt the kid was rethinking his latest career move. Green was tempted to rethink his own decision to examine the body, but just as he was about to retreat, Cunningham saw him. With a weak smile, Green approached.

"What have you got?"

"Male, medium height, five-ten or so. Weight—who knows? Skin colour ditto, although I'm guessing white, because there's some hair left on his head that's brown and long." Cunningham was moving carefully around the body and pointing things out as he spoke. "The guy was wearing a tie and what looks like it might have been a grey suit—one of your higher class mob affiliates, maybe?"

Grey suit, medium height, long, brown hair... Green stared at the body in bewilderment. One man fit the description perfectly, a man last seen wearing a grey suit and tie on his way to a meeting with the CAS eleven days ago. Yet how could Matthew Fraser have died long before Billy Whelan ended up dead in his rooming house?

The pieces tumbled around in his mind as he searched for a new theory to contain them. What if Billy Whelan had killed Matthew Fraser the very day he'd set off to see the CAS, long before Janice Tanner ever reported him missing? Billy must have been desperate once he realized Fraser was about to reveal the truth. Perhaps he'd been following Fraser for days, and when he saw him going to the CAS with a briefcase, he realized he had to act. So he followed Fraser back to his apartment that afternoon and knocked on the door, and for some unfathomable reason no one will ever know, Fraser let him in. Then Fraser either fled or was forced to this secluded river hideaway, maybe hoping Billy would spare him if he handed over the briefcase. But once here, and knowing his secret would never be safe unless Fraser was dead, Billy killed him and threw him off the bridge.

Poor, stupid Billy. He hadn't found the briefcase after all, and in the end he too had ended up dead. Who had killed him? Had his own criminal past finally caught up with him, leading him afoul of the wrong people?

Green pondered the explanation with dissatisfaction, for there was one too many murders for comfort. It made sense that when Billy had discovered Fraser was about to expose him, he had killed him. However, it was too damn convenient that someone—perhaps a Hell's Angels' enforcer—had stepped up to the plate to burn Billy to a crisp just a few days later. In Fraser's rooming house, no less! Random coincidence aside, Green sensed a loose thread dangling just out of reach in his mind, but it eluded his weary grasp. Later, when he'd slept and had a chance to go through the briefcase, perhaps he'd make more sense of it. He was dizzy with fatigue, and a dull ache had settled behind his eyes. He could see the Ident team erecting lights along the shore to help them with their search. Every minuscule cigarette butt would be bagged and tagged, every footprint cast. Up on the bridge, the second Ident team was setting up to examine the railing for prints. A long shot, perhaps, but hopefully enough to explain the mystery if anything were found.

He walked back along the bike path towards the car, where

Sullivan was just wrapping up another conversation with Criminal Intelligence. Wearily, Green filled him in on his half-baked biker gang theory, which Sullivan embraced with few of Green's doubts.

"Well, you were at the meeting," Sullivan said. "You know the biker gangs are stepping up their operations from Montreal. They're trying to hook up with the local clubs, but they're also flexing their muscles to make sure the locals know what happens if they don't play ball. My guess is if Billy was trying to retire, he was a liability. He had entries in his day book that Criminal Intelligence will be salivating over."

Green opened the passenger door of the Taurus, longing to sit down, shut his eyes and do nothing for ten whole minutes. His eyes fell on the briefcase in the back. He looked at it blankly a moment, bothered by that elusive loose thread. Something did not fit. Then finally his sluggish mind connected. Janice!

"Wait a minute!" He jerked upright again. "If Fraser's been dead since the week before last, and Billy's been dead since Tuesday, who the hell called Janice this morning to ask her to go get the briefcase?"

"Do you know for sure it was the briefcase?"

"It doesn't matter. Her exact words were 'Fraser wants me to get something for him'. But that was obviously a lie or at least an untruth, since Fraser was already fish bait."

"Do we know for sure that someone did call her?"

Green nodded. "Another woman at the shelter took the call. Couldn't identify the voice as male or female, but said Janice seemed definitely happy to hear from them. Someone was either posing as Fraser or claiming to call on his behalf."

Sullivan propped himself against the police car and stretched out his long legs with a thoughtful air. "Strange.

Those emails you asked me to look at? Looks like this mistwalker character was helping Fraser with his inquiries. Helped him find the room in Vanier too."

Green leaned on the roof of the car. If mistwalker wasn't Billy, who was it? 'Friend, not foe...' Was it someone who pretended to be a friend, but who'd been after the briefcase all along? Green rested his chin in his hands, letting the breeze off the water ruffle his hair. God, he was tired. "Well, whoever it is, it looks like they were playing both sides of the fence. Although I'm damned if I can think why."

"Seems pretty far-fetched, Green. You already have Fraser out to implicate Whelan, and Whelan knocking off Fraser, and Hells Angels locals torching Billy, and now you want to drag in...who?"

Green turned the question over and over in his mind, sensing the futility of it. Until a vague, preposterous idea dawned. *She's friend, not foe. Remember that.*

She...

Maybe Fraser had it all wrong. Maybe danger had lurked where he hadn't expected it at all. As Sherlock Holmes said, once you've eliminated the impossible, then whatever is left, no matter how improbable, must be true.

"Unless..." he said. "Unless Janice made the whole thing up—made up being followed, the attempted break-in at her house, the phone call this morning—to create a diversion. To make it look as if Fraser was still alive."

"Why?"

"To divert suspicion from the fact she killed him herself."

Sullivan cast him a sidelong glance of such incredulity that Green doubted the soundness of his own mind. Had his concussion finally scrambled his brain?

"Why the fuck would she do that?" Sullivan said.

Green didn't answer. He had no idea. Not until he'd read through all the emails himself, dissected the rest of the material, and done some independent background research on Janice. At the moment he knew almost nothing about her beyond what she'd told him herself. "Do me a favour," he said. "Check if any of the surveillance teams have spotted her."

While Sullivan put in the calls, Green stared into the gathering dusk, his eyes scanning the cluster of bystanders who stood in the road, forming a tight circle around a female news reporter he recognized from the local news channel. Camera lights were trained on her, and off to the side sat the TV channel's van with a roof satellite for a live feed. Green groaned. Soon the reporter would be looking for a sound byte from the police, and he had barely a coherent thought in his head. Why did the public have such a thirst for the macabre? Pressing close to the reporter so they could hear, the solemn crowd was caught in the strobe lighting of the police cars.

He was so distracted that he almost missed the other woman and had to do a double take. On first glance, he caught only a brief shimmer of red in the panning TV lights. On second glance, a tall, angular redhead hovering on the fringe of the crowd, her face frozen with horror as she strained to hear. Just as Green recognized her, she suddenly turned and thrust her way out.

Grabbing Sullivan's arm, Green pointed and ducked into the shadow of the trees so that she wouldn't see his approach. Without question, Sullivan followed. Crouching low, they ran towards the crowd, elbowed their way through and picked up pursuit. The woman glanced back, caught sight of them, and began running straight down the middle of the darkened Parkway. Their shouts only made her run faster. As they gained, she seemed to panic and veered off the road onto the grassy verge towards the neighbouring residential streets. Green felt himself flagging, but she was no match for Sullivan, who caught up with her halfway across the grass. When he touched her arm, she shrieked, tripped and fell, flinging her arms over head in supplication as she landed. She thrashed around on the ground, wailing.

"Janice, Janice," Green gasped when he caught up. "It's Inspector Green. Stop, we won't hurt you."

She took her arms from her face and peered at him. "Inspector Green! Thank God. I was afraid you..." She began to hyperventilate, her eyes white with fear. Not a guilty woman running from capture, he realized, but an innocent one seized by terror. What was it Sharon had said about her? That she sees danger in every shadow? He gripped her hands.

"Janice, what's going on?"

"I just heard on the news...they found a body...I was afraid it was..." She gasped and her eyes brimmed with tears. "Is it Matt?"

Green hesitated. "We don't know."

"I tried so hard. I wanted to help, but I couldn't think where it was! I looked everywhere, and then I remembered this place..."

"Janice, I don't get it. Help who?"

"Matt!"

"You saw Matt?"

"Not, not him. His friend. He's in hiding, and he asked her to call me."

"What friend?"

"The one who called me! When we met at the lake this morning, she said Matt said I'd know where it was—"

"Where what is?"

"The briefcase! I'm supposed to bring it to the Stone

Head." She was beginning to get agitated, as if he were being particularly dense. In truth, he felt it. The Stone Head was a cutting edge bar on the fringe of the Byward Market, hardly the place favoured by an over-thirty, very unhip recluse.

"Janice, what is this friend's name?" Sullivan broke in, ever practical and calm.

"I don't know. Not the type of friend I'd expect. She was very young and fashionable. Pierced everywhere. Crazy hair."

Green's mouth went dry. "Crazy how?"

"She looked like a large green floor mop."

Seventeen

Sullivan careened the Taurus around the corner on two wheels and accelerated up the Parkway towards downtown. With both hands glued to the wheel, he radiated an intensely focussed calm. Beside him, Green was much less calm as he yelled into the radio.

"No visible presence," he repeated. "We need to catch her unawares, not spook her. Just give me two cars on the street covering the exits and a team outside the club to await my orders."

Even as he issued orders, Green's thoughts scrambled to make sense of this new twist. Was it Rebecca with whom Fraser was communicating? Rebecca who was helping him with his quest? Was she mistwalker? But that didn't make any sense. If she wanted to help Fraser nail her molester, why wouldn't she simply tell the truth?

What was it Quinton Patterson had said earlier? That Rebecca was a little out of control? How out of control? Enough to have invited her brother to the rooming house for a drink, slipped him a drug and then calmly set his lifeless body afire? As payback? After all these years of simmering, unfocussed rage, was it payback for her robbed childhood? Or for a more recent crime of betrayal? Patterson said she was finally showing signs of healing. Was that because she was finding peace within herself, or because she had finally figured out a way to right the wrong?

So many questions, but Green couldn't concentrate on any of them. Not now. Only two questions mattered. How deadly was she? And with Hannah in tow, what was she planning next?

On a Saturday evening in June, the Market of old Bytown was alive with people, and its narrow streets were clogged with cars, most circling the blocks in search of parking. They fought with spirited pedestrians for supremacy of the streets. Horns punctuated the cacophony of music issuing from the cafés and shops along the way.

The Stone Head was shoehorned into the basement of a red brick Victorian rowhouse on Murray Street. In the winter, it was confined to a long, crowded room hammered by punk rock and lit in neon purple. Luminol purple, the police often joked. In the summer, it spilled out onto half a dozen tables on the patio out front, whose patrons served as an early warning system to the heavy drug dealers inside. The police paid regular visits but rarely netted anything but underage drinkers and a few hapless recreational users. Plus the Billy Whelans of the underworld, who were too stupid to know when to get out of the way. Green knew the police couldn't expect a warm reception and a spirit of cooperation from the owners of the bar. To make matters worse, even though he and Sullivan were dressed in casual attire, Sullivan's ramrod back and linebacker physique screamed cop from a hundred feet away.

A quick pass by the bar revealed no activity out of the ordinary, as well as no green or blue hair on the patio outside. They parked the Taurus around the corner out of sight, confirmed that the patrol units were in position and set off on foot. As they walked, Green spoke as much to reassure himself as to curb Sullivan.

"Remember, she's sixteen and presumably unarmed. She's not expecting trouble, she's just expecting Janice Tanner to show up with the briefcase. She knows you but not me, so I want you to hang back and watch my back. I'm going to try approaching them as Hannah's father, get my daughter safely out of there without tipping Rebecca off. Then you can move in and nab her. If I encounter trouble, be ready to move in fast."

Just before the door, Green hesitated. Rock music pulsed into the street, overlaid with the din of voices and laughter from within. He felt he was entering alien territory, not just the dominion of youth and sex and drugs, but the world of a teenage daughter he had never met. How would Hannah react, and whose side would she take when he came bulldozing in?

Drawing a deep breath to focus himself, Green tousled his hair to enhance the frantic father look and descended the stone steps to the bar. Inside, the smoke hung as a grey pall over everything in open defiance of Ottawa's new anti-smoking bylaw. Green drifted through the crowd, scanning the dark haze. He saw hair of all shades and styles, silver flashing off all visible body parts, chains, studs and tattoos everywhere, but no one looked like the pixie picture Ashley had sent. He passed through the bar several times, scrutinizing the tables closely, but she was not there.

Disappointment and apprehension hit him in twin waves. He accosted a harried waiter balancing eight beers on a tray and waved Hannah's picture in his face.

"You seen her in here tonight? With another girl with green hair?"

The waiter flicked his gaze over the picture then looked at Green, about to shake his head. Green pulled out his badge.

"Think carefully, buddy. She's only sixteen, and unless you want trouble..."

The waiter jerked his head towards the bar. "She might have been here. Ask the bartender, he might have been talking to them."

Over at the bar, a small television set hung high on the wall broadcasting the Blue Jays game, and the sound competed with the cacophony of rock. The bartender was popping cherries into an cluster of drinks on a tray, and he did not miss a beat when Green showed him the picture and his badge.

"I get lots of kids."

"I'm sure you do," Green replied ominously. "And you're busy tonight, so you wouldn't want trouble. This kid, however, is my daughter, and I suspect you know the other one as well. Rebecca Whelan."

The bartender thrust the tray aside and dried his hands deliberately. "They were just minding their own business. They weren't doing anything wrong."

"Did I say they were? They're in serious danger. Rebecca— she seemed spooked about something, didn't she?"

The man frowned. "Not then." He seemed to debate, and a tiny furrow of worry crinkled his brow. "Is something wrong?"

"You heard about Rebecca's mother from the news?" Green said. "Becky is taking it really hard, and frankly I'm worried what she might do."

The bartender sighed. "They were here till about half an hour ago. Sitting at the bar eating wings, drinking cokes, joking around and watching TV. Becky was a little wired, but then she always is. Then all of a sudden they picked up their stuff and split."

Green felt a twinge of trepidation. "What were they watching on TV?"

"Blue Jays game. Becky often does that here, knows every player in the game. But tonight they split right after the news update came on."

The news, on which that goddamn reporter had probably

aired her live feed on the discovery of the floater. Green forced back fear. "Where did they go?"

The bartender shrugged. "I was loading glasses."

Green banged the counter. "This is important. Think!"

Sullivan drifted over. "Trouble?"

"They've gone. Anything from outside?"

When Sullivan shook his head, Green caught the bartender's arm. "This may be life or death. Where else might Becky go?"

From beside them at the bar, an unshaven youth sporting suburban punk attire piped up. "They might've gone to the river. They scored some pills, and I heard Becky say something about an awesome place for their *grande finale*." He shrugged blearily. "Last score of the night, or something."

"Or something..." Green fought panic as he dashed out of the club with Sullivan on his heels. Sullivan caught his eye as he reached for his radio. "Major's Hill?"

Green weighed the idea rapidly before rejecting it. Major's Hill Park was an urban mix of trees, lawns and flower gardens situated on a bluff overlooking the locks and the Ottawa River. Until recently, it had been a naturalist setting meant for festivals and picnics, but its hidden crannies and shadowy nooks proved equally well suited to clandestine exchanges of all sorts. However, with the arrival of the security-conscious American Embassy across the street, the park had been given a facelift. Now a brightly lit promenade meandered through its centre, and floodlights splashed into every corner, driving the sex and drug trade off into the dingy back alleys of the Market. If Becky was looking for privacy, she wouldn't find it at Major's Hill.

Sullivan reached their car and yanked open his door. "But there's no other riverside park of any size before Rockcliffe, which is way too far for a couple of kids on foot."

Green's thoughts raced as he jumped into the passenger seat. He'd grown up in Lowertown a mere half dozen blocks away, in a time when the Byward Market had bustled with farmers' stalls in the daytime and rough bars and prostitutes at night. He knew every inch of the area and had played in every secret nook along the river's edge.

"Bordeleau Park!" he exclaimed. "Not the Ottawa River, but the Rideau, and only a few blocks on foot."

Sullivan stared at him in confusion, revving the engine but not engaging the gears. "Mike, that's way off the beaten track."

"That's exactly what Rebecca wants! She's gone someplace where no one will see her, and no one will think to look. Nobody uses that park at night but a few teenage gropers and pot-heads. Drive, Brian!"

Reluctantly, Sullivan threw the car into gear and squealed out onto Murray Street. As they raced east toward King Edward Avenue, Green hung on to the dash and ordered back-up units to seal off both ends of the park. Subtlety was gone now. He didn't even want to think what Rebecca had planned. He wanted to wrench Hannah from her clutches before she could so much as offer Hannah an aspirin. Hedging his bets, he requested an additional unit to swing by Major's Hill. A slight smile twitched Sullivan's lips as he rocketed around the corner and headed north toward the bridge to Quebec.

Green ticked off the blocks in his memory as they passed, looking for the little side street that would lead them to the park. It was only a few blocks from the ramshackle tenement of his childhood, and as boys, he and his friends had played in the park all the time, shooting one another from forts in the trees and racing make-shift boats in the river. But Green hadn't been there in over twenty years, not since he'd carried his mother down to the water's edge for their last family picnic before she died. He a brash, invincible young rookie, and she a mere eighty pounds of cancer-ridden bones. Even the memory of it made his pulse hammer with irrational fear. Hannah had his mother's name, his mother's pixie face...

Sullivan extinguished his lights, and they coasted to a stop at the side of the road that bordered the park. Up ahead was a bike path lit at twenty-foot intervals by street lamps. Beyond those splashes of light loomed the grey and black patchwork of grass and trees that ran down to the river. Lamplight glistened off a black expanse in the distance, where Green knew the river to be. He and Sullivan leaped out of the car and ran lightly on the balls of their feet across the bike path and down toward the darker brush.

Crouching in the shadow of a massive spruce, Green searched the silence for the sound of girlish voices. Nothing but the rumble of traffic over the nearby bridge, the screech of crickets in the thick grass, and the swirl of water. Above them, the moonless sky was spattered with stars. The two detectives scanned the darkness, straining to distinguish the faintest shadow of movement in the feeble light. All was still. But beyond the grey patch of grass, the shoreline was overgrown with clumps of brush which provided perfect cover. On Green's signal, they headed toward the nearest clump. As they drew close, Green slowed to listen, and thought he could hear the low murmur of voices. A faint giggle.

He and Sullivan exchanged glances. Sullivan inclined his head faintly in signal, and they rushed the clump of brush. Nothing. In the next clump of trees they startled two young men locked in a naked embrace. The men sprang apart with muffled cries and dove for cover in the bush. Without a pause, Green and Sullivan raced past them into the open stretch ahead. Beside them, the river gurgled softly as it swept along the bank.

A massive willow loomed out of the darkness ahead, its boughs thrust far out over the water. In the silence Green felt goosebumps rise on his skin. Something was there. Faint smudges of pale grey against the dark. Silent, still.

Too still.

Green rushed forward. Almost tripped on the first girl, who sat propped against the tree trunk, dressed head to toe in white, with silver glinting in the light and her mop of green hair cascading over her face. She stirred and moved her head. Giggled.

"Well, well, well. The fucking cavalry."

Green barely heard her as he scrambled over the tree and tripped on the empty beer bottles littering the shore. The second girl lay on a bough that hung over the water's edge, her outstretched hand trailing in the water and a faint smile on her pixie face. At his touch, her eyelids flickered, and her eyes met his briefly before they faded away.

Green yanked her roughly onto shore, grabbed his radio and screamed for 911.

Afterwards he knelt over her, checking her pulse and airways, slapping her face to revive her. Sirens wailed through the night, distant and forlorn, but time stretched endlessly as they waited. Green wrapped Hannah in his jacket and lifted her off the damp ground, rubbing her limbs. She was so tiny! A fragile, blue wraith beneath his clumsy hands. He had a vivid memory of his mother, mere bones in his arms the last time he'd embraced her. Through the roaring fear in his head, he was only dimly aware of Sullivan bent over Rebecca until she spoke, her voice throaty and slurred with imminent sleep.

"It won't do any good. She's history, man."

"What did you give her?" Green demanded.

"Wanted to watch her, see her smile, watch her die."

"Why!"

"So the cop would bleed. Know how it feels. He doesn't give a fuck about her anyway."

Green scanned the darkness. Shouted. Where the hell was everyone! He looked at Rebecca listing towards the grass, her eyes at half mast, but the secret smile still on her lips.

"What did you give her!"

"Roofy specials. Make you soar. So peaceful, so warm, you just leave your body behind. It's what I gave Billy. Promised him the best high he ever had. That's justice, don't you think? The only kind he'll ever get."

Green felt Hannah's pulse slowly fading beneath his touch. She was so grey! The sirens had howled to a stop and red lights strobed the distant trees. He could hear men calling in the dark.

"Brian, go get them. For fuck's sakes, hurry!"

Sullivan bolted into the darkness, and when Green caught Rebecca's eyes, he saw they were fixed on his, alert with a strange, intense light. "When he killed Mr. Fraser, I knew it was over. No more cops, no more trying to fix things. I was alone, like I'd always been."

He saw a shimmer of tears in the dark. She was slipping under, losing her hard edge. "Rebecca," he said. "Your mother and father would have helped you. Why didn't you just tell the truth?"

The voices grew closer and flashlights danced through the trees. But Rebecca seemed oblivious as she shut her eyes and giggled. Just as she answered, the first of the paramedics crashed through the brush, so loud that Green could barely believe what he'd heard.

*　　*　　*

Almost an hour elapsed before Green was ready to put in a call to Quinton Patterson. He had let Sullivan take charge of the investigation and follow-up, but even once the girls were whisked from the ambulance into the hospital and out of sight, there were forms to fill in at Emergency and questions to answer. As soon as he had a spare moment, he slipped outside the Emergency entrance so that he could use his cellphone. It was nearly midnight by then and the phone rang five times before Quinton's foggy voice broke through. When Green filled him in, Quinton was instantly awake.

"Are they going to be all right?"

"I don't know, they're unconscious. The doctors are with them now, and I expect they'll pump their stomachs and give them some drug to counteract the effects. Then we'll have to wait and see. Quinton, you should know this was a deliberate overdose. But Rebecca was conscious till near the end, so she has a good chance." He didn't add that Hannah had the worst of it, all because Quinton's stepdaughter had wanted to watch her die.

"This is all your fault, Green! This was all behind us till you barged in!"

Like hell it was, Green thought, clenching his teeth. How could he explain to the idiot over the phone about the incest in the family, about the murder of his stepson and the power of his wife Anne to destroy lives through her own moral cowardice?

"I think you need to come down," was all he said.

"Well, if she's unconscious and I can't visit anyway, I guess I can wait till morning."

"Quinton, your stepdaughter may die. And take my daughter with her!"

"But Anne can't be left alone yet, and I can't get anyone to relieve me at this hour."

A fury welled up in Green so strong that he wanted to throttle the man. Why was everything about Anne? Not about the children, or even Matthew Fraser, the other real victim in this case.

271

"Fuck Anne!" he yelled and hurled the cellphone across the lawn.

Five minutes later, he was still wrestling his rage under control as he sat in the back of a squad car, speeding through the empty streets towards the Glebe. The young constable he had commandeered kept glancing at him nervously in the rear view mirror but had the sense to say nothing. Green knew he looked a sight, with his left temple gradually ripening to purple, his clothes in dirty disarray, and more than a hint of hysteria in his demeanour.

Quinton Patterson was fully dressed when Green pounded on the door, and he jerked it open with a scowl.

"I only just got her back to sleep," he snapped. "She knows something is up."

"Then get her. She needs to hear this."

"Absolutely not. She's too fragile—"

"She's not fucking fragile! And if you don't get her, I'll move the meeting upstairs."

He had reached the foot of the stairs by the time Quinton grabbed his arm to block his path. "Inspector! Haven't you done enough to her? I've called my sister, and we can leave as soon as she gets here."

"I want Anne to hear this. I want her, for once in her self-serving life, to face the whole bald truth about what happened."

Quinton blocked the stairway and folded his arms. "What truth?"

"Point one. Did you know it was Billy who molested Rebecca?"

Quinton's jaw dropped.

"Point two. Did you know Anne knew all along, but let Matthew Fraser take the fall? Point three. Did you know Rebecca was trying to help Fraser set the record straight? Point four. Billy found out and killed Fraser to prevent—"

Quinton found his voice. "Matthew Fraser's dead? I thought you said the body was Billy."

"It was. Billy threw Fraser off a bridge. It was Rebecca who set Billy on fire."

Quinton sagged onto the steps, his colour draining. "Becky...? Killed her brother?"

Green nodded. "Quite a few things you didn't know, aren't there?"

"Oh...God. Poor...poor kid."

"Which one?"

Quinton looked up at him. Tears shimmered in his eyes. "I don't know. Both."

The man's utter desolation, his bleak and buffeted look, gave Green pause. He felt his rage slowly seep away. This was not the enemy. "Yes. Both. Billy's already paid for his crimes, but Becky still has to face what she's done. She's one hell of a bitter young lady, and no matter what she's done, no matter what sentence she'll have to face, nothing will be worse than the hell she's already in. She's going to need all your help."

Quinton rested his head in his hands and shook it slowly back and forth. "How could I not have known this? Why didn't she tell us? Why didn't she tell someone?"

"That's the most damning point of all, Quinton. Because your wife, your precious, fragile Anne, told her if she ever breathed a word of it, she would kill herself."

There was a loud thud from upstairs, and Green realized Anne had been awake and had heard every word. He felt some satisfaction that Quinton, after leaping instinctively to his feet, turned to gaze up the stairs for a moment, and then slowly turned away.

*   *   *

273

Dawn was washing the hospital grounds in pale light when Sullivan dropped by on his way home from the station. Green had spent the last few hours on a vinyl cushioned bench, listening to Quinton on the pay phone calling in favours and mustering his defences for the battle ahead. Psychiatrists, social workers, crown attorneys, even Josh Bleustein were rounded up, all before his daughter was even off the critical list. Green let the sounds and smells of the ER flow over him and was just drifting into a fitful sleep when Sullivan arrived with two cups of fresh Tim Hortons coffee and a grim update. After all the paperwork and official briefings were wrapped up, he had settled down to examine the contents of the briefcase Matthew Fraser had been so desperate to hide.

As Green had surmised, Fraser had been trying for years to piece together enough evidence to identify Rebecca's molester and to clear his own name beyond a doubt. He had contacted a couple of Rebecca's old classmates by email, and suddenly two months earlier Rebecca herself, using the code name mistwalker, sent him an email asking to meet. They had met on a secluded bench at Dow's Lake, where she told him she had been trying to locate him for over a year because she wanted to apologize. During the past two years, she'd finally been facing her past and looking for a way to set things right. She'd not been confused, she'd not been too young to understand or remember; she had outright lied, because with the police and the CAS all demanding answers, she needed to think of someone else to blame, and his was the first name to come to her lips. As a little girl, she'd never thought her lie would suck them all into the vortex of the legal system. She'd expected Fraser would get sent to the principal's office, and her mother would fuss over her more closely.

In that first meeting, Fraser had asked her if she'd be willing to go to the police and the Children's Aid to clear his name. He told her he'd learned through research that most pedophiles didn't stop by themselves, and that she could help right the wrong by stopping her abuser from victimizing other little girls. She said that she wanted Billy to pay for what he'd done and that she would help Fraser every step of the way, but that he would have to build the case without her testimony. She had sent him to see Billy's former girlfriends and warned him of Billy's gang ties. In the end, it was she who warned him Billy was on to him, and helped him pick the rooming house where he could be safe.

Green tried to imagine her fear when she discovered Fraser had never checked into the rooming house. Her dawning realization over the ensuing few days that Billy must have gotten to him. Her rage and utter despair that justice had been snatched yet again from her grasp.

"No wonder she took things into her own hands," he said. "What other hands did she have?"

Sullivan sat picking fretfully at his coffee cup and twisting it in his large, rough hands. "There is one other thing, Mike. Don't know if this is the right time. Or if I should tell you at all. When the allegations first came out, Anne Patterson apparently asked the school psychologist to change her story."

Green grunted. "Small wonder. Anne knew it wasn't true. But that's the psychologist's problem, not ours."

"The thing is, the psychologist told Devine. And Devine never put it in the record."

Green rested his head wearily back against the wall. "Fuck."

"If the Crown had known, or the rest of the team had known, they might have looked further."

"Might have. But might not have. There was a real lynching mentality going on back then. Someone had to pay, and Fraser was the man in their sights."

"But we might have looked further. I mean us—the cops on the ground, who don't give a fuck about lawyers and press."

"A couple of cops even quit the force when he got off, Brian. That's how detached they were."

"Okay." Sullivan squinted at the floor. "So what are you going to do about Devine?"

Green hadn't the least idea. All he knew for sure was that he wasn't going to deal with it now. Once he knew Hannah was safe, once the crises were over and his family back to normal, once he'd slept for a month, then he'd figure out what to do. It had been buried for ten years; it could stay that way a little longer, while he mustered the strength to deal with the stink if he exhumed it.

He remembered the raw outrage on Devine's face when she recalled the case. She had believed Fraser to be guilty, and after years of watching pedophiles waltz through the courts unscathed, she had cut a small corner to try to even the odds. She had been wrong, and that mistake had cost an innocent man his future and ultimately his life. However, ten years later, both the innocent and the guilty man were dead. Blowing the whistle would not change that nor allow history to rewrite itself, but it would ruin the career of a woman who had once been a good cop.

After Sullivan left, Green looked at Patterson, still on the phone and in full damage control mode, and wondered what the man would do if the information ever fell into his hands. But before he'd begun to envisage even half the trouble it would cause, the entrance door opened, and Sharon came in. She looked as tired as Green felt, and with a flood of relief, he enveloped her in his arms. For a moment, he could say nothing.

"How is she?" Sharon asked.

He disengaged himself and drew her down beside him.

"Alive. So far."

"That's good, Mike."

"I guess." He avoided her eyes. "Did you call Ashley?"

She shook her head. "I figured I'd wait till we knew, one way or...no point panicking the poor woman when she's four thousand kilometres away, and there's nothing she can do but bite her nails."

He pulled her back into his arms. "Wise lady," he managed.

"Mike, what the hell happened?"

He told her. When he'd finished, she shook her head with a mixture of helplessness and outrage that mirrored his own. "And to think no one did anything."

"Three people did something," he corrected grimly. "They made a pact of silence, and they've maintained this sick love-hate triangle ever since. If I'd had my wits about me, the tattoo should have given me a clue. I think Medusa was how Billy saw his sister. A beautiful girl turned deadly."

"Oh!" she said in surprise. "That tattoo is not Medusa, it's a Fury. After you left last night, I did a search on Mist Walker in Greek mythology. As two words instead of one. The Mist Walker was a name for Erinys, one of the Furies who roamed the underworld avenging wrongs that had gone unpunished, especially within the family. They had hideous faces and snakes coiled in their hair."

Despite his exhaustion, he felt a grim satisfaction to see the final piece of the jigsaw fall into place. He didn't know much about classical mythology, but enough to know that the Greeks and Romans had filled their myths with rapes, incest, betrayal and endless spilling of blood. For some reason, their epic themes of heroism and villainy had captured the imagination of today's disaffected teens in countless fantasy games and tales.

He thought of Rebecca, the self-styled avenger in the hazy

netherworld she roamed. "Billy probably knew that Rebecca called herself the mistwalker. I wonder...sounds crazy, but in this sick family, I wonder if he chose the tattoo to remind himself of what he'd done to her."

She made a skeptical face and reached for his coffee. "That presupposes he felt guilty about it, or even knew who the Furies were."

Green had no doubt of the latter. Billy had been a poet and a player of fantasy games, who saw himself as Love caught on the shores of the River of Death. He had written lyrics about dark temptation and desolation. Not only did he know who the Furies were, but what wrong Rebecca was out to avenge. "Beneath it all, Billy was an intelligent and mystical man. I think the tattoo was his private confession. Or perhaps his private admission of fear."

"Or maybe both. It shows how much he was still obsessed with her."

Out of the corner of his eye, Green saw Patterson on the phone again, still marshalling the troops for the legal battles ahead. What had Rebecca said? That Quinton relied on the law to keep evil at bay. Green knew she held no such hope. He leaned his head on Sharon's shoulder. "Do you think she'll ever get through this?"

She didn't answer right away, then sighed. "I don't know. She would have survived the abuse, she might even have survived her mother's betrayal and Fraser's death. But murdering her own brother..."

"If I hadn't investigated—"

She silenced him with her finger to his lips. "It wouldn't have mattered. The damage was done."

He leaned back, closed his eyes and contemplated all the people whom Billy had made victims two-fold. Janice,

Matthew Fraser, even...

He opened his eyes again. "Oh God, that crazy dog. Janice won't be able to keep her in the shelter, will she?"

Sharon shook her head and a slow smile spread across her face. "I've been thinking, once we get through all this stuff, we'll have to take a serious look at Mary's latest grand old manor. With all these additions to our family..."

A little joy seeped into his exhaustion, but before he could muster a reply, a nurse padded quietly up behind them. "Mr. and Mrs. Green?"

Green spun around, his spirits plunging.

"Your daughter's awake. You can see her now."

They followed the nurse through the doors and down the hall past a series of cubicles. She pulled back the curtain, then backed discreetly away as they stepped inside. Hannah lay on her back, propped up by a huge pillow. Her spiked hair was flattened into a poorly spun bird's nest, and her face was waxen against the white sheets. But her large elfin eyes were alive and watched him without expression as he approached. He didn't know what he'd expected. Love? Tears? A residue of shock from her close brush with death? Certainly not this flat, appraising stare.

He hadn't any idea what he should do or what he should say, and was just leaning forward gingerly to kiss her forehead when she pulled away.

"Hello, Mike," she said.

"I'm your dad, Hannah."

"Fred's my dad. You're just a sperm."

He raised his eyes helplessly to look at Sharon across the bed, and he thought he saw a faint smile twitch at the edges of her lips.

"Well," Sharon said, "after you've lived with this sperm for a while, maybe a few other names will come to you."

Barbara Fradkin's work as a child psychologist provides ample inspiration and insight for murder. She has an affinity for the dark side, and her short stories haunt several anthologies and magazines, including *Storyteller*, the New Canadian Noir and Ladies' Killing Circle anthologies.

Mist Walker is the third in the Inspector Green series. The first, *Do or Die*, was published by RendezVous Press in 2000. The second, *Once Upon a Time* (2002), was shortlisted for an Arthur Ellis Award for Best Novel.

Barbara lives in Ottawa and is an active participant in Canada's crime writing community. In her spare time, she is working on Green's next case.

The Inspector Green Mysteries

Inspector Green is obsessed with his job, a condition which has almost ruined his marriage several times. When the biggest case of his career comes up, his relationships and many lives are put into danger. A student is found expertly stabbed in the stacks of a university library, and no one seems to know why. But as Green probes into the case, a web of jealousy and intrigue is revealed. He finds himself emboiled in a rivalry in the delicate arena of university politics. When the killer strikes again, Green realizes that he must quickly solve the case, no matter what the consequences may be.

ISBN 0-929141-78-4, $11.95 CDN, $9.95 U.S.
264 pages, 5 1/8" x 7 1/2"

When an old man dies a seemingly natural death in a parking lot, only Inspector Green finds it suspicious. Why did the victim have a mysterious gash on his head? A search of his house turns up an old tool box containing a German ID card from World War II. Was the victim a Jewish camp survivor or a collaborator who had sold his own people into slavery and death? Could someone have tracked him down for revenge? The second Inspector Green novel is not only a tightly plotted mystery, but a compelling tale of unhealed emotional wounds from a time of unspeakable atrocity.

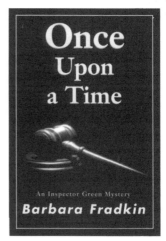

ISBN 0-929141-84-9, $12.95 CDN, $10.95 U.S.
264 pages, 5 1/8" x 7 1/2"